THE LAST SUNDAY IN MAY

THE LAST SUNDAY IN MAY

A Novel

KATE CLARK STONE

LAKE UNION
PUBLISHING

Published by Lake Union Publishing, Seattle

www.apub.com

EU product safety contact:
Amazon Media EU S. à r.l.
38, avenue John F. Kennedy, L-1855 Luxembourg
amazonpublishing-gpsr@amazon.com

ISBN-13: 9781662533525 (paperback)
ISBN-13: 9781662533532 (digital)

Cover design by Emily Mahar

Cover image: © Fayethequeen / Getty; © CuteCharacters, © Wise ant / Shutterstock

Printed in the United States of America

For my dad. See you in Turn 3.

How could I give up that white heat, that ferocity
without malice, that infinitely sharp focus on each
indefinitely small segment of time? How could I
renounce that mysterious access to abilities beyond
what the conscious mind or will could accomplish?
For . . . years, racing had been an obsession. The
prospect of giving it up loomed like a kind of death.
—Janet Guthrie

CHAPTER 1

Ten years ago

Mack Williams was born with her foot on the accelerator.

At least that's what her dad said nearly every day of her life. He'd said it when she was four and rode a bike down the metal slide at the city park, breaking her arm in two places. And he said it when she was eleven and won her first dirt track race by half a lap. And every single time she made a podium, which was often. He said it tonight too, as she buckled in for the biggest race of her life so far.

But she intended to do more than just mash her foot on the throttle; she was going to win it all.

She closed her eyes and absorbed the low growl of a dozen V-8 engines revving in preparation for the Kings Royal at Eldora, arguably the most famous sprint car race in America. Even through her helmet and earplugs, the sound of multiple nine-hundred-horsepower engines screaming mere inches away made her ears ring. She would probably be deaf by fifty, but she didn't care. That sound flowed in her ears, through her blood, into the very core of who she was.

She'd qualified midfield, a surprise but nothing she couldn't handle. Her dad teased that she'd done it on purpose: "You love showing everyone you can pass them without sweating. Such a damn spectacle." He wasn't right, but he wasn't entirely wrong either. Mack loved passing cars and winning races, and she loved the attention that came with putting on a good show.

Above her, giant stadium lights illuminated curtains of dirt sweeping through the air and clinging to anything within reach, including the visor of her helmet. She didn't bother to clear her line of sight; soon she would be completely peppered in a fine layer of rich, fragrant clay. Two dozen aluminum-tube-frame sprint cars circled the track on the last warm-up lap before the green flag waved and all hell broke loose. Petrichor filled Mack's nostrils and her heart hammered with anticipation of the ear-splitting, filthy, revving-up-to-fight-every-second beginning of a sprint car competition.

And after she won this race, she'd channel her energy into pure debauchery, like she had the night before and the night before that. For another driver, her lingering hangover and aching thighs might be a distraction, but for Mack, racing and partying were twin flames. She'd stumbled into her bed around three in the morning, buzzed and high and well laid by a motorcycle racer she hooked up with when their paths crossed. And tonight, if she won, *after* she won, she'd treat herself to another night of booze and smoke and sex. Just the thought of how she'd celebrate made her adrenaline spike.

In the span of two short seconds, the cars ahead of her bunched tightly together and accelerated toward the start-finish line. A hot current flooded Mack's body, and she reacted before her brain registered the sweep of green from the flag stand, slamming her right foot down hard on the accelerator, full throttle.

Time to show these little boys what a big bad girl could do.

Electricity traveled her body until it reached her head in an incandescent rush. She was going to win this damn race. It didn't matter that she was only twenty, or that she was the only woman on the track. Since she'd first hopped into a quarter midget car, she'd raced against men, most of them ten, twenty, sometimes even thirty years older than her. Age and gender meant nothing to a race car, and Mack had more talent in her pinkie finger than most people had in their entire bodies.

But more than talent, she had desire. No one wanted to win more than she did, and she'd busted her ass to get to the top of her field before she could legally buy a beer. She may party hard, but she worked harder.

She raced through the field, swerving and pushing and throwing her elbows all the way out, barging her way up to fifth place before the race was half over. With three laps to go, she'd ticked her competitors off her list until she was in second place. A decent enough finish for some but not nearly good enough for Mack Williams. She'd win or wreck out trying.

Her blood pumped in time to her heartbeat as she hunted down the driver in front of her, Ricky Russo. The white flag waved, signaling the final lap of the race, and Mack pulled within inches of Russo's back tire. Steadying her front wheels, Mack stomped down on the throttle as if the V-8 had anything more to give. When Russo went high at the entry of turn two, Mack let her car drift up from the inside line to the middle of the track, forcing Russo to either stay up high in the dirt or release the throttle and fall in behind her.

It wasn't a dirty move; it was racing.

Mack was strong, but her legs shook with the effort to keep the pedal even with the floorboard. Placing her left foot on top of her right, Mack slammed down on the throttle and shot toward the start-finish line. Her front wheel hit the line an inch before Russo's.

She'd done it. She'd won Eldora.

First woman to win it, and the youngest ever.

The electric current in her body exploded into a lightning bolt of ecstasy, and Mack felt tears of joy smart in her eyes before she quickly stopped them. There were many rules for women in motorsports, but the golden one was *don't ever cry*. It didn't matter if she won the biggest race of her career or broke every bone in her body, if she let tears fall, she'd be forever known as The Girl Who Cried.

Mack steered her car to the center of the famous track, unbuckled her harness, and pulled herself out of the car. Using the roll cage, she hoisted herself onto the wide panel on the top of her car, ten feet in the air. The crowd roared and Mack screamed back, drawing energy from the noise and lights and movement. Up here, she was a queen, a goddess, unbeatable. Her dad called her Spectacle, and she loved the nickname. She wanted everyone to see her, and to see her win in spectacular fashion.

Eldora was the biggest win of her career so far, with a six-figure purse, prestige on a national scale, and hopefully, the attention of more fans, more teams, more races.

She looked toward the grandstands and spotted her dad, cheering like a madman. He'd lost out in the heat races earlier in the night, but she knew that her win was as good to him as one of his own. He was a seven-time series champion, but Mack was beginning to beat him more and more often. She also spotted in the crowd the motorcycle racer she'd been hooking up with, holding a handle of Old Fitzgerald. Her mouth watered in anticipation of the celebration to come.

Tonight, she'd party until she was naked and hanging her head in a toilet. Tomorrow, she'd hit the gym and the phones, playing up her victory to get something bigger and better.

She was so close to getting everything she wanted.

She thrust her fists in the air and absorbed the cheers of more than twenty thousand fans into her body. She'd known she could win this race, she proved she would win, and soon she would prove that she could win at any track, against anyone.

CHAPTER 2

Present day
4 weeks until the Indianapolis 500

Mack parked near a row of brightly lit garages, unclipped her seat belts, and shut off the engine. Her body ached, tired from fighting an unfamiliar car through the corners, and her hands shook with the adrenaline crash that came after a race. From the grandstands behind her, Mack heard the announcer calling out the heat order and she gave herself exactly one second to feel sorry that her name was swallowed in the ruckus of the next wave of cars taking to the track.

There'd been a time when she'd known how to use that energy—channeling it into another race, another man, a stupid prank—but now she winced as she set her feet on the gravel. Her knees buckled and she caught herself before falling forward.

"Mack? We got a problem in garage six." She jumped and turned toward where a longtime employee waited. "Small fire, got it put out with the extinguisher, but it burned a hole in the siding. Needs fixing before it rains next."

Don't cry.

Tucking her helmet under an arm, she thanked the employee and avoided any conversation by taking the long path around the outside of Haubstadt Speedway. She made her way to the track office, a narrow space tucked into a corner under the bleachers, where she surveyed the mess and renewed her vow not to cry. She'd filled in for a sick driver, a one-time opportunity to race some laps, but this dingy room was her real life, the bills and work orders and schedules, even the damn plunger leaning against the wall. She used to run in the biggest races, and now she simply ran her family's small dirt racetrack in little Haubstadt, Indiana.

Her mouth tasted like soil and sorrow.

She gently wiped dirt off her helmet and set it on the shelf above the ancient desktop computer, next to a faded photograph of herself with Laurie, back when she and her sister had still been friends. Two dusty reminders of what she'd lost.

"Good night, huh?"

Her father stood in the doorway, leaning heavily on his cane. The right corner of his mouth drooped slightly, but the lopsided grin only added to his charm. A near-fatal wreck couldn't take away the Wes Williams charisma, or his reputation in racing. A sizable chunk of their ticket sales came from fans who wanted to meet the GOAT of dirt track racing.

"Ticket sales are decent for opening night, lots of close races for the spectators, and concessions were up three hundred dollars last time I checked. Might start our season in the black," Mack said.

"I meant your race."

Mack rocked her head from side to side as she pulled off her racing coveralls—borrowed, six sizes too big—and threw on a hoodie, cutoff jean shorts, and work boots. She wasn't faking humility; she had raced well, pulling herself from the back of the pack to finish a respectable fourth in her heat, but the race tonight left her feeling melancholy and bitter.

"I'm out of shape," she said as she laced her boots. She needed to get out of the office and check in on everything. It had been calm when she'd ducked out for her heat race, but running a small business meant she was the race director, the accountant, human resources, a bouncer, and more often than she liked, the plumber.

That's who she was now, not a race car driver.

"Hard to stay race ready when you don't make any effort to put your butt in a car."

Mack gave Wes a sharp side-eye as she pulled her long blond ponytail through the back of her worn Hoosiers cap. She knew Wes encouraged his buddies to call her to fill in for a sick or injured driver, but lately those sporadic races felt like punishment, not pleasure. Like lashes from a whip, woven from the threads of the dreams she once had.

"Stop telling your friends to call me," she said sharply.

Wes managed a smirk, unbothered by her tone. "Stop saying yes when they call."

They'd barely spent a single day apart in the entire thirty years of her life, and it pissed Mack off that her dad knew she'd say yes to any chance to race. She grabbed her keys off the dusty desk. "I gotta go check in on ticket sales. You shook all the hands and kissed all the babies tonight?"

Ten years ago, her dad had been in the lead in Kentucky when he tangled tires with another driver, flipped end over end, and only stopped flipping when his car struck a light pole. Wes still struggled with the aftermath, a traumatic brain injury and chronic seizures, and he'd slid into the role of ambassador for the track while Mack took over actual operations. Wes liked to pretend he was still in charge even though he mostly schmoozed with spectators and advertisers.

"I can do the load out tonight," Wes offered. "You leave early and get Shaw into bed at a decent hour."

"The parking lot is one giant tripping hazard, it's so soft and wet from all the rain." She waved him toward the door. "Go shoot the shit with the fans. The young guys love that. Like a blessing from the Pope."

Wes groaned. Sometimes Mack couldn't tell if his disappointment was in his own limitations or in her. He lifted his chin toward the photo behind Mack. "Heard from your sister yet? She get moved in okay?"

Mack suppressed a flash of irritation. She was the conduit for communication between her father and sister, both of them too pigheaded to pick up the phone and call the other. "She texted to say that she was in her new apartment. She seems okay."

It was a total lie; Mack had no idea how her sister felt about anything, or even why she'd left her cushy job in DC to move to Indianapolis, which was still four hours away from Haubstadt. Growing up, she and Laurie had shared confidences but now they only traded bland, transactional text messages: Did Dad's knee surgery go okay? Do you know how to file for SSDI?

"At least Indy is in driving distance. Maybe she'll come visit."

The hope in her father's voice stoked Mack's barely banked frustration. Wes and Laurie remained stuck in a toxic match of who-was-the-most-stubborn, and Mack felt like the eternal loser in their game in which Wes wouldn't call and Laurie wouldn't visit.

Mack sighed, watching as her breath disturbed the sooty office air. Her whole life was coated in dust.

"Uh, Ms. Williams?" A teenager they'd hired for seasonal work poked her head in the doorway. "Someone came to concessions saying the men's toilet is plugged and spilling on the floor."

Mack grabbed the plunger. Make that dust *and* shit.

~

Three hours later, the last teams had ambled out of the parking lot, the grandstands were empty and swept, and Mack flipped the master switch to turn off the lights encircling the track. A tension-dehydration-dust-ponytail headache bloomed along her forehead, and Mack rubbed her temples as she tabbed through her mental checklist one more time. Her hands and face were filthy, her feet throbbed, and the persistent smell of popcorn and disinfectant would haunt her forever.

At her side, her daughter turned cartwheels, pausing here and there to inspect the patchy grass for four-leaf clovers. Her clothes were grubby and her tangled blond hair was dotted with grass.

"You need a bath tonight, Shaw Westly Williams."

Shaw paused long enough to wrinkle her freckled nose. "Mama, do you think mermaids have to take baths?"

Mack pretended to think it over. Shaw had recently turned ten, still a little girl, but occasionally Mack could see the early signs of puberty popping through when Shaw rolled her eyes or sassed. Anytime she could indulge the childishness in Shaw, she tried. "Mmm, they live in the ocean and swim underwater all day, so probably not."

"Then I definitely want to be a mermaid!" Shaw giggled a second before turning serious. "Can we go to the ocean? Pretty please?"

Her light voice hit Mack with the force of a heavyweight punch. They managed to get by on the income from the track, Wes's social security, and the occasional odd jobs Mack pulled in the winter when money was tight, but they'd never had the funds to take any kind of vacation. Ten years ago, Mack would have left right then, driving until they reached the surf, windows down and blasting music. She'd lived for the moment, drunk on the wildness of doing whatever she wanted whenever she wanted. But now she had to be solid and more stable for her daughter. Shaw needed a schedule and sleep and the foundation of home and family, not a midnight trip to Florida.

"Someday, baby."

"Daddy lives near the ocean. Maybe he could take me."

Mack jerked, as if Shaw really had hit her. Shaw had stayed with her father exactly once, and Mack would never, ever allow her to go anywhere alone with him again. Not that he would make time for her anyway. Saying so would only hurt Shaw, so she nodded and said, "He does."

"I have to swim in the ocean so I can learn to be a mermaid."

"Solid logic," Mack said as she swept strands of fine hair off her daughter's forehead. She was long-boned like her father, and had only a few inches to grow before she matched Mack's height. Recently she'd lost the chubby cheeks of younger childhood, and Mack could see glimpses of the teenager Shaw would be far too soon. Time truly was a goddamn thief.

Mack gestured at two suspicious red parentheses on each side of her daughter's mouth. "Were you sneaking candy again?"

Shaw was a track kid through and through, roaming the grounds on race nights and wrangling free snacks from the septuagenarian who'd worked concessions since the mid-nineties. Shaw smiled and Mack saw remnants of popcorn in her teeth.

"Bath, brush, and floss."

"I know, I know. Track night, bath night," Shaw grumbled.

As she watched Shaw skip away across the parking lot, Mack tried to appreciate the youthful energy of her daughter instead of giving into the weariness that seemed to be her only remaining personality trait. She packed snacks, washed load after load of clothes, cooked bland but nutritious meals, practiced spelling words, and drove Shaw to dance class and softball practices, all while keeping the track solvent and Wes in good health. Next week there'd be another race, another load out, more bills and bathrooms and bleachers to hose down.

Mack wasn't ungrateful. Shaw was a great kid, her dad survived an accident that should have been fatal, and she could pay their bills. But on nights like tonight, when everyone needed something from her at the same time, when she could hardly feel her feet inside her worn boots and she knew she still had work to do, and when the mundanity of her future stretched out like a rural country lane, she had to shove away her grief for the life she might have had. She hated herself for being unsatisfied with a good life.

"Mack Williams?"

Mack turned to see a tall woman with wiry gray hair leaning against the ticket office. She wore a wrinkled man's shirt, ill-fitting jeans, and the Merrell slip-ons favored by old men. She shifted, as if she'd been standing in the same place for a while.

"We're closed for the night. Sorry."

"I already saw the races." The woman held out her hand. "Janet Joyner."

Holy shit.

Mack hadn't recognized the woman at first, but the instant she heard her name, memories clicked into place. She was more weathered, with grooves at her mouth and starbursts by her eyes, but the woman in front of her was definitely the same woman whose autographed picture still hung on Mack's bedroom wall. In the 1990s, Janet Joyner broke gender barriers in multiple forms of racing, from the Daytona 500 to the Indy 500, and now she owned a small IndyCar team. Suddenly, Mack was eight years old again, standing on top of an aluminum riser and screaming at the top of her lungs as a silver-and-blue car zoomed by her. *That's the girl driver,* she'd told her dad. *I'm going to race in the Indy 500 just like her!*

Embarrassed by her grimy appearance, Mack wiped her hands on her shorts and shook Janet's hand. "Oh wow. It's . . . an honor. I . . ." She almost started spouting random facts about Janet's career at her. Mack's face felt sticky and hot. "Like I said, we're done for the night but we run races every weekend from now until the fall. I can give you some tickets."

Janet looked at her oddly, as if she'd said something amusing. "You're Wes's girl, right? Mackenzie Williams?"

Mack returned her frown. "It's Mack. You know Wes?"

To her surprise, Janet grinned, revealing straight, coffee-stained teeth. "Me and Wes go way back. I always said I'd visit and—" She held out her arms in an impressive wingspan. She looked more like a retired WNBA player than a race car driver. "I'm here."

Mack gestured toward the infield, surprised her dad never mentioned that he went *way back* with one of her heroes. They generally told each other everything. "Dad's home for the night. It's only me and . . . um . . ." Mack looked around for Shaw and saw her sitting in the cab of Mack's car, pretending to drive. She held up a finger. *Just a sec.*

Janet grinned again. "I'm not here for Wes. I'm here to talk to you."

CHAPTER 3

4 weeks until the Indianapolis 500

Janet gestured toward the lumpy patch of gravel connecting the corrugated metal garages and the main grandstand, then turned and marched up the path without waiting.

Mack followed, her mind churning. Why the hell did someone like *Janet Joyner* want to talk to *her*? At midnight? At a dirt track in the middle of nowhere Indiana? Mack once dreamed about talking with the woman she'd hero-worshipped, had even thought she'd earned it, but that was a long time ago and her life was a far cry from racing stars and heroes now. She was dead on her feet, dirty, and so hungry her stomach stopped growling hours ago. She trudged after Janet, wondering if maybe she was already home in her bed, having a bizarre dream.

Janet waited until Mack caught up, no easy feat when Janet stood at least a foot taller than Mack's five feet even. "Your dad never mentioned me?"

The smell of wet spring grass rose up as their feet crushed the stubborn shoots that pushed through the gravel. Mack made a mental note to spray herbicide, and immediately decided against it. Crappy for the environment and crappy for her budget. The grass would be dead by the third or fourth weekend of the hot Hoosier summer anyway.

She exhaled heavily, finally understanding the woman's presence. "Oh." She tried to keep her voice casual and kind. "No, sorry. My dad's had a lot of girlfriends."

Her dad dated women the way he'd once smoked cigarettes—any brand, no loyalty. Mack had seen dozens of girlfriends come and go, and she saw it as a kindness to warn any woman that got involved with Wes Williams not to get too comfortable because he'd change the sheets tomorrow.

Janet threw her head back and laughed heartily, her voice both husky and loud. "I was never one of your dad's girls. But I knew him in his skirt-chasing days. We weren't close enough to stay in touch after his accident."

Mack closed her eyes against the memory of almost losing the only parent she'd ever had. Wes was more than her father, he was her best friend, her coach, a beloved grandpa to Shaw, and the only person who'd ever really understood Mack. She'd thought she and her sister were close, but turned out that Laurie didn't care much about who Mack was at all.

"So y'all raced together?"

"A bit. I didn't stay in dirt long. Always had bigger plans."

Unconsciously, Mack murmured a tone of agreement. She'd had bigger plans, too.

Janet's smile fell, and she blatantly studied Mack. She didn't seem like the type to care about dirt and sweat, but Mack swiped a hand over her face anyway.

"You race often, Mack?"

Mack rubbed at the grass with her boot, kicking up more of the spring fragrance. "Nope. Subbing for a friend."

"Hmm. I met a little girl at the concession stand who told me her mama was racing tonight. She yours?"

They'd reached the dark area between the garages and the grandstand, and Mack could no longer make out the features of Janet's face. She walked a few feet over to the large chain-link fence bordering the parking lot and leaned back against it, facing the racetrack. It was nice like this, quiet and empty. "Yeah. Shaw's my daughter."

"I figured. She's got that wide Williams mouth." Mack squinted at Janet through the dim light but could barely make out the line of her profile. "Cute name."

Mack nodded, wondering if Janet could guess that she'd named her daughter after the famous three-time winner of the Indianapolis 500, Wilbur Shaw, who'd also saved the famed Speedway from becoming a housing development in the 1940s. She'd stared down at her newborn daughter and wanted a name that made her feel hope, not the desolation she'd actually felt in that moment.

"I'm surprised you don't still do winged sprints. I know you've got the kid, but you could run races in the Midwest."

Mack cracked her neck from side to side and lifted her waist-length ponytail off her sweaty neck. She was too tired to come up with a lie. "We sold the car during a rough patch. 2020 nearly did us in." It broke her heart to sell that car. She'd won so many races and had some of the best moments of her life in that machine, and selling it felt like the final death blow to her racing career. But the car was just an excuse; even if she still had the sprint, she couldn't race and keep everything going.

Mack's shoulders sagged with fatigue. She should get Shaw home and tucked into bed. Hero or not, Janet needed to get to the point. "Ms. Joyner—"

"Janet."

"Um, okay. It really is nice to meet you. You were my hero as a kid." Mack looked down at her feet, mortified that she'd said it out loud but too tired to be anything less than honest. "It's late and I need to get my daughter home. Did you need something from me? Or . . . want to talk to Wes?"

The older woman stepped away from the fence and faced Mack. She looked at Mack for an awkwardly long time, then seemed to come to a decision. "You ever think about the Indy 500?"

Mack startled. How could she ever forget it? The question confused her. "We watch it every year. Your driver Leo Raisman is my daughter's favorite."

Janet shook her head impatiently. "No. Do you ever think about *racing* in the Indy 500?"

Mack's skin flushed, quick and hot, at the shameful memory of her long-ago dreams. She didn't think about racing in the Indy 500, she dreamed about it.

She relaxed the tightness in her throat before answering in what she hoped was a cool, unaffected voice. "Uh, not really."

"Hmm. That's a shame. I came here to see if you wanted to qualify for this year's race."

Around Mack, the air froze and her senses shut down. The darkness covered her eyes completely, and the smell of the grass and motor oil receded.

The Indianapolis 500—one of the most storied car races in the world—had been her dream for twenty years until she ruthlessly made herself excise it.

Except she hadn't. Not entirely.

During the day, Mack was consumed by her to-do list—making pediatrician appointments, fixing the ancient washing machine, painting the track grandstand—running ragged, too busy to remember any part of herself that still had racing ambitions. She even felt content at times, proud of the stability she'd built for her small family. But at night, her traitorous brain reminded her of what she'd once spent every moment working toward: being the first woman to win the most famous car race in the world.

Try as she might, she could not work that dream out of her mind.

Behind them, a small voice called out. "Mama, can we go now?"

Mack straightened and held up a finger once more. "Be right there!" she called back, her voice shrill and overloud. She stayed facing the distant figure of Shaw, trying to focus. She was so tired that she'd imagined that Janet Joyner had asked her to drive in the Indy 500.

"I'm sorry," she said. "I kinda spaced out there for a minute. It's been a long night. What was it that you said you wanted?"

"I'm entering a second car into the race this year. I want you to drive that car." Janet's face was still unreadable in the darkness. "Call me crazy, but I don't think your racing days are over."

"You are fucking crazy."

"Probably," Janet conceded, a cluster of small wrinkles formed around her wry mouth. "I know your history, and I know what I saw out there tonight. You went from last to fourth in a B-feature heat. One more lap and you'd have had first." She paused and lifted her hands in a lackadaisical gesture. "But if you're not interested, I can find a hundred other people who are."

Ten years had passed since Mack raced at an elite level. Janet was right: There were dozens of young drivers, all of them more prepared than she currently was, hustling to find a ride with an IndyCar team. She could fill the grandstands full of talented drivers who didn't have the baggage of a kid, a father who needed full-time care, and a struggling family business. Those were the people who got IndyCar rides, not washed-up single moms who drove carpool and watched the Indy 500 from the sofa.

"I'm not giving you anything for free," Janet said. "I'm offering you the seat, but you'll have to find sponsorship like any other driver. Offer is open for twenty-four hours. Qualifying starts in less than a month and there's a shit ton to do."

Janet held out a paper rectangle. A dormant surge of hope flooded Mack's nervous system and her breath quickened with the possibility that the offer was real. She pictured herself standing on the dais at Indianapolis, waving to three hundred thousand fans before rocketing down the track at two hundred miles per hour. She hated how she wanted to believe Janet, hated the pinprick of optimism puncturing her usual pragmatism. Wanting something you couldn't have was a weakness, and Mack didn't indulge in worthless wishes. She held her hands in tight fists at her sides.

Frowning, Janet grabbed Mack's hand, slammed the card into her palm, and strode off toward the back of the parking lot.

Mack closed her eyes and tried to calm her breathing.

"Wait!" The word escaped her mouth without her brain approving the message. Janet stopped and turned back, but Mack panicked, scared of her own longings. "Why me? I haven't really raced in . . . a while."

In the darkness, Janet's expression was opaque, and she stood without speaking for so long that Mack thought she wasn't going to answer. "I'm finally able to fund a second car. I want a woman in that car."

"But why *me*?"

Janet muttered something that sounded like "Fucking millennials, always needing a gold star" as she walked back toward Mack. "I remember you from when you were younger. At first I watched you because you were Wes's girl, but then I watched because I couldn't look away. You had that fire. Anyone who watched you knew you were something special. And I saw you out there tonight. You had no business gunning for the front but you drove like you still had something to prove." She glanced down at her feet, seeming to search for words. Finally she said, "Janet Joyner Racing isn't the biggest team at Indy and I don't have the time or cash to fuck around. I want someone who will fight for the front even when they're ten laps down, and that's what I see in you. I saw it then and I still see it now."

Mack's skin was clammy even though her insides were on fire. She squeezed her eyes shut and shivered in the cool spring air. Was she really still that person? That part of her felt, if not dead, buried under the crush of her daily responsibilities. For nearly a decade, she'd transformed herself from *Mack Williams, fastest woman on four wheels* into *Mack Williams, quietest woman in the carpool lane*. How could a stranger see fire in her when all Mack saw was ash?

When she opened her eyes, Janet was gone.

INDIANAPOLIS COURIER-JOURNAL

April 26

The Ultimate Guide to the Indianapolis 500

It's almost May, which means it's almost time to go racing! Most of our readers have attended the Indianapolis 500 at least once, and many attend the race annually, but in case you're new to the city or new to the Indy 500, here's a primer for our city's biggest event.

The History

The Indianapolis Motor Speedway was built in 1909 as a testing facility for local automobile manufacturers. Over the years the Indy 500 grew into The Greatest Spectacle in Racing, known for fast speeds and as the largest single-day spectator sport.

Month of May

- The Indy 500 is run on the last Sunday in May.
- Qualifications for the Indy 500 take place the weekend prior to the race.
- Practice takes place on four consecutive days before qualifications begin, and is the first time teams are allowed to test their speed on the oval during May.

Indy by the Numbers

- 1911: The first Indy 500, won by Ray Harroun (who used a rearview mirror instead of a driving mechanic).

- 33: The maximum number of cars in the Indy 500 field. Cars are lined up in eleven rows of three at the start of the race.

- 200: Number of laps it takes to complete 500 miles. Each lap of the famous oval covers 2.5 miles.

- 250,000: The number of permanent seats at the Indianapolis Motor Speedway. Infield fans, Snake Pit, teams, or track and support staff add up to an additional 100,000 spectators on race day.

What's up with All Those Traditions?

- Yard of bricks: The original track surface was built from over three million paving bricks (hence the nickname *The Brickyard*), but as time and technology advanced, the track was converted to asphalt. A yard of bricks remains at the start-finish line in homage to the original "Brickyard."

- Winners drink milk: After his win in 1936, Louis Meyer requested a glass of cold buttermilk, and a tradition was born. Indy 500 winners are given a liter of milk, a wreath of orchids and a sizable winnings purse.

- Borg-Warner Trophy: Each winner has their name and likeness sculpted onto the iconic Borg-Warner Trophy, valued at over $1 million (but we think it's priceless).
- "Back Home Again in Indiana": The race doesn't start until over 300,000 people, led by Jim Corneilson, sing the beloved state song.

Whether you're a die-hard race fan or just someone who loves a good party, there's something for everyone at the Indy 500. We hope to see you there!

CHAPTER 4

4 weeks until the Indianapolis 500

"Dad, I made oatmeal!"

Mack yelled down the hallway of their tiny post-war bungalow while Shaw plopped into a worn kitchen chair and glared at the steaming bowl in front of her. Mack poured a glass of orange juice for Shaw while checking the clock. The bedroom door yanked open and Mack startled at the sight of her dad's newest girlfriend wearing skinny jeans and a fuzzy white sweater. At seven thirty in the morning, Billie's glossy brown hair was perfectly curled and her makeup photo ready, including . . . was that a temporary tattoo of a butterfly on her cheek? On a Monday morning?

"Oh hey, Mack," Billie drawled in her thick East Tennessee accent. "We're running a little slow this morning. Nothing an allergy pill and a little Tylenol can't fix. D'ya need me to help get Shaw ready for school?"

Mack grimaced at Billie's casual use of *we*. Billie hadn't officially moved in but she was at the house more mornings than not, and her things were slowly taking over. Last week, a blender appeared on the counter "for Wes's green smoothies" as if her dad regularly chose pureed produce over Fritos. Wes and Billie may be cosplaying newlyweds, but Billie hadn't been there in the days when Wes couldn't use the bathroom alone because the seizures came so often. When she realized the full extent of Wes's health needs, she'd leave. None of Wes's many girlfriends lasted for long, before or after his accident.

Proving the point, Mack grabbed a large plastic pill sorter from the countertop and shook it in Billie's direction. "Dad needs to take his medicine first thing in the morning, and he can't take it on an empty stomach. He should be eating by now." She cringed at her own harsh tone. No one should be yelled at before eight a.m., even grown women who wore glitter. It wasn't Billie's fault Mack tossed and turned last night as Janet Joyner's words lashed her over and over.

You had that fire.

I saw it then and I still see it now.

When was the last time someone had spoken about her like a driver? Like a competitor and not a caretaker? It was humiliating how much she wanted to believe Janet's words, how much she wanted to be that person Janet thought she saw.

Mack held out a bowl, contrite. "Oatmeal?"

"It's kinda gross but I added grape jelly," Shaw offered helpfully.

Billie gracefully accepted a bowl of lumpy porridge and doctored it with maple syrup—she'd replaced their crusty bottle of Log Cabin with the kind that comes in a real glass jug—before speaking around dainty bites.

"Why don't I take Shaw to school today and give you a little solo time?" She turned to Shaw with a wink. "You wanna listen to more of the Go-Go's?"

"Yes!" Shaw shouted. "Can we put the top down on the convertible? Can I have a butterfly sticker on my face, too?"

Shaw's enthusiasm for all things Billie irritated Mack; no need for her daughter to get attached to someone temporary. "Don't you want me to walk you in?"

Shaw wrinkled her nose. "Ew, Mom. My friends will think I'm a baby. I'm a fourth grader now."

Billie rested a manicured hand on Mack's arm. Her long acrylic fingernails had tiny three-dimensional unicorns and rainbows. "Take a little time for yourself. I'll stop at the IGA and grab groceries to make tofu tacos for dinner."

Mack jerked her arm away from Billie's touch. She didn't need mothering from a stranger.

"Morning," Wes mumbled as he shuffled into the kitchen. Mack heard the screen door slam as she poured her dad a cup of coffee and glimpsed the blur of Shaw's purple backpack through the window. Billie blew Wes a quick kiss and followed Shaw out the door before Mack could protest. Wes accepted the phantom kiss and placed it on his own lips. *Gross.* Wes tipped his chin toward the door. "Let Billie take Shaw to school. We gotta talk."

"We gotta talk," Mack mocked in a deep voice as she poured a second cup of coffee for herself. She refused to admit that the kind Billie bought tasted better than their usual bargain brand. She jammed two slices of bread in the toaster. "Are you going to nag me about changing the oil in the Bronco? I told you, I'm going to—"

"You seen the news about Kelley?"

Mack's mouth snapped shut. Hearing the name of Shaw's absentee father made her feel a dizzying combination of rage and nausea. Shortly after she'd peed on a stick, Kelley received a full-time offer to race in MotoGP, the most prestigious circuit for motorcycle racing, and moved to Spain. He wasn't there for Shaw's birth, and had been mostly content to communicate with their daughter only when he felt like it. In her ten years, Shaw had stayed with Kelley for exactly two weeks, and in the aftermath, Mack vowed it would never happen again.

"The MotoGP ride?"

"Yep. Shit floats. That asswipe managed to get another ride in motorcycle racing's biggest series." Wes took a bite of the buttered toast she plopped in front of him and spoke with his mouth full. "Can't decide if I'm disgusted or impressed."

"Would have been nice if he'd told Shaw himself." Mack didn't want her daughter living with Kelley, but she also didn't want Shaw to grow up without knowing him. Kelley's approach was more scattershot.

They mostly got information about Kelley the way everyone else did: the internet. Last year, they'd found out he'd been injured in a massive wreck on ESPN's evening highlights.

"His loss." Wes scowled. "I would have missed out on the best part of my life if I hadn't raised you and your sister."

"Better than winning the Knoxville Nationals?" Mack raised a brow, relieved to be teasing her father instead of talking about Kelley. Wes pretended to consider her question and Mack threw him a playful middle finger. "Too bad our mom died and you got stuck with me and Laurie."

Mack meant it as a joke, but Wes sobered and shifted forward to grab both of her hands. His worn fingers used to steer finicky cars and now the right palm hardly exerted any pressure against her own. "Listen to me, and listen good. When your mama died, I could have walked away but I learned that parenting is a choice. Both you and Shaw deserve a lot better than that jackwad."

"That's what you wanted to talk about?" Mack waved an impatient hand through the air, embarrassed Wes still felt he had to protect her from Kelley. "I'm fine, Dad. He is who he is."

An alarm split the quiet and Mack quickly silenced her phone. She reached across the narrow gap between the table and countertop, grabbed the pill organizer, and handed Wes two tablets. She refreshed their coffee and sat back down as Wes dutifully swallowed.

"That wasn't all," he said as he struggled to pull something out of his pocket. It was the small white paper rectangle Janet had given her last night, inscribed Janet Joyner Racing.

To: Janet@JanetJoynerRacing.com
From: HollisWhitfield@hartley.com
CC: CarolinaFarmington@hartley.com
Subject: Meeting request—Urgent [4/27, 8:16 a.m.]

J—

Contact my assistant immediately to schedule a Zoom about this new driver you want to hire. As you'll recall, we've discussed several more marketable prospects that provide ROI for our sponsorship investment. I appreciate the publicity stunt of "the only girl in the race" but Hartley is more interested in results than spectacle.

Carolina get this scheduled ASAP.

Hollis O. Whitfield
VP of Marketing
Hartley Harvester Manufacturing, Inc.
A Fortune 500 Company

CHAPTER 5

4 weeks until the Indianapolis 500

"Found that on the floor in the hallway. Not a speck of dust, so it's pretty damn recent."

Mack picked at her bottom lip as she stared at Janet's card. He hadn't technically asked her a question.

"How did you get this?"

Mack was torn between telling him everything and telling him nothing, so she deflected instead. "Did you ever race against her?"

"Nah, never that lucky. She was a hell of a driver. Shame she never went further in IndyCar. There was lots of folks then who didn't think a woman belonged."

"Look at it now, Dad. That attitude hasn't grown mold yet." Not a single woman competed in the Indy 500 last year. In the entire history of the race, only nine women had started. "How come you never told me you knew Janet Joyner?"

"Shit, Mack, I knew everyone back then. You know that. Don't change the subject. How did you get this? Did you see her?"

There was no point in telling him about something that couldn't happen. Even if she admitted to herself that she wanted to accept Janet's bizarre offer—geezus, she wanted to accept—she couldn't leave her family. They needed her, and the business would fall apart without her. She'd spent years pretending she didn't mourn her racing career, hiding the hurt so that Wes and Shaw would never think they were the cause. She couldn't up and *leave*. She picked at her cold oatmeal, letting the soft cereal muffle her voice. "It was nothing."

Wes banged a fist on the faded table, rattling the dishes. Mack was used to his match-strike temper; it flared quickly but never held a flame for long. "You gonna start lying to me now? Why was she here?"

She didn't lie to him. They'd been through too much together and Wes knew all of her tells. She simply . . . kept her feelings to herself. So she surprised herself when she blurted, "She wanted to talk about a ride. But it's not going to work out."

Wes's left eyebrow shot up and he leaned forward, bracing his weaker elbow on the table. "What kinda ride?"

"It won't work out, Dad. Let it go."

"Why won't it work out?" His voice got louder. "What kind of ride?"

"Let it go!"

Wes stood up surprisingly fast for a man who had limited use of his right leg. "What kind of fucking ride?"

"The Indy 500!"

Shock highlighted Wes's face and he fell back into the chair. Mack felt her cheeks turn hot and she hastily cleared the table to avoid facing him. She didn't know which would be more devastating to see on his face, pity or excitement. Wes had always been her biggest cheerleader, but he knew better than anyone why she couldn't accept Janet's proposal. "I have no business thinking I can handle an IndyCar. And we have races booked at the track every other weekend until October and Shaw has the end-of-year field trip and you've got that new physical therapy assessment—"

"Don't you dare use me and Shaw as an excuse!"

Mack turned and held out both hands. "It's not an excuse, Dad, it's reality." Even if they didn't have the track, even if she hadn't taken almost a decade away from full-time racing, there would always be Shaw. Her daughter deserved a childhood of calm stability. "I'm not Kelley. I can't leave everything behind on a whim."

They fell silent, both waiting each other out. Mack wanted her dad to agree with her, to tell her he understood she couldn't take Janet's offer. She wanted his complicity, not his blessing to chase an impossibly wild idea. Her life changed direction ten years ago and she saw no point reversing course now.

At least that's what she tried to make herself believe.

"The daughter I raised would have left rubber streaks on the driveway on her way out of town. Wouldn't have even said goodbye. Like that time you were already racing at Sebring by the time I knew you were gone. Always such a spectacle."

Mack bit her lip. She'd thought about taking off in the night, getting on the road before she thought over the details. Instead, she'd crept into Shaw's room and watched her daughter sleep to remind herself that she was steady now. Sturdy. Not someone who rushed off on a whim. "I'm still the daughter you raised, just less stupid."

Please tell me not to do this, she begged him silently. His words threw gasoline on the spark that had started in her chest last night when Janet had thrown the words *Indy 500* at her. A long-buried wildness, the restlessness she could never quite kill off, kindled inside her.

Wes jabbed a careless hand toward the center of her chest. "Shaw has everything she needs right here. You love that girl. You'd give her a good life whether it's here or in Indianapolis. Hell, you'd probably give her a better life there."

Panicked, Mack tried to throw cold water on the fiery hope curling in her body. "You think it's better for Shaw to leave the only home she's ever known? During the last month of school? To live . . . geezus, where would we live?"

Why was she even talking about this? It couldn't happen.

Wes grinned wickedly. "Ain't that somethin'? You got a sister who lives in Indianapolis now." Mack shook her head. Following this lark and uprooting her daughter was one thing; asking for a favor from Laurie was another. "Anyway, Shaw can stay home with me and Billie. She's an easy kid. We can manage her for a few weeks while school wraps up. You've got to take this chance, Spec. Might be your only shot at the Indy 500."

Mack frowned even as her heart rate picked up. Was her dad really considering this as a real opportunity? Did he believe she could make it all the way to the Indy 500?

No. It was impossible.

"Stop it," she snapped at Wes. Her body was so overheated now that she felt her forehead for fever. Moisture dotted her hairline.

It had been too long. She couldn't just dive back in, going from cleaning urinals to driving an IndyCar.

She couldn't.

Could she?

Ten years ago, she'd been young, aggressive, and the daughter of legendary Wes Williams. People in the racing community had whispered that Mackenzie Williams had *It*: The rare combination of physical stamina and mental acuity that seemingly reacted to the car before it even moved. By the time she was twenty, she'd won some of the biggest sprint races in the country and topped podiums at sports car endurance races, but she pursued one dream with single-minded focus: a chance to race at Indianapolis. And by January of her twentieth year, she almost got what she wanted when Ampersand Autosport invited her to test drive for their IndyCar team.

As bold as she'd been on track, she'd been even wilder in her free time. As a teenager, she regularly spent late nights playing euchre and drinking Jack and Cokes with men three times her age. She laughed as she rode on the back of motorcycles with no helmet, swam with friends in abandoned strip mines, and drag raced down city streets. At nineteen, she'd started hooking up with motorcycle bad boy Kelley Caruthers. They didn't even try to keep it quiet, and when Mack canceled her IndyCar test because she was sixteen weeks pregnant, no one was surprised except herself. She'd been hot-blooded, living for the moment, and stupid enough to trust a man ten years her senior to wear a condom properly.

That choice irrevocably changed her life. She'd spent years working to retrain herself: She was no longer impulsive, taking hours or days to make decisions on the smallest things. She didn't drink, didn't date. Her life was about Shaw and preventing her from making the kinds of decisions Mack had made herself.

She walked to the sink and washed her hands in cold water, an old trick her dad had taught her when she needed to calm her heart rate. It pissed her off that he knew exactly what she was doing. He always knew because he'd always been by her side. She dried her hands and turned to face him. "That door closed a long time ago, Dad."

Wes squinted at her. "Because you closed it, Spec."

She used to love the nickname he'd given her, but right now she *hated* it. Her hands were already hot again, her armpits damp with the anxiety of the conversation. She gave into the anger, let herself be pissed off. It felt so much better than the swirling terror of possibility her dad's words had caused.

Shaw was only five weeks old when Wes had the accident that left him with headaches, seizures, memory loss, and a pinned and patched body. Mack spent the first years of Shaw's life in a day-to-day subsistence of single parenting, caring for her father, and learning how to run a small business. By the time Shaw was three, Wes's health had mostly stabilized, but those first years had been so stressful that when Kelley offered to bring toddler Shaw to Spain for two weeks, Mack jumped at the chance to have a break. She would never make that mistake again.

She hadn't slammed the door on racing because she'd wanted to; she'd had no choice but to push it softly closed. Shaw needed a parent who would focus on her safety, not one who chased down empty hallways.

"Stop," she rasped.

Wes stood and shuffled to where she leaned against the sink. The house was small but blessed with an embarrassment of windows, and pastel light filtered through the kitchen, highlighting the dull linoleum floor. Her dad tipped her chin up, forcing her to make eye contact. "I know you're scared, but Shaw will be safe and happy with me and Billie, and I can run my own damn track for a few weeks. This is the *Indy 500* we're talking about, Mack. You will never, ever forgive yourself if you let this one pass you by. Shaw will be fine, I will be fine, the track will be fine. But if you don't get your ass to Indianapolis . . ." He swallowed, and his voice came back thick and high. "If you don't give the Indy 500 a shot, I worry you'll never be fine again, Spec."

She closed her eyes against the burning tears that came out of nowhere. She worked so hard to hide her boredom and regret from her dad. She chugged through her responsibilities at the track, went to every PTA meeting and school function for Shaw, dutifully took Wes to medical appointments, and she thought she did it all with a smile. She didn't know if she was crying now because he was encouraging her to go or because he knew the truth of her unhappiness.

But of course he did. He knew the truth of *her*, that the wildness wouldn't die no matter how hard she tried.

Of course she'd think about this lost opportunity every day until she died. She'd stayed up half the night replaying her conversation with Janet, obsessing over every word. Maybe she could take this one chance and bury the wildness forever. She could go to Indy, chase checkered flags, and come home and shut the door on racing for good, but this time she'd turn the key in the lock.

"Even if it wouldn't leave you and Shaw in a lurch, you're forgetting that I'd have three weeks to learn how to drive a car I've never driven before," Mack whispered. She was afraid to look at Wes's face.

"Now that," Wes grinned as he lifted her chin, "I ain't gonna worry about. If it's got an engine, you can send it."

TEXTS BETWEEN MACK WILLIAMS AND BILLIE SUMMIT

MACK [4/29, 11:34 a.m.]: hey I forgot to tell u about Dad's inhaler. he should take it anytime he's doing any kind of physical exertion. It's in the basket on the kitchen counter.

MACK [4/29, 11:34 a.m.]: U should probably add that to the list I gave you under PRN meds

BILLIE [4/29, 11:35 a.m.]: Got it! 👍

MACK [4/29, 11:35 a.m.]: he should take it even to the grocery if he's going to walk the aisles.

BILLIE [4/29, 11:36 a.m.]: Okay honey! I'll take good care of everyone ❤️ 😘

BILLIE [4/29, 11:36 a.m.]: Take care of yourself and drive safe! 🏎️

MACK [4/29, 11:37 a.m.]: Did u see instructions on how to refill the Rxs? And for Shaw's allergy med? She won't take the liquid. It has to be the chewable.

BILLIE [4/29, 11:38 a.m.]: Why don't u give me a call ☎️ and we can talk thru it 1 more time. U can make sure I've got it down crystal clear. 💎

TEXTS BETWEEN MACK WILLIAMS AND WES WILLIAMS

Wes [4/29, 12:47 p.m.]: goddammit stop calling billie

Wes [4/29, 12:47 p.m.]: i wiped ur ass and taught u to drive. we're fine here.

CHAPTER 6

3.5 weeks until the Indianapolis 500

Wes always said country was country and city was city, no matter the place, and Mack felt the truth of those words as she stood in the foyer of her sister's downtown Indianapolis condo. The warm oak floors, soft white palette, and wall of windows in her sister's twenty-second-floor condo seemed closer to Manhattan than the wood paneling and shag carpeting in her Haubstadt house. Mack looked down at her feet to make sure her worn sneakers were free of dirt, and toed them off just in case.

"You can come all the way in." Laurie impatiently gestured her inside.

"Your place is nice," Mack said as she studied the home her sister had made. Everything was neutral: A white upholstered chair and white linen couch sat upon a pristine jute rug, beige linen chairs flanked a large whitewashed trestle table, and Mack could see through to the equally colorless kitchen. Shaw could ruin this place in less than thirty seconds.

"Thanks. Are you hungry? Thirsty?" Even in the comfort of her own home, her sister wore a crisp shirtdress and gold jewelry.

"No, I'm good." Mack patted her messy braid, suddenly feeling childish in her ancient Wes Williams #88 airbrushed sweatshirt and cutoff jean shorts. Thirty years old and still Mack felt coarse and plain—too short and too much of the Williams chin—next to her sophisticated older sister. She'd somehow forgotten what a knockout Laurie was, with her dark glossy hair and ridiculously long legs. Once they'd hit puberty, the adults around them couldn't stop pointing out their differences. *My god, Laurie, you could be the next Cindy Crawford! And Mack, you look so much like your dad.*

Their mother died two days after Mack's birth and left no information about the father of her four-year-old daughter, Laurie. Without much thought, Wes brought Mack home, adopted Laurie, and went from a rowdy bachelor to the parent of two young girls overnight. From the start, Laurie was physically the odd person out, tall and warm-toned and beautiful even as a child, where Mack and Wes were short and solid with wild tangles of wavy hair. It wasn't until she was older, and Laurie was long gone, that Mack realized Laurie probably never heard these comments as compliments, only speculation on their parentage.

"God, this is awkward," Laurie said with a tense laugh. "At least get out of the entryway. Are you sure you don't want a drink?"

Without waiting for an answer, Laurie went to the kitchen and began reaching for glasses. Mack perched on a clear stool at the white marble island. Her sister placed a glass of ice water in front of Mack and then poured herself a large glass of red wine. A tender pain of familiarity tugged at her belly that Laurie remembered Mack never drank wine. Then again, she was the only witness to thirteen-year-old Mack's disastrous Boone's Farm incident.

The room was so austere that sounds echoed off the marble, and they both jumped when Mack cleared her throat. "Um . . . thank you. I couldn't have done this without you . . ." Mack gestured vaguely in Laurie's direction instead of finishing with *I can't believe you said yes.*

Laurie took a gulp of her wine before clinking the glass down on the counter. "Geezus, Mack. What were you going to do, come to Indianapolis and not stay with me?"

A thousand different defenses bloomed at Mack's lips but she chose the most honest one. "I didn't know if you'd want me in your space."

"I have never not wanted you in my space." Laurie huffed out a breath and swiped her hand across the counter, searching for imaginary crumbs. "But I couldn't stay in that place."

Mack frowned. They'd mostly lived in a pull-behind trailer attached to the same old Bronco Mack drove today, and the sisters only had each other for company while Wes chased checkered flags across the country. He'd give Laurie a ten-dollar bill and instructions to stay away from strangers, and they'd stuff their bellies full of hot dogs and soda and somehow not get abducted. Laurie made it clear she hated the dirty, noisy tracks but never left Mack's side, always there to fix whatever trouble Mack got herself into. They came home to the house in Haubstadt and attended school just enough for the girls not to get sent to the county truancy office. They'd been happy, Mack thought. She was fourteen when she'd made the podium in Kansas and come home to find Laurie clutching a giant envelope and crying; she'd been accepted to Georgetown. Neither Mack nor Wes had any idea Laurie had such ambitions. She left that summer for college, then stayed gone for the last sixteen years.

"Uh, am I keeping you from anything? You don't have to babysit me. I need to get to bed anyway. Early morning tomorrow."

Laurie twisted her wineglass on the counter. Her short fingernails were perfectly shellacked with neutral polish. She shrugged. "Not really. I'm working on a brief for a senior partner. I should let an associate do it but these recent grads are worthless. I can finish it later."

Her sister had always been smarter than most of the adults they knew. Mack was grateful that racing came to her easily because school had not only been difficult, it had been downright embarrassing next to Laurie's straight A's. "I don't even know what you do, to be honest."

Laurie leaned forward to rest her forearms on the counter, still twisting the wineglass between her fingers. "I'm in mergers and acquisitions. Basically, I help corporations make money and avoid taxes. A keeper of capitalism."

She'd always assumed Laurie loved her job—she used work as her excuse to avoid coming home—but her sister didn't sound very enthusiastic. "But you like being a lawyer?"

Laurie sighed. "Firm culture is extremely competitive and the majority of my clients are spoiled megalomaniacs. Mostly white boomer dudes who've never been told no and still struggle to take a woman's brain seriously. It's intellectually stimulating work but . . ." She shrugged and the silence stretched between them.

"But the money is good." Mack nodded toward the expensive stainless steel appliances. Laurie glanced around as if she'd just noticed them herself.

"It would be even better if I didn't have so many student loans, but it's nothing to sneeze at. They call them golden handcuffs for a reason." Mack's brows rose in surprise. She never once thought about how her sister paid for college and law school, but of course she'd had to take out loans. It wasn't like Wes had any money saved for education. For the first time since Laurie had left, Mack felt sympathy for her, and a little guilt. She'd had to make it on her own without any support, unlike Mack, who'd always had Wes by her side. As if Laurie had heard her thoughts, she drained her wineglass and asked, "How's Dad?"

"Good. Hasn't had a seizure in a few months."

Laurie waggled her fingers in a tell me more motion, and irritation killed Mack's moment of empathy. If Laurie wanted to know about their dad, she could call him herself.

"He's still with Billie?" Laurie prompted. "She seems sweet. Texts me pictures of Wes and Shaw."

Mack pulled a face.

"You don't like her because . . . ?"

It was annoying how well her sister could read her, especially because Mack didn't know a damn thing about Laurie anymore. She hated that Laurie could turn her into a petulant younger sister in less than ten minutes. "Her perfume is aggressively floral. She makes something called 'maca powder pancakes' that taste like sawdust. She owns an alarming number of robes with feathers. Obnoxiously cheerful. So not Dad's type."

"His usual type is there for one night only."

Mack huffed but couldn't find the right words. She didn't know how to say that with Billie always around, Mack felt lonelier than ever in her own house. So she went for common ground.

"Yeah, well, you're not there to see them drool over each other. Dad practically pants when she's around."

"Ugh. Wes is pathetic around women."

They shared a smile, and then an awkward silence filled the kitchen, neither of them good at pointless chitchat. In the quiet, Mack thought about Shaw. It had been unnervingly simple to scrape together a plan for the next few weeks. Mack may not buy into Billie's long-term commitment, but even she could admit that her daughter would be safe and well cared for, and Shaw seemed more excited to ride to school in Billie's convertible than sad about her mother's departure. Mack spent two days prepaying bills, making event schedules and extra keys, and reminding her dad where they stored spare parts. In the end, the ease with which she left her life behind scared her.

"How are you feeling about it?" Laurie asked after she'd washed, dried, and put away both of their glasses.

Still thinking about her daughter, Mack said, "Leaving home was hard. I can't believe I left Shaw. And Dad. And if—"

"Shaw and Dad will be fine," Laurie interrupted. "It's about time you got out of Haubstadt anyway."

Mack rolled her eyes. Laurie was such a snob, always making snide comments about Mack's small-town life. Just because she hadn't run off to a big city didn't mean her life wasn't *real.*

"How would you know anything about what my dad and daughter need?" Mack snapped.

Laurie's olive cheeks flushed, and she straightened the already perfect alignment of dish soap, hand soap, and scrub brush by the sink.

Instantly, Mack felt guilty. Hadn't she spent her whole life convincing Laurie that Wes was *their* dad? That DNA didn't matter; it mattered who had raised them? Her sister could be an elitist but Mack truly believed Laurie was her full sister in every sense of the word. So why did Laurie always bring out the worst in her?

"I'm sorry—"

"Well, you're here now so best to focus on that," Laurie said, her face implacable. "What's the plan for tomorrow?" Behind her, the fading afternoon light flooded the kitchen and reflected off the shiny surfaces.

Ashamed, Mack let Laurie make the pivot. "Tomorrow I go to the shop and get fitted for a seat, learn the basics of the car controls, and meet the team. Friday, I try out the car at the Speedway. If it goes well, I can do my rookie test the same day. If I pass . . ." She trailed off, not willing to let herself imagine the moment when she received a special license to qualify and run the Indy 500. "A week of learning the car on a simulator and trying to find a sponsor, then four days of practice before qualification starts."

The achievement of a lifetime, all boiled down to a handful of days in the car.

Laurie reached out and squeezed Mack's hand. She was embarrassed by how much she wanted the physical contact to continue. Other than a hug from Shaw, Mack couldn't remember the last time anyone touched her. She'd grown used to being lonely but her body had not.

Mack's inner child wanted to keep hold of Laurie's hand and confess the cluster of emotions bouncing through her mind: nervousness, impostor syndrome, hope. But it was the last one that terrified Adult Mack.

Her own yearning was shameful. The minute Janet put that crisp card in her hand, Mack's own hands throbbed with desire for a tight steering wheel and a twin turbo V-6 at her back. She shouldn't want that. She should care about what she was doing to her daughter, her father, her family business. She wasn't only nervous about learning the car and making the race—she was terrified she'd fall in love with it and forget the little girl who waited at home for her, forget the father who'd given her everything. She was scared shitless by how very much she wanted the Indy 500, afraid of what she'd do once she got a taste of the life she'd missed out on.

She was afraid she'd want to stay.

Years ago, she might have told Laurie all those things, but now she pulled back her hand.

TEXTS FROM WES WILLIAMS TO MACK WILLIAMS

WES [5/1, 8:51 a.m.]: want u 2 know how proud I am.

WES [5/1, 8:51 a.m.]: don't overthink it. full send, throttle on the floor, like you always do.

CHAPTER 7

3 weeks until the Indianapolis 500

Mack pulled her gear bag from the battered Bronco and looked up at the towering glass building in front of her, the iconic Indianapolis Motor Speedway Pagoda. The ten-story glass and steel building was a far cry from the single-story wooden grandstand at Haubstadt, and Mack felt like Dorothy in *The Wizard of Oz*, suddenly lifted from her grayscale life and dropped into a Technicolor dream world. Dorothy spent her time in Oz trying to find her way home, but as Mack took in the enormity of the Speedway—not so different from Oz, really, with its bright colors and magnitude—thoughts of home quickly faded.

"You get the helmet?" Janet said by way of greeting. Generously, Janet paid in advance for Mack to have a new helmet fitted since her own was painfully outdated, without the connection points for a water straw or cooling hose. Many drivers put elaborate designs on their helmets, but Mack asked only for a bright blue helmet with her initials and the number of the car she'd be driving, the same style she'd used throughout her career.

Mack held up her bulging bag. "Thank you."

Without another word, Janet turned and headed toward the long, low rows of garages known as Gasoline Alley. The sharp tang of renewable ethanol fuel seared Mack's nostrils and she allowed herself to stop for a moment and breathe in the cool, acrid air. She'd once been an insider in this sport, walking through tracks and taking for granted the joy of being part of something she loved so much. She inhaled and let herself feel the honor of being one of the few drivers to walk this infield.

The weather was cold but clear, every driver's dream, and a charged stillness pervaded the infield. IMS was the largest sporting venue in the world, with 250,000 seats surrounding the two-and-a-half-mile oval track. Inside the giant asphalt loop were a museum, a golf course, a regulation dirt track, a concert venue, the pagoda-shaped media and control tower, multiple parking areas, and over one hundred garage bays. Come race day, the track would be teeming with almost a half million people and the chaotic energy of spectators, teams, sponsors, officials, and drivers, but today it was empty but for the JJR team.

Mack's back pebbled with goose bumps as she took in the three long, low concrete buildings that stretched farther than she could see, each with a bold black number painted over the garage door. From this angle, Gasoline Alley appeared to stretch on without end. Janet strode silently in front of her, and as Mack watched her boss march forward, she remembered the old racing superstition that women in the garage area were bad luck. Only fifty-five years had passed since the first woman was allowed in Gasoline Alley, and Janet raced here not long after, when men still routinely spat on and shouted death threats at any woman who dared walk on this grease-stained concrete.

It was a prejudice many young women imagined as long past, but Mack knew that if she qualified she would be only the tenth woman to start this race in one hundred years.

"You actually read all that lawyer paperwork?" Janet asked over her shoulder.

Mack nodded in acknowledgment of the massive deck of information Janet overnighted to her house. Background information on the team, insurance riders, waivers of liability, and Mack's contract with JJR. With no time or money to find an agent and desperate for the chance, Mack signed it all. Last night, she'd warily asked Laurie to read it over, and to her surprise, her sister examined the contract and explained it in regular words without making Mack feel stupid. Her translation: Mack was at Janet's mercy.

"So you understand that our main sponsor, Hartley, is supporting a share of both cars, but the eleven machine is still blank," Janet said, using the practice of referring to a car by its assigned number. "You're responsible for securing additional funding for your ride. If you can't cover the final cost of running the car, you'll owe me. Any additional income you want from this opportunity, you'll have to find through sponsorship."

Mack's throat tightened at the reminder of the risk she was taking. Not only was she not making any money on this endeavor, she could potentially put herself deeply in debt if she couldn't find sponsorship. A single car for the Indy 500 cost upward of $1 million, and Janet was only providing the physical car. Mack needed to raise six figures alone to support the cost of her team members and supplies. She was too scared to ask Laurie if she was putting the family business at risk, and she couldn't even begin to think of the consequences for Shaw if Mack brought a load of debt on their heads. It had been so long since she'd courted sponsors, and back then she'd had it easy, coasting on her youthful success and, admittedly, Wes's reputation.

Janet pursed her lips, seemingly reading Mack's mind. "Kissing ass for cash is hell on earth, but the Indy 500 is worth it. You working on sponsorships?"

Mack hummed a nonanswer. She saw no point asking for money until she passed the rookie test.

"Well then, here we are." Janet stopped at an open garage and Mack gasped at the work of art in front of her. The shiny machine looked more like a spaceship than a race car. A long, narrow nose cone flared into a sleek, low body, topped by a cockpit-like capsule where the driver sat, and thin bilateral wings bookended the front and back of the vehicle. The low-slung car measured only three feet high but stretched almost seventeen feet long. Mack could smell the fresh rubber of the wide tires even twenty feet away.

Janet placed her thumb and index finger on her lower lip, filling the garage with a shrill whistle. “Some of you met Mack Williams at the seat fitting yesterday. The rest of y’all come say hi to our new driver.”

Mack recognized a few faces from the previous day’s visit to the JJR team garage for a seat fitting—a laborious process involving sitting in a puddle of poured foam to create a custom fit—and a crash course on the controls and features of the race car. Mack greeted the other team members and tried to memorize their names.

She did not need to memorize the name of the man smiling at her from the front of the garage. Leo Raisman was the star driver of JJR and one of the most popular drivers in IndyCar. His laid-back California attitude, charming yet self-deprecating YouTube channel, stint on a reality TV dancing competition, and a near-win at last year’s race vaulted him from niche sports star to national fame. On track, he was a captivating combination of steady yet aggressive, and he’d racked up enough wins to take tiny JJR from obscurity to a competitive threat. He was Shaw’s favorite driver and for good reason: Leo Raisman was an all-American star.

He was also alarmingly good-looking in person.

Dark hair brushed his shoulders in loose curls and several days of beard shadowed his suntanned face. Leo lazily chewed a piece of gum while studying her a little too long, like he was trying to keep his eyes on her face but couldn’t stop himself from flicking his eyes down to take in all of her, her compact frame and tight jeans and the freckles across her cheeks. His perusal didn’t make her uncomfortable, but she fought the urge to fidget anyway.

“Hey, Rookie,” he said, grinning. He had tan lines at the corners of his eyes, like he spent a lot of time squinting in the sun. She would *not* think about how he looked like a model for a sporting brand, or how his joggers and team polo fit *juuust* right. Her focus here was the Indy 500, not Leo Raisman.

She straightened her spine. “I may be a rookie, but you’ll be chasing me down the track.”

Leo threw his head back and laughed with abandon. His teeth weren't perfectly straight and Mack was annoyed that it worked in his favor. "I look forward to it." He held out a hand. "Leo Raisman."

His hand was warm and calloused, how Mack liked a man to feel. *Nope, nope, nope.* She did not date men who raced. Ever. She would not let his unusually dark eyes make her forget that hard-earned personal rule.

She dropped his hand and rolled her eyes. "I know who you are."

He nodded. "Likewise. Sick win at Perris a few years back. I saw that one from the stands."

Mack blinked in surprise. She'd won at the California track eleven or twelve years ago.

"Moving on," Janet said as she flicked her fingers dismissively in Leo's direction, but her tone held obvious affection. Mack was grateful for her intervention. She needed to focus on what was important, and Leo Raisman wasn't it. She turned so she couldn't see him and gave Janet her full attention. "Lucie and Jimmy are JJR's engineers. Lucie is with Leo, and Jimmy will call strategy on the eleven car. On race day, he's the voice in your earpiece and he makes decisions about fuel strategy, tires, pit stops, and the like."

Jimmy, a stocky Black man in his sixties, gave Mack's hand a perfunctory pump before returning to the rows of computers at the back of the garage. Mack took no offense; she knew she had to earn respect from her team. Nothing in racing was given, and even drivers with deep pockets had to prove themselves on the track.

Janet pointed to the restroom outside the garage bay. "You may be in the big leagues now but the locker room situation is the same. Get changed and the crew will tow the car out. I'll wait for you."

Women were still an anomaly in racing and most tracks had little incentive to add separate locker rooms. Mack had changed in countless bathroom stalls, and in this one she quickly stripped and replaced her clothing with fireproof everything—underwear, tight-fitting long-sleeve top, and borrowed fireproof coveralls. She'd brought her own worn racing boots, and she couldn't decide if she felt embarrassed or proud of the rusty dirt stains.

Mack exited the bathroom in time to follow the team toward pit lane. Premier race cars were towed from the garage to the track, both because it was important to conserve every drop of fuel on race day, but also because firing up a turbo-charged engine inside an enclosed space could burst eardrums. Janet and Leo chatted easily ahead of her, but Mack lagged behind, too anxious for chatter. Today of all days, she did not need distractions, and Leo Raisman was definitely a distraction.

Instead, she focused on every detail of the moment: the hard concrete under her soft-soled boots, the chilly spring breeze in her face, the crackling sound of the rubber tires on pavement. There was a time in her life when she'd used this exact moment as a visualization technique for success, an image she'd used to motivate herself to work toward her goal of racing at Indianapolis Motor Speedway. In her dreams, she'd walked confidently down Gasoline Alley, but now she had to grip her helmet tightly to hide the shaking of her hands.

God, she wished Wes were here to see this. He'd know exactly what she was feeling, what it meant to stroll down the same pit lane as her heroes, what it meant to be here after she'd thought she'd lost her chance. He'd know how to calm her, how to say the right thing to wipe away distractions. She bit her lip, letting the pain confirm that it was real, that she was really about to drive an IndyCar. She looked all around her, at the enormous metal grandstands, the scoring pylon that jutted almost a hundred feet into the air, the colorful flags that bordered the exterior of the track.

The sight of those signal flags flapping in the breeze brought back a long-buried habit. *Ray Harroun. Joe Dawson. Jules Goux . . .*

She hadn't recited the list for almost a decade, but superstition won out over pride.

Johnnie Parsons. Lee Wallard. Troy Ruttman. Bill Vukovich . . .

She said the names of the former Indy 500 winners, still remembering each one in order.

Mario Andretti. Al Unser, twice in a row. Mark Donohue . . .

The exercise settled her breathing like it always had. She finished the list, naming last year's winner as the crisp air ruffled her hair, and she felt a fizzle move through her blood. She used to feel this way before every race: electric with energy, full of her own potential, certain she belonged, exhilarated by the challenge. Only now, anxiety mingled with excitement. If she couldn't handle the car today, her Indy 500 chance would be over before it even started.

Muscle memory took over, even while her nerves jangled. She wove her long hair into a quick braid and stuffed the end down the back of her coveralls. Her pulse reverberated in her ears as she inserted earplugs, pulled her fireproof balaclava over her head, eased on the new helmet, and wiggled it into place. Silently, Jimmy helped Mack connect the awkward HANS device, the head and neck restraint that prevented fatal spinal cord injury, and Mack pulled on her gloves. They were new, and she flexed her fingers against the stiff fabric. Beneath her fire suit, Mack's body erupted in a fine layer of moisture. She would be drenched after a few laps, but she hoped Janet didn't see her sweating like a rookie before she even took a turn.

The helmet muffled sound, and Mack belatedly realized there were two people in suits walking toward her. Janet watched them, hands on hips and scowl on her face. The man looked nondescript—suit, tie, glasses—but the woman was effortlessly stunning in a light gray suit and black pointed-toe pumps. As she came closer, the woman removed oversize sunglasses and tucked them into her hair.

The woman was her sister.

CHAPTER 8

3 weeks until the Indianapolis 500

"Sorry!" Laurie huffed as she came within a few feet of Mack and the crew. "I tried to get here earlier, but security thinks I'm suspicious." She glared at the man next to her and pointed at Mack. "See? That driver is my sister. A woman. On track. Like I told you."

Janet gave an irritated wave in the direction of the security guy, and he turned and walked back toward the pavilion without a word. Mack's heart bounced between embarrassment and elation, and embarrassment at her elation. She could count on one hand the number of times she'd seen her sister in the last sixteen years, but now Laurie was here on the biggest day of Mack's life.

"What's wrong?"

For her sister to show up randomly, something had to be catastrophically wrong. She hadn't showed up when Mack was feeding Wes through a straw, or when Shaw's colicky cries were so intense that Mack wouldn't pick her up for fear of shaking her.

Laurie scowled as she pulled out a tissue to dab at the tiny beads of sweat on her forehead. "You think I'd miss this? I left a pathologically needy associate in charge of a deposition, but I'm here." Laurie shifted in her four-inch heels and glanced quickly at the half dozen crew standing around the car, watching her. She motioned at the concrete pit wall. "I'll . . . tuck back here. Out of the way." She looked pointedly at Mack. "But I'm here."

Mack was grateful her helmet smushed her face too much to reveal her emotions. Her earliest memories in a race car involved Wes, but also Laurie. How had she forgotten that her sister was woven into the very core of her racing life? Just seeing her now caused tears to build behind her eyes.

No crying, she reminded herself. *Women don't get to cry here.*

"Williams, focus." Janet's tone was tight. "Feel that breeze? Seems small but you'll feel it like hell in turn two. Ease out there and get a feel for the car. We have plenty of fuel and tires for today. I'd rather see you take it slow than slam the car into the wall. Keep the throttle where you're comfortable, I don't give a shit if it's one-thirty or one-eighty. The first pass is about getting comfortable in the car. We won't start the rookie test until you're ready."

Nerves fizzing, Mack nodded.

"Make sure the seat feels good before you take off. Jimmy and the boys built a special extender for the pedals to accommodate your height." Mack was grateful; at IndyCar speeds, even the smallest discomfort could be debilitating.

Again, Mack nodded, a growing sense of disquiet building inside her.

"The back end is going to swing out hard when you first accelerate, and I mean hard."

Another nod. Did Janet expect her to screw this up?

"And the—"

"Damn, Janet, let the girl try it for herself. You picked her, now you gotta trust her." Jimmy's voice sounded surprisingly low and soothing, like Peter Coyote.

"Yeah, yeah, tell me that when you've put your own money on the line."

From the wall, Laurie called out, "Go fast! Be safe!"

Since her very first race, it was the last thing Laurie said to Mack before she buckled in, and she hadn't even known she needed to hear those words today. For her early races, Laurie had always been right there at her side, and now Laurie was here, and *here* was the Indianapolis Motor Speedway. Mack tried not to give in to nerves but her chest clenched with something dangerously close to panic.

Jimmy gestured toward the cockpit and held out a hand to help Mack over the high, clear safety shield, known as the aeroscreen. The step distance from the ground over the screen was much longer than Mack's legs but she was all too aware of the crew—and Leo Raisman—watching her, so she shrugged off Jimmy's offer of help and gripped the side of the titanium and polycarbonate windshield. She lifted her right leg but her foot only made it halfway up the screen. She hopped on her left foot and stretched her right leg farther but got no closer to clearing the lip of the cockpit.

Behind her, Jimmy cleared his throat.

"You can use the sidepod as a step. You're light enough, it won't hurt."

Gingerly, Mack stepped on the wide flange at the side of the car and slid down until her rear settled inches from the ground. The cockpit was extremely narrow and tight, so much tighter than the open cage of a sprint car. Her arms could expand no farther than the width of her own body, the close sides of the car squeezed her hips, and foam safety panels lightly pressed down on her shoulders. Even more disorienting was the reclined forty-five-degree angle of the seat, making her momentarily feel as if she couldn't see out of the car. Panic took over her body and she fought the urge to flail like a wild animal.

Fear had absolutely no place inside the car. The day a driver succumbed to fear was the day they should retire. Fear created mistakes, and at two hundred and thirty miles per hour, mistakes could be deadly. But Mack couldn't deny what she felt in that moment was sheer terror.

She felt gentle pressure on her shoulder and looked up to see Leo. He held her eyes for a long moment, and she worried he could see the stress on her face. But he calmly pointed at the steering wheel—a compact oval that comically resembled a video game controller with multiple buttons, dials, and two paddle shifters—and started rattling off the functions as another crew member helped buckle the four-point harness. Leo cracked jokes along the way, gently teasing the crew for the nonsensical layout of control buttons and telling her a silly story about how he couldn't figure out the built-in drinking straw for his first two races.

"You got this, Rookie. Only thing you really need to remember is to never turn right." He winked, actually winked, and Mack rolled her eyes at the tired joke. It wasn't until Leo had given her a fist bump and walked away that she realized he'd distracted her from her panic.

Jimmy gave her a quick thumbs-up before slapping her helmet with two quick taps. "Radio check. You hear me okay?"

Before Mack could answer, Janet said, "Show me that I'm not stupid, Rookie."

"Heard that loud and clear," Mack answered.

A crew member started the engine and the machine growled to life all around Mack. The bassy rumble was a living thing: She could feel the vibration deep in her body and her ears flooded with the low moan of the engine. The car was pure energy, designed for the singular purpose of going as fast as humans could manage. Mack's lizard brain briefly took over—*It's been too long, I can't see, what if I wreck on my first try?*—and she ruthlessly shoved the thoughts away.

She wasn't scared of the car; she was scared of failing and losing this last chance at Indy.

She flipped down her visor and thought again of Wes. She'd told him not to come today, wanting to keep both of their expectations in check, but now she wished she could share the moment with him. If Wes hadn't discovered Janet's business card, Mack might not be sitting in this race car getting ready to take her first laps on the track that had haunted her dreams. From her first race, he'd been right there when she closed her visor and there again when she flipped it back up. It felt wrong that her dad wouldn't see her first—possibly only—laps at Indy.

A crew member swept his arm in the universal release signal, and Mack's brain simultaneously flipped into go-mode, a bolt of energy zipping up her spine as her right foot slammed the accelerator. She peeled out exactly as Janet warned her not to do, swinging the back end of the high-strung car in a wide arc and screeching the tires. *Shit.* The throttle was more sensitive than anything she'd ever experienced.

She caught the fishtail and steered the car off pit row and out onto the track. Cool air reduced friction between the tires and asphalt, so Mack took her time bringing the car up to speed even though her foot itched to slam down. She'd be damned if she shamed herself by slapping the wall on the first lap. She steered onto the warm-up apron, a small lane below the main racetrack that kept slower traffic safely away from at-speed cars, then out onto the main track. Above her, the empty grandstands towered over the track, casting laddered shadows on the pavement. It was eerily silent, only the sound of the engine and wind filling her ears, but she'd heard part of the magic of the Indy 500 was driving through the sensory onslaught of hundreds of thousands of people cheering in surround sound.

For a split second, she let herself feel the magnitude of what she was doing, feel the awe and honor of driving at the Indianapolis Motor Speedway, to imagine the fans on race day. And then she tucked her sense of wonder away and got to work.

She left the short chute and eased into the sharp ninety-degree bend of turn two, the most notorious of all corners at this track. She exhaled in relief as she left the turn and headed down the long, straight backstretch. IndyCars had no power steering, and her arms already ached from forcing the wheel to turn. She pushed the accelerator down the backstretch, gaining a little more speed before downshifting into turns three and four. In less than a minute, she crossed over the famous yard of bricks and completed her first lap at Indianapolis Motor Speedway.

"How's it feel?"

Mack jumped at Jimmy's gravelly voice, unused to radio communication while driving. She was used to being isolated in the car. "Spirited," she said into the microphone of her helmet.

Slowly Mack built speed, and with it, confidence. This car was as different from a sprint midget as the creek near her house was to the

Ohio River, but cars intuitively made sense to her in a way that nothing else ever had. Traditional learning had been a frustrating slog, full of tears and book throwing. Now that she had a school-age child, Mack suspected she had some form of dyslexia, but in her teens she'd thought she was stupid. Every time Shaw asked a question—*Why do we eat pigs if they're really smart? Why does that sign say Black Lives Matter?*—Mack wondered if she fumbled the answer and screwed Shaw up for life. She was an impatient, imperfect nurse to Wes, she hated housework and cooking, and she worried that Shaw would only remember her exhaustion and short temper. Even running the family dirt track confused her because she didn't understand why she was bored doing something she should love. Everything else in her life was full of confusing contradictions.

But this, *this*, she knew.

From an early age, she could drive anything: raw sprints, nimble go-karts, heavy stocks, and finicky sports cars. The best drivers had a unique skill, a little something that allowed them to step above the field, and Mack's was versatility. She could figure out a new car twice as fast as most drivers, and IndyCar was no exception. Only a few dozen laps and she was zooming into the two hundred miles per hour range. She slipped, almost spun, but even then her body hummed with euphoria as she wrestled the car around the track. Nothing in her life had ever felt as good as wind in her face and an engine at her back.

How would she walk away from this moment and ever think that anything else was enough?

From: HollisWhitfield@hartley.com
To: Janet@JanetJoynerRacing.com
Subject: Promos [May 1, 3:33 p.m.]

Let's hold on promo materials for Mack Williams. I want to see better metrics before additional engagement.

Hollis O. Whitfield
VP of Marketing
Hartley Harvester Manufacturing, Inc.
A Fortune 500 Company

CHAPTER 9

3 weeks until the Indianapolis 500

Two hours later, the sun cast a golden halo behind the Pagoda as an official signed off on Mack's rookie test, a grueling sequence of increasing stints at increasing speeds, ending with laps at over two hundred fifteen miles per hour. In the car, she'd been too focused on the work to process what she was accomplishing, but now Mack sat on the low wall of pit lane in her sweat-soaked coveralls, holding her helmet between her legs and blinking back tears.

Don't be the girl that cries.

When she'd watched the Indy 500 on television last May, she had to turn away for a second, choked with regret that she'd never get to race at Indianapolis. She'd watched other drivers cross the start-finish line and felt a jealous pain that made her hate herself. Now, a year later and despite all improbability, she would be vying for a spot on the grid.

Indianapolis was so much more than a sports arena. It was grit and passion and endurance amplified, the spirit of hundreds of drivers who'd attempted to win the world's biggest race. It was over one hundred years of history, each race day tradition honored and beloved by devoted fans. It was her own history too, the memory of attending races with Wes and Laurie, and the dreams she'd birthed in these very grandstands.

She was so busy keeping her own feelings in check, she'd forgotten Laurie perched next to her on the concrete wall until she heard a sniffle. Oversize sunglasses covered most of her sister's face. Mack didn't know much about fashion, but she knew the interlocking pearl *C*s on the side of Laurie's sunglasses meant they were worth a month of rent. Laurie laced her fingers through Mack's and squeezed. Her nose looked suspiciously red. "I bet you wish Dad was here."

No longer able to contain her dammed emotions, Mack dropped her head back to stop the tears from running down her face. Good god, did she wish Wes was here. She could imagine what he'd say: *Stop crying and get celebrating!*

"Hope you have plans to celebrate tonight, Rookie. You cooked it out there."

Mack snapped her head up, the moisture in her eyes disappearing instantly at the sight of Leo Raisman and his perfectly imperfect smile. Was he a fucking mind reader or had she said that out loud?

"Welcome to the month of May." Leo laughed and the sound bounced off the empty venue before the vastness of the area swallowed the noise. "Rest and hydrate tonight. Monday, we start Body Work."

Mack blinked.

"Pardon?" Laurie said crisply.

A charming little blush crawled up Leo's neck, but he covered it with an easy laugh. "Body Work is a gym, with specialized exercises for drivers. Janet has us go three days a week. And we'll race on the simulator as often as possible, lots of promo stuff for the series, events with our main sponsor."

"Sounds like a lot of time together," Laurie said. Mack hoped Leo didn't hear the warning in her voice.

Mack shot Laurie a look that told her she could take care of herself. "Can't wait," she said to Leo.

"It's nice to finally have a teammate. See you tomorrow, Rookie." She watched him walk away, joggers hugging all the places they should, feeling like a total creep perving on her teammate.

"Stop," she warned before Laurie could say anything. Laurie had been giving her that same side-eye since they were kids, the one that said, *you know this is a bad decision, right?*

Mack grabbed her helmet and stood up, but the inevitable adrenaline crash slammed into her and she suddenly felt hot and cold at the same time. Afraid she'd vomit or pass out or both, she clawed at the Velcro closure on her fire suit. The cool air soothed the worst of the nausea, and Mack let the sleeves dangle at her waist as they walked to the parking area. By the time they reached the rusty Bronco, Mack felt steady enough to balance on one foot while peeling off her coveralls and pulling on athletic shorts. If they wouldn't give her a locker room, they could deal with a parking lot strip show.

Laurie swept an arm toward the rust-speckled car door. "I'll drive. Hop in, passenger princess."

They drove east down Sixteenth Street as the sun finally settled below the horizon. Central Indiana got a lot of shade for being so flat, but Mack thought the endless horizon was beautiful in its own way, with wide-open views that made anything feel possible. The sky gleamed purple and majestic through the windshield, and as her nausea faded, Mack finally let herself smile as she replayed the test drive and thought about the days to come.

"I guess I have to get serious about sponsorship now."

"About that," Laurie said, sitting up straighter. "I started playing around with a slide deck. We'll need to get numbers on JJR's ROI and potential hits per view. I think your best move is to target women-centered companies—"

"I can do it," Mack interrupted.

"Yes, yes, you don't need me, you're strong and tough and don't need help," Laurie snapped.

"Because you're always right there offering?" How dare she act like the martyr when Mack had been drowning for the past ten years without so much as a paddle from her sister.

"Oh my god, we are not having this argument!" Laurie banged her palm on the steering wheel in an uncharacteristic show of temper. Mack and Wes ran hot, mouthy and quick to react, but Laurie was eerily icy. She once caught Mack reading her diary, and instead of blowing up, she'd silently removed the journal from Mack's hands and doused the book in the shower. Laurie settled her shoulders. "I was shitty when I left home. I know that. I left you alone to deal with Dad and I regret it. So much." Laurie's voice wobbled and Mack could hardly hear her over the wind. "I can't change the past, Mack, but I'm here now and I want to help. Please."

They drove silently as the city scrolled outside the windows, hospitals and high-rises and tidy rows of houses with green lawns. It was the *please* that killed her. In all the years they'd been apart, during all their battling and bickering, it never occurred to Mack that their separation might hurt Laurie, too. Laurie left first, but had Mack ever let her sister back in?

"Because I have lots of ideas," Laurie pushed on. "Think of what Pippa Mann did with the Komen Foundation, or Lyn St. James with JCPenney. We need to look at companies that specialize in skincare, athleisure, organization, home goods. Period vitamins or a coffee chain, anything targeted at women. But nothing icky like weight loss tea or waist trainers."

"I don't use any of those things."

"Of course you don't." Laurie groaned. "Don't worry about the brands. They'll give you free stuff, show you how to use it, and tell you how to post it on social media."

"I don't have any social media."

"I'll set it up and manage your accounts." Laurie waved dismissively. "The point is that no current drivers target women-centered businesses, but women have always been race fans and continue to be a growing sector of spectators. Evidence shows women are more likely to align with brands supported by their favorite athletes. There's a huge market space available."

"I need to make sure we don't overlap with any of Leo's sponsors."

"Got it." Laurie peeked a glance at Mack, that same sideways warning. "Speaking of Leo . . . if I remember correctly, he's your type? Tall, good hair, drives fast . . ."

Mack shot Laurie a scathing look. "I don't date race car drivers. Or anyone. I'm a swipe-right-on-a-stranger type of woman."

"With a condom, I hope?"

"And a goddamn IUD firmly in place."

"So," Laurie said, arching her perfectly laminated brows over the top of her sunglasses. "You're Wes."

"There's no time for a relationship when you have a family and a business to take care of. I scratch the itch, then go home."

"That sounds lonely." Laurie slammed the ancient brakes as a railroad crossing arm lowered over Indiana Street. They both jerked forward with the force of the sudden stop. Laurie turned to face her sister, but Mack stared at the train as if she were driving the damn thing herself. "Have you ever even been in a relationship?"

The soft sympathy in Laurie's voice irritated the hell out of Mack. How dare Laurie judge her for the choices she'd made? Laurie had no idea how often Mack was barely treading water, swimming from one crisis to another. "Nope. You?"

"A few." Laurie swiped at the coat of dust on the dashboard. Her hand came away covered in thick copper dirt, and Mack dug in the glove box for a napkin. "Nothing that lasted."

"That sounds lonely," Mack mocked. The glare Laurie shot across the cab was so familiar that Mack saw the ghost of the teenager her sister had once been, could almost imagine Laurie was angry because Mack used her tube of Revlon Fire and Ice to mark tires.

"Relationships aside . . . you wouldn't do anything stupid like start something with Leo, right? Because you won't get a chance like this again."

The words pressed down on Mack more than the g-forces she'd weathered on track. Mack knew Laurie judged her for taking up with Kelley and getting pregnant. She'd made it clear since that first phone call when Mack told her sister about the two blue lines on the pee stick. She'd even loaned Mack the money to get an abortion in Illinois and had refused to take it back when the clinic turned Mack away for being three days past the legal cutoff. In a mortifying moment, Mack had sobbed on the phone to her older sister about how she hadn't known she was pregnant. They'd used protection, every time, and she'd had no idea until it was too late. She'd confessed to her sister that she didn't want to have a kid, she wanted to race. *Please, Laurie, fix it, please fix it, please,* she'd begged. Laurie had listened in stony silence. They'd never spoken about it again.

Graffiti-covered boxcars lumbered across the tracks in front of them. Mack felt the grubbiness of her skin and badly wanted to wash away the dried sweat and tiny rubber particles. A certain truth about life in Indiana was that a train would come whenever you were desperate to be on the other side of the tracks. Mack closed her eyes and rubbed her gritty eyelids. As much as she wanted to say something mean and sharp to hurt Laurie right back, there was truth in her sister's words.

Mack couldn't afford to lose racing over a man. Again. Even if she'd be spending a lot of time with Leo Raisman's dark-lashed doe eyes. She could still picture him holding her gaze while she panicked in the cockpit.

"I know better now," she said, humiliated.

The crossing arm lifted and Laurie slowly accelerated, as if she knew the bumps of the track would further unsettle Mack's stomach. They rode in silence as Laurie turned right on Meridian Street. Ahead, the Soldiers & Sailors Monument peeked over the surrounding buildings, the wings of the bronze figure of Victory at the top glowing with the final rays of the setting sun. The defining feature of the Indianapolis skyline, the monument reminded Mack of where she was. Reminded her to keep her head screwed on right and remember why she was here. For the Indy 500, nothing else.

TEXTS BETWEEN BILLIE SUMMIT AND MACK WILLIAMS

BILLIE [5/3, 8:14 p.m.]: check out the pic—everyone loved my lentil burgers with vegan sriracha mayo! 🍔❤️🔥

MACK [5/3, 8:14 p.m.]: wow, really? can't believe dad and shaw ate that. is she still awake? i'll call to say goodnight.

BILLIE [5/3, 8:15 p.m.]: no, poor thing fell asleep during family movie time! 😴. Yard work wore her out! She's been asleep for over an hour.

MACK [5/3, 8:15 p.m.]: yard work?

BILLIE [5/3, 8:16 p.m.]: a little spring fresh up! I'll send pic when the knock out roses bloom. 🌹

BILLIE [5/3, 8:18 p.m.]: P.S. I looked online but can't find any Mack Williams fan swag! Do you have any t-shirts or banners?????

CHAPTER 10

3 weeks until the Indianapolis 500

Light barely broke the horizon when Mack walked into Body Work. It smelled like a standard gym, disinfectant and stale socks, and even looked like a regular gym, but the exercises were uniquely designed to support race car drivers. Most people assumed that driving a race car was physically undemanding, but staying in control of a seven-hundred-horsepower engine embedded in a carbon fiber frame required strength, focus, stamina, and extraordinary reaction time.

Mack wasn't afraid of the workout, but she was unsettled by what she saw near the bank of cubbies at the back of the gym. Or rather, *who*. Leo Raisman stood talking with two other drivers, both famous enough that any American race fan would recognize them, and they were all looking at her. Mack smoothed a hand down her cutoff sweatshirt and snagged leggings and tried not to show her self-consciousness.

"Williams, you made it! Come meet the slowest guys on track." Leo waved her over, way too chipper for five in the morning. Morning people were the worst.

Jericho Blair, or Jericho Junior as everyone called him, needed no introduction. The spitting image of his father, a Scottish Formula One legend who died racing the Nürburgring shortly after Jericho Junior's birth, he won last year's Indy 500, edging out Leo by half a car length. The crowd had gone positively mad celebrating the win of a beloved son. The shorter, stockier man was Boomer Compton, the son of yet another racing legend, quietly chasing down his father's championship records.

The three men glanced from Mack to each other, and she braced for a barrage of either sexist bullshit or coded questions about her inexperience.

"Okay, I gotta ask," Leo said, eyes sparkling. "Your dad is Wes Williams, right?"

Mack blinked in surprise. "The one and only."

"Ho-lee shit!" Jericho hooted. "A damn legend!"

"Trust me, he knows it." Mack rolled her eyes as she tightened her ponytail. A palpable energy filled the gym as more people rolled in. She recognized a JJR crew member and the logos of several other teams.

"I met him once in Charlotte," Boomer said. "After he won the Outlaws Showdown. 2002, maybe? I was a kid and he was so cool. Tried to give me a beer."

"Sounds like Wes. It was 2003, I think," Mack said. "He hated that place. So hard to pass on the outside."

Leo frowned thoughtfully. "Is he still racing?"

Mack hesitated, protective of Wes's privacy. Someone as vibrant as her dad wanted to be remembered for winning races, not living in a La-Z-Boy. "He retired awhile back."

"Well," Jericho said, "nice to meet a fellow kid of a legend. Heavy is the head, and all that."

Mack pointed at the giant Indy 500 winner's ring on his hand. "Pretty sure you're making out okay with your crown."

"Okay, people!" Behind them, a Black woman with chiseled biceps clapped her hands. "This is not social hour. Get warmed up and then rotate stations. Go!" The trainer pointed to Mack and Leo. "Y'all team up. Start with treadmill sprints. Don't cheat, Raisman."

A row of treadmills lined the back wall, and they hopped onto adjoining machines. Leo began to run at a sedate pace. "Bertie is by far the hardest trainer. So much running." Mack grinned and pushed up her speed, and she had to admit she liked the admiration in Leo's eyes. She pushed the speed up again.

Leo groaned but pushed his treadmill one increment higher. Mack clicked her toggle even higher, expecting a pissing match from Leo, but he tipped his head back in laughter and raised his palms in surrender. He'd pulled his hair back with a thin elastic headband and she could see the tender skin behind his ear.

"You're a sadist," Leo huffed. "Cracked my kneecap at Iowa two years ago and it's never been the same."

From two machines over Boomer called out, "Excuses, excuses! I broke a hand in Saint Pete and still beat you!"

Injuries were another part of their unusual job, but the way Leo slowly blew out his breath, the way he obviously bit back a retort, told Mack that Leo was frustrated with his injury.

"Broke my collarbone twice in one year and I've never done a plank since without it aching," Mack said.

"Twice?" Leo grimaced. "Tough cookie, Rookie."

Mack scoffed at his bad joke but couldn't stop her smile as they finished their sprints.

A whistle blew and Leo hopped off the machine before the sound quit echoing. He turned toward an inclined bench where Bertie waited for them. A TV screen hung on the wall above the bench. "When you come up from a crunch, tap the green light. Green only, even if other colors flash. We're training the mind to react to visual cues while the core works to maintain body position." She smiled mischievously and pointed at Mack. "You do burpees while Leo does this exercise. Gets the heart rate up. Switch for a total of three rounds."

Leo dove in, completing an impressive number of crunches and dot taps before Mack took a turn. She was grateful the pain of the burpees stole her attention away from the outline of Leo's abs under his T-shirt. They were perfect, straight out of a *Men's Health* magazine. She'd told Laurie she swiped right when she needed to, but with all the work to get ready for the dirt track season and the chaos of Shaw's school activities, it had been way too long since Mack had let a man put his body on her own. Clearly, she needed to redownload her hookup app if she was ogling her teammate at the gym.

I know better now, she'd told Laurie, and Mack said it over and over to herself as she completed her own crunches.

Jericho, Boomer, and Leo distracted her with their friendly ribbing, and they included her in their shit-giving like they'd been friends for longer than an hour as they cycled through upright erg pulls, round-the-world squats, and a particularly evil machine that strengthened the neck muscles. Mack was a runner but not in racing shape, and halfway through the workout she kept up with Leo only from sheer willpower as he carried the bulk of the conversation. He kept her entertained during the workout without interfering with her concentration. When she hummed the chorus of John Mellencamp's "Hurts So Good" during a round of lunges, Leo sang the next few bars of the song until everyone joined in.

By the time they stretched on the rubber floor, her muscles were full of lactic acid, screaming with use, and she could feel the blood pumping through them as she pulled off her soaked sweatshirt and wiped her dripping face.

She looked up to find Leo watching her.

Had she thought she was hot before? Because now she felt positively inflamed from the inside out.

Boomer snapped his fingers in front of Leo's face, but Mack was the one who blushed. The look between the two men was mortifyingly obvious, one giving the other a pointed warning. Mack couldn't look at Leo as he handed her a cold bottle of water.

"Bertie!" Jericho called, breaking the awkwardness. "Why do you hate us?"

Bertie stood, hands on her hips, looking like a goddess in red spandex and waist-length box braids. "If you want to win, you have to work. When it's one hundred degrees and you're stuck in a car during the ninth caution flag of the day and you still have forty laps to go, you'll thank me for your strength and endurance. You'll be tired, you'll be sore, but you'll finish the damn race. Maybe one of you whiners will even win. Now get out of my face and go eat some protein."

Mack pushed out of the gym door soaked in sweat. Her muscles were sore and spent in a way that felt encouraging, and she'd genuinely enjoyed getting to know Boomer and Jericho. They exchanged numbers and she waved goodbye to the two IndyCar stars who were maybe her new friends.

But Leo . . . She'd thought her attraction was one-sided, a product of her too-long dry spell, but the way Leo looked at her made her wonder if he felt the same unavoidable attraction.

She needed to bring them back to professional ground, so she said, "I am so gassed. Probably feels ten times worse after the race?"

Leo rubbed a hand through his thick curls, pulling when he hit a snag. Mack tried not to watch his long fingers against his glossy hair. Behind him the sky was the pale blue of a perfect spring day. "The dehydration is insane, no matter how much you drink. And exhaustion on a scale you've never experienced."

Mack arched a brow, wondering if Leo Raisman had ever dealt with a newborn who refused to sleep. She knew little about Leo's personal life but she was pretty sure he wasn't a parent . . . or if he was in a relationship . . . and why was she even wondering about that anyway?

"But," Leo continued, one half of his mouth tipped up. "It's also the best feeling ever, knowing you made it through all five hundred miles."

"Even if you lose by half a car length?"

She'd said it as a tease, but his smile melted into a grimace. The Indy 500 had no podium because nothing other than winning mattered.

"Sorry," she said as she leaned against the door of her car, tipping the dregs of her water bottle over her head to cool down before getting in the stuffy vehicle. The AC quit sometime around her twenty-fifth birthday but she'd never had a good enough reason to fix it. "That came out mean but I genuinely meant it as a question. It's worth it, even if you lose?"

Leo turned serious. "Indy is always worth it, Williams. Always." He rubbed a palm over his scruffy cheek. "Ever had someone you couldn't get over? Even if you know there's only a one percent chance you'll work it out?"

She refused to think of Kelley. How she'd seen more in their relationship than was really there. To this day, she didn't know if she'd loved him, but she had wanted him to stay, to choose her. To want her the way she'd wanted to be loved. Maybe she'd just loved the idea of being in love with him. She shook her head.

"Ah. Well, Indy is a lot like that. You know it will break your heart but you do it anyway because the chance that it will work out is worth any other pain."

Leo turned and opened the door of a shiny blue F-150, and Mack wondered if he'd had his heart broken, and if it had happened recently. He tossed his sweatshirt and water bottle on the seat, and the sweet smell of new leather upholstery drifted out of the car. "Want to grab a coffee? Maybe some kind of breakfast? There's a great spot not far from here that serves smoothies, too."

She'd eaten a protein bar and a banana every day for breakfast since Shaw was born. She wasn't about to start drinking pureed sludge through a straw, and she told Leo as much. But now she understood how he'd gotten those abs. "Plus, I probably need to go home and work on sponsorships."

"Any luck? I bet companies are crawling all over themselves to put you in an ad."

Mack cut Leo a look. "Hardly. I know this is shocking, but no one wants to give money to a nobody. Especially not a *girl* nobody."

She said it mockingly, but it was the sad truth. Motorsports sponsors weren't willing to gamble on what they believed was an unproven product: a woman.

Leo returned her cutting glance. "You're not nobody. You drove the damn wheels off the car at the test. You've made the podium at endurance races and you won at *Eldora*." His voice almost sounded like it held a note of awe.

And why shouldn't it? She *had* kicked ass at Eldora, and many other races. Over the past two days, she'd felt that old self coming back to life, the one that drove too fast and made crass jokes and beat the boys at their own damn game. She'd felt more alive during the test drive, and even in Bertie's workout, than she had for a decade.

She swallowed a surge of shame. What kind of mother felt wholly alive away from her child?

"Plus, you . . ." Leo was looking up at the sky but waved a hand toward her, from head to toes.

She raised her brows, wanting to hear him say it out loud. "I'm what?"

He shifted uncomfortably, shaking his head, but his discomfort told her he felt the same pull, the line of gasoline that could easily ignite if either of them struck the match.

Ten damn years of Mack playing it quiet and safe, turning down anything that might look like trouble, but that one glance made her impulsivcly curious. Mack didn't know if Leo Raisman was a risk, but she couldn't get burned from a little investigation.

She pulled herself into the driver's seat and cranked the engine. "So where are we going?"

From: DevDhillon@Simpson.com
To: MWilliams@email.com
Subject: RE: Unique Indy 500 Sponsorship Opportunity! [May 6, 9:01 a.m.]

Dear Ms. Williams,

Thank you for contacting Simpson Carpet Company with your request for sponsorship. Since 1976, Simpson has been committed to the community, the country, and carpet care.

We believe our people are our best asset, and it follows that our marketing work is best done through our personnel. We're sorry we can't provide you sponsorship but we do wish you best of luck in your noble pursuit!

Yours in flooring,
Dev Dhillon
Chief Marketing Officer
Simpson Carpet Company
Duluth, Georgia

CHAPTER 11

2 weeks until the Indianapolis 500

"I don't understand why I lift in the corners when I know it's not real. My brain thinks I'm actually going to slam into a concrete wall."

Leo took an enormous bite of his burger and hummed in appreciation before unselfconsciously wiping grease from his chin. "The simulator looks like a hyped up video game, but the impact on the brain is real. You're lifting in the turns because that's what you'd do on track."

They'd spent time together every day in the week since her test drive—racing on the simulator machines, team engineering meetings, or doing promotional work for the IndyCar Series. Afterward, they'd grab a bite to eat and talk racing for hours. Today, they'd had a three-hour media session at the Speedway, followed by two hours of racing on the simulators at the JJR garage and a Zoom interview with a well-known sports reporter. By the time they left the JJR garage, Mack was hangry so Leo brought her to Workingman's Friend, a burger dive bar that smelled like a hundred years of grease and smoke and beer. It was heaven.

It was also packed on a Friday night. Mack and Leo snagged seats at the bar, but people kept bumping into Mack's back as they leaned forward to order drinks. She shifted closer to Leo to avoid a giant man with body odor ordering a staggering number of PBRs.

"I wish we could get actual practice on track. I love kicking your ass on the sim but would like to do it for real," Mack said through a mouthful of crinkle fries. She washed it down with a sip of beer, feeling only slightly remorseful. Leo told her it was tradition for Indy 500 drivers to get beers and burgers at Workingman's during the month of May, and if this was going to be Mack's only Indy 500, why not go all in? She'd never had a problem with alcohol; she'd simply stopped drinking when she'd stopped partying. And damn it if an ice-cold beer didn't taste incredible after a hard day of work.

She used to do this after her sprint races, eat greasy food and drink too much and shoot the shit at bars all over the country even though she was underage. After Shaw was born and Mack took over the business, every choice she made put her daughter and dad first, and she took whatever was left. Which was usually not much at all. It felt indulgent to do whatever she wanted without thinking of the consequences. To be Mack, the woman, not just Shaw's mom.

The thought made her feel guilty, so she checked her phone. No messages. She hated that she felt relief.

"You'll get to drive soon enough, Rookie," Leo said, tapping the sticky Formica counter. He had a splotch of mustard on the corner of his mouth, and when Mack handed him a napkin, she felt the calloused ridge of his palm. Under the bar, she shook off the feeling of his touch.

They'd fallen into an easy pattern, a quick friendship based on common interests and the long hours they spent together. They both loved Sturgill Simpson ("'Water in a Well' makes me cry every time") and hated Florida ("too many reptiles"). Leo never took her seriously when she ran her mouth. If she wrecked on the simulator, Leo broke down her errors in a way that was helpful, not insulting, and cheered her on when she made good passes. He challenged her at the gym without being a douchebag and answered her many questions without making her feel stupid.

And yet, there was something more, an undercurrent of interest that Mack couldn't shake no matter how many times she told herself that attraction to her teammate was a no-go. Laurie was right: Leo Raisman *was* her type, in all but one regard.

"Tell me something, Leo Raisman. How are you so damn nice?" She hadn't meant to say it out loud—the beer went straight to her head—but there it was. He *was* nice. So far, Leo Raisman lived up to his guy-next-door reputation, both thoughtful and playful, and it was baffling how his kindness made him even more attractive.

Leo laughed, a little self-consciously, and took a long pull from his beer. Someone had cranked up the music, and she had to lean in to hear him over a ZZ Top guitar solo. He smelled fucking amazing, like detergent and motor oil. "My parents are incredibly nice people."

"Of course they are," Mack said dryly. "You've got that whole Americana thing going on." She raised a mischievous eyebrow. "And yet, you're so shady on track."

"Shady?"

"Sneaky. Stealthy. That little over-under move you pulled at the Barber race? Shady as hell."

He grinned and she had to look away from his mouth. *Stick to racing.* "You should have been my hype woman during media day. 'Leo Raisman, sneaky, stealthy, shady.'"

Their day had started early with IndyCar's mandatory media day—a long series of headshots, recorded interviews, and promo videos that appeared on television and social media throughout May. Media day was also the reason Mack now had makeup melting down her face. She'd let Laurie slather her in cosmetics even though they'd sniped at each other the entire time. Their cohabitation wasn't so different from when they were teenagers, rooted in petty arguments. Laurie was still bossy and high-handed, and Mack still responded in defiance. When Laurie suggested Mack use a smoothing balm on her hair, Mack teased her untamed waves even higher. Her sister bitched about a wet towel on the floor, so Mack added some underwear and socks to the pile even though she griped at Shaw for the same thing back at home. They never talked about Wes or the family track or the dark circles under Laurie's eyes when she dragged in the door after work, exhausted and dispirited. They never talked about anything deeper than who left a glass in the sink. But each little spat felt weighted with their history. Getting ready for media day had been no different. Mack knew Laurie wanted to help her and yet she felt her sister's censure in every brush of eyeshadow and swipe of lipstick. *You won't get a chance like this again.*

Mack dipped her napkin in her untouched glass of water and rubbed at the itchy makeup. She didn't want to think about Laurie or any part of her family. "Media day was weirdly fun. I almost pissed my pants when Jericho told that story about crowd-surfing after his win last year. And I am thrilled to have lots of new information on little Leo."

As part of the interviews, teammates played a round of twenty questions, and Mack now knew that Leo still slept with his childhood blanket, had thrown up in the cockpit at Texas and still made the podium, and cried at the sight of roadkill as a child.

Leo lifted a finger to her cheek, stopping just before touching her. "Good to see your freckles again."

"Fuck you," she said, but there was no heat in it. "No one else had to wear lipstick or have their nose touched up with powder. It's bullshit."

"It *is* bullshit. You don't need it."

She didn't like Leo's tone, warm and soft. Or maybe she liked it a lot. She looked away, pretending to study the neon signs while swigging her beer.

They were sitting so close together, unconsciously scooting nearer as the bar filled up, that Mack could see a dimple on his right cheek, barely visible under the scruff of his beard. She pushed her beer away. Used to be she could slam a six-pack and still walk a straight line, but half a schooner was giving her stupid thoughts about her teammate.

She swiped one last mouthful of fries, intending to head back to Laurie's before she could say or do something reckless, when a heavy weight slammed into her back. The fries flew out of her hand, and her stool went out from under her body, sending Mack flying forward. Her chin smacked the sharp edge of the bar, but strong arms caught her and pulled her upward before she hit the floor.

"Hey, careful." Leo's voice was as even as always, but Mack could feel his chest vibrating with irritation. The warmth of his body felt even hotter compared to the cold beer streaming down her back and into her shorts.

"Sorry," a voice slurred behind her. Mack turned to see the huge PBR guy teetering over the tray of shattered beer steins that had rammed into her back. She started to cuss out the drunk jerk, but Leo held her tightly to his side with one arm while the other tilted her chin up. "Shit. You're bleeding. Give me some napkins," he hollered at the bartender.

"I'm fine," Mack protested. Her chin didn't hurt much, but she felt powerless to move away from Leo's embrace. Her body fit neatly under his shoulder, and she could feel those calluses on her waist where her shirt didn't quite meet her cutoffs. It had been so long since she'd pressed her body against another body, and Leo Raisman had an unquestionably good body. Warm, firm, and that damn smell. She could not stop herself from leaning in a little more, just for one more second.

Leo compressed a wad of paper napkins against her chin, watching her with concern. It was adorable how worried he looked, as if she hadn't shattered random pieces of her body in a million worse ways. "You might need stitches."

She gave him a look.

"Yeah, yeah, you're tough but you at least need a butterfly bandage. The skin is split pretty good. Let's get out of here."

He settled their tab with the bartender, who comped their food for the trouble, and they were in the parking lot before Mack realized she shouldn't drive. Not drunk, but even in her wildest days she'd never gotten behind the wheel after drinking. She said as much to Leo.

He led her to a pristinely restored cherry red Corvette and held open the passenger door. She could feel blood soaking through the napkin and beer dripping from her back down through her cutoffs. "I'll ruin your upholstery. What is this, 1992?"

"1990 ZR-1," Leo said, voice tighter than usual. "I'm not worried about the car, Mack."

He'd never said her real name before and she did not want him to say it like that, so reverently. "It's a small cut, Leo. I've had way worse injuries."

"You chose those, I'm guessing. That asshole was so drunk he could have hurt you a lot worse. Get in."

She slid in the car, cringing as her wet back met soft leather, promising to pay Leo for any damage. She pressed both hands against her stinging chin to keep any blood from leaking out. He was probably right about needing a butterfly. "Bossy. You always get all caveman with women in bars?"

To her surprise, a flush crept up Leo's neck, so bright it was obvious even under his dark beard. "It's not caveman," he said, reversing out of the lot. "I know you can take care of yourself. You kick my ass at the gym every day. But yeah, it pisses me off to see you get hurt because someone else was careless."

Mack didn't know what to say, so she simply nodded. They drove silently and when Leo passed downtown and headed east, she didn't protest. He punched the clutch and shifted through the gears, occasionally glancing at her. At first his looks were concerned, checking in on her, but soon they turned into something else, something that told her that he also felt the way the air had changed. She was hyperaware of the small distance between them in the car, Leo's long fingers on the gearshift so close to her thigh. They passed Geist Reservoir, eventually turning into a winding driveway that ended not at the McMansion she'd expected but at a charming bungalow. Ferns hung from the porch and Mack could see water glistening behind the house.

She followed Leo inside, passing a cozy living room and tidy kitchen, down a hallway toward what she assumed was the primary bedroom. It looked like Leo, warm and casual with lots of earth tones.

He went immediately to a linen cabinet stocked full of medicines, creams, and bandages, staple items for every driver. Neither spoke as Leo wiped her chin with antiseptic. He was so close, his hands so gentle on her face. She closed her eyes, trying not to gasp or cry at the feeling of someone touching her. If the cut hurt, she couldn't feel it over the riot of sensation throughout her body as Leo stood so close to her. Was she imagining it or did he ghost his thumb down the line of her jaw?

When he pulled the cut together and carefully placed the bandage, she hissed and opened her eyes. His eyes flicked to hers, inches away, and she remembered how his hand felt on her skin, rough and right. She wanted to feel wanted, wanted someone else to make her feel good. She was so fucking lonely, so tired of giving and giving and never getting, and Leo was right here, so kind and warm and so close, his eyes asking hers for guidance.

She could stop this, make a joke or ask for Advil. Anything to keep from making the same mistake she'd made years ago.

I know better now.

But the old wildness zinged through her lonesome body, her mind and skin and all of her insides desperate for feeling. She *ached* for touch. She lifted the chin he'd so carefully bandaged a fraction toward his own, but still he waited, so damn nice even as his eyes flicked down to her mouth.

She leaned forward an inch more and there was Leo, surrounding her with warmth and gentleness. His beard rubbed at the tender cut on her chin but she pressed harder, wanting the pleasure-pain, wanting connection and contact. Leo kissed her softly, humbly, as if he knew this may not last and he'd savor each second they were connected. Mack tried to hurry the pace but Leo wouldn't let her, holding her steady and keeping the kiss slow.

He pulled back, his hand still holding her chin. The look on his face was regretful, already apologetic. Mack didn't give him a chance to say the words. She stepped back and stripped off her beer-soaked shirt. His eyes followed her, the debate in them turning to liquid heat as she took off her shorts and underwear. She walked to the shower, turned it on, and prayed he would join her.

~

Mack slowly pushed the front door to Laurie's condo closed, holding the knob to dampen the snick of the lock. The soft sunrise cast a dim glow on the open space, everything clean and quiet and perfectly in place. Laurie often went to the office early, but Mack toed off her shoes and tiptoed toward the hallway in case her sister was still sleeping.

"Have a good night?" Laurie sat at the kitchen island, a small white mug steaming in front of her.

Mack flinched and self-consciously touched her messy hair as her sister looked her up and down. After their shower, she and Leo had moved to the bedroom for a second round of brain-melting sex before falling asleep. Like the coward she was, Mack snuck out and nabbed a rideshare while Leo was still asleep. She knew her sister could draw only one conclusion from her shambled state.

"Hungry?" Laurie looked as elegant as ever in a silky white robe but Mack could see puffy, dark circles behind her stylish black glasses.

Mack sat gingerly at the kitchen island as Laurie stood and poured her a cup of coffee. Awkward silence vibrated between them as Laurie sliced a fresh loaf of brioche, then whisked eggs with milk and added a dash of vanilla. She asked in a flat voice, "Was it Leo?"

Mack blew on her coffee, not looking Laurie in the eye as she nodded.

Laurie inhaled sharply but didn't say anything. She soaked the bread in the egg mixture and added it to a buttered pan, the sizzle reminding Mack of how her sister had made this same meal over a camp stove twenty years ago, back when their biggest argument had been over who ate the last of the Cap'n Crunch.

Laurie set a plate of perfectly cooked French toast in front of Mack. For several long seconds she leaned against the counter, holding Mack's gaze. "Why do you do this?"

How could Mack answer when she didn't know the reason herself? There was nothing she could say that would take the judgment off Laurie's face, no explanation that would make her feel less shame than she did. Mack didn't need her sister to tell her she was thirty years old and still pulling the same stunts.

Instead of answering, Mack shoved a giant bite into her mouth, and then another, and another.

Laurie closed her eyes, looking for a moment like she might cry or scream or both, before she turned and walked down the hallway without another word.

TEXTS BETWEEN BILLIE SUMMIT AND MACK WILLIAMS

BILLIE [5/10, 2:11 p.m.]: Have you ever given Shaw colloidal silver drops for her allergies?

MACK [5/10, 6:12 p.m.]: Absolutely not.

CHAPTER 12

12 days until the Indianapolis 500

The volume of people and gear swarming the Indianapolis Motor Speedway on the first day of practice befitted the world's biggest sporting event. Teams descended like grit sucked into the intake filter, swiftly filling the infield with semitrailers, buses, equipment, and crew. The biggest teams took up entire acres of the infield, corralling their coordinated trailers-turned-offices, catering buses, and haulers filled with million-dollar race cars. The full-season drivers all had their own motor homes, lined up together like a subdivision, complete with patio furniture and inflatable hot tubs. The elaborate setups would stay in place until race day, unless someone failed to qualify for the race, in which case they would quickly slink away, shuttling back to wherever they'd first hatched their Indy 500 dreams.

At Janet's urging, Mack arrived at the track an hour before the Tuesday orientation meeting, but her nerves felt like one of Shaw's little stretch toys pulled in opposite directions. She was ready for the track at dawn, eager to get in the car and see what she could do, but the weaker part of her wanted to sweep in at the last minute so she wouldn't have to face Leo. She hadn't seen him since the dark hours of Saturday morning when she'd called a rideshare and snuck away from his house like a stupid, scared mouse. He'd texted, a simple did you get home okay? and she'd responded with a cowardly yup.

A hookup was one thing, but a hookup with her teammate was a relapse into behavior she could no longer afford. She'd held herself so tightly since Shaw was born, made safe decisions, done everything she could to create stability . . . and yet she'd come to Indianapolis and lost her damn mind in less time than Shaw's holiday break from school. Laurie wasn't wrong in her silent censure. Thank god Shaw was two hundred miles away, home and not exposed to her mother's chaos.

What Mack hadn't been able to articulate to Laurie was that she hadn't acted out of sheer recklessness. In the past, she would have found any man at all, anyone willing to make her body feel good and her mind go blank. She used to crave that adrenaline rush the same way she'd craved fast cars and winning races. But Leo was different. She wanted *him*. The way he put other people at ease and had a connection with every person on the team. The way he built her up instead of knocking her down. The way he'd gripped her thighs and told her she was *so fucking beautiful.* He made her feel like she was a woman, someone worth knowing, and she could grow addicted to that feeling.

But Leo Raisman wouldn't help her win the Indy 500, and when this was over, she would go home to her daughter and close the window on racing for good. Mack was here for one reason only, and that reason had nothing to do with a man, Leo or otherwise.

Even though it was early, the track already buzzed with palpable energy and hundreds of people—mechanics, engineers, support staff, hospitality, sponsors, and more—hustled purposefully around the infield. So many people, all with a singular purpose: to qualify a car to race on the world's most famous racetrack on the last Sunday of May. JJR had a hauler each for Mack's and Leo's cars, a semitrailer of tools and electronics, and a large trailer that served as office, meeting space, respite for the drivers, and lunch cart. In the JJR garage, the mechanics and engineers were fine-tuning the car before practice began, but Mack avoided them. What if Leo had mentioned their extracurricular activities?

Antsy but not willing to brave her own garage, Mack walked around the infield, taking in the buzz of activity. Near the media center, news stations and reporters and YouTubers spread in serpentine lines, and drivers moved along the asphalt from one interview to the next. In the past, she'd loved media attention, the fans scrambling to meet her, being Wes Williams's daughter, the perks and invites and free gear, and most of all, being known for being very, very good at her job. But now she gave the media area a wide berth, too afraid to find Leo there.

She hated that she'd ruined this moment for herself. This wasn't how she wanted to experience her first and only Indy 500—no sponsor, no recent accomplishments, avoiding everyone because she'd slept with the wrong guy. Turning her head to look up at the Pagoda, she tried to think about the good things to come, not the mistake she'd made that weekend with Leo Raisman.

Too bad she walked smack into him.

Everything suddenly felt big and small at the same time. The wide Indiana sky, the towering Pagoda, the immenseness of the track surrounded her, but all she could see were the tight lines around Leo's mouth. She had no idea what to say.

He stared at her a beat too long, then tilted his head toward the long rows of RVs and haulers. "We need to check in at the team trailer."

She'd just come from the JJR hospitality bus but followed Leo anyway, assuming he knew something she did not. They walked quickly, exchanging bland conversation on the day's schedule and Mack found herself hoping they'd never talk about Friday night. That they would both pretend it never happened and go forward as teammates only.

When they reached the JJR coach, Leo held the door open for her before following her inside and closing it.

"What the—"

"You left," he said, his voice as even as always. She whirled around to look behind her. "It's just us," Leo assured her. He gestured for her to move to the center of the bus, away from the windows. "Why did you leave?"

Mack pushed forward toward the door. "If someone saw us come in here . . ."

"They'll think we're two teammates grabbing a snack. How did you get home?"

"Rideshare." She sounded like her daughter, petulant and irritated. She crossed her arms for good measure.

"How's your chin?"

She pressed on the cut, needing the small sting. "Healing."

"I would have driven you home. I wanted to drive you home."

"It wasn't a fucking date, Leo." He startled, and if their situation was different, she might have thought she hurt his feelings. "I'm sorry I fell asleep at your house. Must have been the beer."

He blinked. "Were you . . . ?"

She shook her head. "Very sober. The dumb decisions were all mine."

His face was perfectly placid, his body language unreadable. She didn't know him well enough to guess what he was thinking. Hell, she didn't even know what she wanted him to say. She felt like that stretch toy again, one side of her wanting him to forget their sexy shower and the other wanting to kiss him again. She needed to get Leo Raisman out of her face and her head *now*.

"Did you tell anyone?"

He blinked several times as his thick brows came together. "Who would I tell?"

She hugged her arms over her chest. "I don't know. Janet. The crew. Jericho. Boomer."

"I wouldn't do that. I would never do that." He shoved a hand through his messy curls and blew out a frustrated breath. "What happened Friday . . . it's between us. It doesn't have anything to do with JJR or the race."

Mack knew she was being a hypocrite. He may not have told anyone, but she'd told Laurie.

"I don't sleep around with people at the track," she told him now. "If anyone finds out . . . I'll be the woman who slept her way into a job and you'll be the badass dude who fucked his teammate."

He dropped his hands from his hair and stared at her as if she were speaking in tongues. "I had nothing to do with you joining JJR."

"I know that, but no one will care if they find out I—" She tossed a casual hand in his direction.

"*We,*" he emphasized, "are two adults. Is it messy that we're teammates and attracted to each other? Sure, but we don't have to say or share anything until we figure out what we want to do."

"What we want to do? There's nothing to *do*, Leo. It was a mistake. Anything more than a professional relationship is a mistake."

Her words reverberated through the small space, made extra loud by Leo's silence. He hadn't looked away from her face since they entered the bus. After a painfully long moment, he said, "So . . . that's it?" He looked at her in a way that made her feel white-hot rage. Like she'd actually hurt him.

"Leo, how many women do you see in the paddock?" Even though her stomach boiled with frustration, she waited patiently for him to answer. He conceded with a shake of his head. "Exactly," she said with fury. "Whether I want it or not, I'm the example of what a woman in motorsports looks like. If I'm anything other than professional with my teammate, I'm proof that women can only succeed if they sleep their way to the top. All it takes is one person finding out to ruin my reputation and the reputations of other women in racing."

She stopped before she said the thing that had kept her awake through the weekend, the other half of why she couldn't indulge in Leo Raisman: No matter what happened in qualifications, even if she made the race, she'd end her Indy 500 bid with a trip right back home while Leo moved on. She'd never introduced Shaw to a man and she wasn't going to start now. In her lowest moments, she realized that she'd never let herself be in a relationship until Shaw no longer lived at home. The one time Mack had let Shaw stay with Kelley, he'd left Shaw with a girlfriend and she'd come home with a fracture and sores. Shaw was older now but Mack would never again trust anyone so easily with her daughter. Wes had dated Billie for months before Mack would let her spend supervised time with Shaw.

"It was a fun night, Leo. But that's all it was. One misguided night."

His eyes moved back and forth between her own, as if looking for a hole in her argument. She uncrossed her arms and hoped she projected more stern resolve than she actually felt. Leo inhaled deeply, bobbed his head in a quick nod, and said, "If that's what you need."

She nodded emphatically. That was what she needed.

"But we're still cool? As teammates?"

The sharp look Leo gave her was gutting, like she'd offended him. "Yeah, we're still teammates, Rookie." He glanced at his watch. "Teammates who need to get to the garage. C'mon."

He led her out of the bus and Mack had the sinking feeling that by choosing what she needed, she'd ruined something she wanted.

No matter, because she couldn't have it anyway.

~

If she thought things would feel less edgy on the track, she was sorely mistaken.

The all-driver orientation was long and intense, full of reminders of all the risks they would face. IndyCar worked tirelessly to increase safety measures both in the cars and on the tracks: using ethanol fuel prevented catastrophic gasoline fires, shock-absorbing SAFER barriers replaced deadly concrete walls, the entire chassis was designed to deflect impact away from the driver, and the relatively new aeroscreen protected the driver's head from flying tires or debris. The safety team walked them through a series of rules and best practices—*never pass the pace car, use the aprons if you're a danger to other cars, flip your visor up to signal that you're uninjured after a wreck*—and Mack tried to commit it all to memory, but she was too keyed up to focus.

After the meeting, the other drivers greeted each other, asking about babies and boats and plans for the summer. Most people in the room spent the entire season racing against each other, making friends or rivals. Everyone she met was polite, even kind, but she lingered only for a moment before leaving by herself. She told Leo she needed to focus on racing and that was what she would do.

But once she was in the car, she was bludgeoned with reminders that she was a rookie. It was one thing to drive two hundred miles per hour when she was the only one on the track, but a different beast when dozens of other cars zipped around her on all sides. The first time another car passed her, she rode so high up the outside of the track that she lost traction on the small marbles of rubber left by degrading tires and almost tank-slapped the wall. Only her quick reflexes and a heaping dose of luck kept her from wrecking. In the pits, she overshot her marks so badly that she almost hit a crew member.

She spent most of the first day trying to not piss herself, barely breaking two hundred eighteen miles per hour. Not nearly fast enough to qualify.

At the end of practice, she parked in her pit box and yanked her seat belts and radio cords with flailing fury. Furious at herself and pissed at her team for giving her a brick to drive, Mack stomped down pit lane, blowing off Jimmy and walking past her crew like she didn't even see them. When Leo called out to her, she gave him double middle fingers and told him exactly where he could go.

Back in the garage, she threw her gloves and kicked her helmet and growled in rage. She knew she was having a temper tantrum but she was too angry to care. Never had she been so disappointed in herself—not when she'd wrecked during a championship race, not when she'd found out she was pregnant, not when she'd messed up the books for the family business. She was infuriated with her performance on track but more than anything, she was pissed off that she'd let a man distract her. She'd heard all the jokes about female drivers: *Don't get too close, she'll wreck you out! She can't go any faster, she's checking her nails!* Mack had wanted to come to this hallowed ground as a fighter, as a real contender, and instead she was no better than she'd been ten years ago, making shitty choices and letting their shitty consequences ruin her career.

"You wanna act like a toddler or talk like an adult?"

Mack was so busy jerking her equipment bag out of the tiny locker than she didn't hear Janet enter the garage.

"I'll be better tomorrow," she said over her shoulder, giving her bag a final tug to release it from the locker. She stood and faced Janet. "I can do better."

"No shit," Janet said. She skewered Mack with an assessing look. "You'd better apologize to every single person on this team for acting like an entitled brat." Janet tucked her sunglasses into her nest of frizzy hair. "Especially Raisman. What happened between you two?"

Mack froze, her entire body going into fight-or-flight mode. *No no no no.* She made sure to keep her face very, very blank as she asked, "What about Leo?"

"The entire paddock heard you tell him to fuck off! He was trying to talk to you about the understeer and you flayed him alive. You might learn something from him if you weren't so busy shouting at him to go to hell."

Her shoulders fell and Mack rolled her eyes to cover her relieved exhale. Mack could handle a reputation as a bitch, but not as a slut.

"I don't need his help," she said, crossing her arms over her chest. She almost meant it. Without exception, Leo had been nothing but kind to her, but she'd been so mad at her inability to manage the car and her lapse in judgment over the weekend that she'd taken her wrath out on anyone in her way. Doubly so on Leo when he'd tried to give her some pointers during a break in his own practice.

She started to shake with the letdown of adrenaline and ego. Janet stepped into Mack's personal space. "If you're going to act like a snotty little girl, I'll treat you like one. Yes, it can be frustrating to learn a new car. Yes, it takes time, and no, we do not have time. But acting like an asshole does nothing to help you or your team. I thought you were a grown up. Act like a professional or you can go back home to Nowhere, Indiana."

Around Gasoline Alley, the sounds of racing churned as teams returned to their garages. Teams laughed and discussed strategy and setup, drivers chatted to mechanics and team owners, crew members industriously moved equipment. In the garage bay next door, Mack could hear Leo talking with his engineer. She stood alone with her attitude and the pile of gear she'd dropped on the ground, feeling like she'd already screwed up her last chance at the Indy 500.

TEXTS FROM WES WILLIAMS TO MACK WILLIAMS

MACK [5/12, 8:10 p.m.]: Thanks for listening. I'm sorry I couldn't stop crying. Today was fucking hard.

WES [5/12, 8:10 p.m.]: u never have to thx me for anything, Spec. I love u

MACK [5/12, 8:10 p.m.]: I'm so embarrassed. I acted worse than Shaw as a toddler. Remember the time she had a meltdown in the snack aisle at Wesselman's? A million times worse.

WES [5/12, 8:11 p.m.]: Did you bite someone?

MACK [5/12, 8:11 p.m.]: Ha! No.

WES [5/12, 8:11 p.m.]: So maybe only 10x worse

MACK [5/12, 8:11 p.m.]: Gee thaaaaaanks

WES [5/12, 8:12 p.m.]: all you can do is move forward tomorrow.

MACK [5/12, 8:14 p.m.]: I wish it were that easy. These cars are harder than anything I've ever driven.

WES [5/12, 8:14 p.m.]: wut about ur team? Raisman?

MACK [5/12, 8:15 p.m.]: What about them?

WES [5/12, 8:15 p.m.]: get to know them. ask for help

MACK [5/12, 8:18 p.m.]: Yeah. Ok I'm going to bed. Goodnight dad. I love you. Kiss Shaw for me.

WES [5/12, 8:18 p.m.]: g'night Spec. u'll figure it out. U always do

CHAPTER 13

11 days until the Indianapolis 500

"Try to release the anti-roll bar as you exit the turn."

Jimmy's instruction crackled through Mack's earpiece and she cringed in frustration. For the second practice day in a row, Mack's speeds were abysmal.

She'd vowed to show up fresh and friendly, but instead she arrived twenty minutes late because she'd forgotten to put her Nomex in the washing machine the night before. Like her clothing, the day stank. The crew treated her with an icy tolerance she knew she deserved, and the car didn't seem to think she was worthy either.

For the last hour, she'd plugged through the same pattern: run a dozen laps before coming back into the pits so the crew could make adjustments to the car, Janet would offer her opinion on what Mack was doing wrong, then she'd go back out to run laps. This time, Mack held her tongue and tried everything, but nothing worked. Somehow her speeds kept getting *slower*. Gusting winds swept the track, and Mack lifted her foot off the accelerator in turns two and four to keep from smacking the outside. On her last run, she'd hardly managed two hundred fifteen, which would not only keep her out of the race, but create unsafe conditions for other drivers on the track. Which she knew because more than one driver had screamed at her spotter, and in one case, directly at her while Mack caught her breath on pit lane.

Meanwhile, Leo was running in the top five, making practice look like a lazy amusement park ride. She knew she owed him an apology for yesterday, and yet she ignored him in the garage that morning, as immature as her ten-year-old daughter when she didn't get her way. Mack suspected he'd be kind and forgiving, and she didn't want his absolution. Did not deserve it. She'd managed to avoid him before practice, but shamelessly watched him on track, admiring his consistent, steady laps.

Back on track once more, her hands hurt from gripping the wheel, her hips ached with the unfamiliar reclined position, and she'd sweat through her fire suit so thoroughly she could feel the moisture pooling in her ass crack. Mack held her breath as she steered into turn two, grimacing as she pushed left as hard as she possibly could, her wrists sore from the previous day's effort. The back end of the car pulled hard to the right, the front end wanting to go directly into the wall. As she headed down the back stretch of the track, Jimmy's voice crackled over the radio.

"How's it feel?"

"Almost lost the back in two but also have push. Understeer still there."

The line buzzed with the quiet line of the open radio. "Better or worse than yesterday, or can you tell?"

Mack wrestled the high-strung car through another two turns before radioing back, "I'm trying not to hit the wall on every turn. Car wants to go straight."

Jimmy's resigned voice filled her ears. "Come on in. Remember the pit limiter."

Ducking into pit lane, she pressed the button that automatically slowed her to the sixty-miles-per-hour speed required by pit lane rules. A blue plastic placard attached to a long metal pole identified her pit box, and she pulled in, overshooting her marks by a foot. She raised her hands in apology to the crew, and Jimmy signaled for Mack to kill the engine. The sudden stillness echoed louder than the low rumble of the big engine, and Mack's ears continued to ring despite the protective earplugs she wore.

Jimmy frowned down at her. "There's no way you're feeling understeer after all the changes we made."

Mack scowled up at Jimmy even as her face flamed inside her helmet. She knew she'd acted like an unforgivable jerk the first day, but goddammit, she understood the mechanics of racing. "I know what push feels like. I'm telling you, this thing wants to drive right into the wall. My arms are crossed just to make the turn."

Jimmy put his hands on his hips, his weathered face stern as he leaned over the cockpit. "That's enough for today."

"What? There's another hour of practice left!"

"Get out of the car."

Too exhausted to put up an argument, Mack unclipped the steering wheel and disconnected the communication and hydration cords, her arms wobbling with fatigue. She plopped on the lip of the aeroscreen, taking a moment to catch her breath. Between the g-forces in the turns, the sheer speed on the straightaways, and the strength required to steer the car, a driver's heart rate often hit one hundred eighty beats per minute for hours on end, similar to marathon running. Mack was gassed.

Yesterday, she'd been livid. Today, she was scared. What if she couldn't find the pace in time for qualifications?

Jimmy seemed to have the same worry. He said little, simply tapped her helmet and sighed. "Get rest tonight and we'll do it all again tomorrow."

Climbing out of the car, she sat on the pit wall to remove her helmet and gloves. She was still catching her breath when Leo smoked in the pits, stopping exactly on his marks and killing the engine. Mack watched as he wriggled out of the car. His speeds had been great all day, and his engineer looked particularly pleased. As she should; Leo was flying on track.

Across the pit box, Leo flipped his visor screen up and caught her staring. *Shit.* She couldn't exactly run away from him with both of their crews watching. Leo sat down on the pit wall next to her and took his time unsnapping his helmet.

"Great practice," she shouted over the noise of the cars still out running laps.

Leo pulled off his helmet and balaclava, and Mack pretended not to watch as he scrubbed a hand through his sweaty hair. Her fingers could still feel the weight of those thick curls.

"Lucie got us set up right," he said, removing his earpieces. She'd only known him for a week and a half, but it seemed natural for Leo to give the credit to his team instead of acknowledging his own skill. His face was creased from the tight fireproof hood they all wore under their helmets, and he looked wrung out, but the signs of his hard work made him more attractive to Mack. "You still having a hard time finding speed?"

"Yeah," she admitted. She heard the defeat in her own voice.

Leo squinted at her as he opened the Velcro tab on his fire suit to let cool air on his skin. It was hot on track, close to ninety degrees with the sun reflecting off the asphalt. "It's a tense few weeks. Worse when you're a rookie."

"I'm sorry," she said, as softly as she could on pit lane. "The way I talked to you yesterday . . . That's not who I am, I swear."

Leo stopped folding his gloves and looked at her. "I know."

She wanted to say so much more, but she couldn't. Not here. They sat side by side, watching the few remaining cars whir by.

"Do you want to talk about it?"

Mack wasn't sure what *it* he meant—their night together, her attitude yesterday, or what was happening in the car—but she chose the safe option. "It's like I have understeer and oversteer. Coming into the turn, it feels like the car wants to go straight. Exiting the turn, I can feel the back begging to snap around. The tools don't seem to help," she said, referring to the minute adjustments a driver could make from inside the car.

Leo considered that, then blew out a breath. The longer she watched him, the more she could see the fatigue in his face. "Do you want to go over the tools again, talk about how you might use them at each point in the turn? I need to grab a shower first but we can talk in the garage after."

"Don't you want to go home and watch SportsCenter and eat carefully balanced macronutrients?"

Leo laughed and Mack felt shamefully proud as she watched some of the tired leave his face.

"We're teammates, right? Let's clean up, get some food, and go over the tools."

She walked with Leo toward the garage, grateful for the help and knowing she didn't deserve his generosity but accepting it anyway. But in her mind, she kept hearing the way he'd said *we're teammates* like it was a consolation prize.

From: KGehlhausen@SunGloHair.com
To: MWilliams@email.com
CC: Laurie.Williams@StoeppelEvansFirm.com
Subject: RE: Exciting sponsorship opportunity! [5/13, 10:18 a.m.]

Ms. Williams,

Thank you for contacting SunGlo Hair Products. We have scaled back our marketing and do not provide sponsorships.

Thank you,
Keely Gehlhausen
VP of Marketing
SunGlo Hair Products INC.
La Jolla, California

CHAPTER 14

11 days until the Indianapolis 500

In the JJR garage, Leo talked Mack through the buttons and levers that adjusted the balance and weight of the car, tiny changes that made the car minutely faster. On qualification day, those fractions of seconds could make careers or heartbreak. Mack didn't think he was teaching her anything she didn't already know, but she was desperate and it was an excuse to spend time with him, so she listened carefully until her yawns grew so frequent that Leo waved her out of the stripped-down practice car tucked into a quiet corner of the garage.

Leo returned her yawn. "You know the tools. You need to have confidence in when you use them."

Mack wanted to snap that she was pretty damn confident for someone who learned the tools a week ago, but she held her tongue. The little lift to Leo's lips made her think he knew what she didn't say. She liked that he wasn't put off by her prickliness.

Mack hauled herself out of the driver's seat and arched her back, pulling her arms overhead to stretch the length of her spine. Her back felt both tight and tender, and she couldn't remember the last time she'd been this physically sore. She knew exhaustion—anyone who'd spent more than twenty-four hours with a toddler understood how truly threadbare a person could feel—but this was a physical drain, a depletion of her body she hadn't felt for a decade. For the briefest second, she wondered how long it would take her muscles to adapt to the unusual angle of driving an IndyCar until she realized it didn't matter because she wouldn't be here long enough for her body to get used to anything.

Soon she'd go back to the usual aches of pressure washing bleachers and helping Shaw with fourth grade math homework. The thought of driving home to Haubstadt if she didn't qualify made her stomach cramp and she jolted upright.

Leo placed a light hand on her back and she turned to face him. Behind him, the wide garage was empty. The oversize fluorescent lights were out in every station but for the small pit practice area where she and Leo were, and the business bullpen, a small loft over the garage, was shut down for the night. When they'd first started going over the in-car tools, there had still been a smattering of JJR crew milling around the garage. She had no idea how long she and Leo had been working.

"Everyone else went home," Leo confirmed. His voice bounced off the wide-open space of the garage. "Are you okay? Backache?"

His hand still rested lightly between her shoulder blades, a soft and comforting counterpoint to her aching spine. She wanted him to rub gentle circles, to ease the aching muscles of her neck, to turn her around and pull her into his arms. She wanted more, more, more. She rolled her shoulders to remove his touch.

"Sorry," he said, withdrawing his hand, shoving them both into his pockets. He wore his usual joggers and a soft-looking San Diego Padres sweatshirt, his still-damp hair curling on his shoulders. "I'm sorry," he said again, softer. He chewed his lip, and Mack realized she'd never seen him look nervous. "I'm sorry about the other night. I'm never impulsive like that. I . . . we were . . . it was . . . You were right. It was a mistake."

She grabbed her elbows. She'd said the words first, and she'd meant them, but they hurt coming from Leo's mouth. It had felt so good, even for a false moment, to be wanted.

Leo looked at her with the same intensity he wore before he pulled on his helmet. "I don't regret anything, Mack. That night was amazing. I think about it when I shouldn't." He pulled his lower lip between his teeth. "When you were yelling at me on pit lane I realized how badly I'd put you in a horrible position. I took advantage of you. You're a rookie, new to the team and IndyCar. I don't regret you, but I regret what I did to you." He dropped his gaze to the floor, and his shoulders drooped. "If you don't want to be on this team with me, I understand."

She squinted at him in disbelief. "So you want me to go?"

"No!" He was destroying his glossy curls, pulling his fingers through them mercilessly. "I'll go. I'll . . . try to find a last-minute ride with someone else or . . . or I'll sit this year out."

Her jaw flopped open.

"You should make a report to Janet. You need to be comfortable here." He kept his eyes on the floor. She suspected he was trying not to cry.

"What the actual fuck, Leo? You're not going anywhere. I'm not saying shit to Janet. If anyone was impulsive, it was me. It's kind of my thing." She waved her index finger back and forth between them. "You did not take advantage of me or any other stupid shit you're thinking. Surely you remember how very, very consensual we were?"

He looked up at her. "I remember."

Mack couldn't stop herself from reaching out and removing his hands from his poor mangled hair. She laced his fingers with her own and they faced each other, hands intertwined. They were so close she could feel the rise and fall of his breaths under his hoodie. "You are going nowhere, Leo. You are going to win the Indy 500 this year, and you're going to do it in JJR's colors. I'm going to qualify and run this damn race and find you at the front. We made a mistake and we both agree it won't happen again."

He stared at her for a long time, his eyes bouncing back and forth across her face, from her eyes to her lips, until finally he nodded. His thumb rubbed over the arc of her own. The empty garage, dark and cavernous around them, felt strangely intimate.

"I'm never reckless," Leo whispered, his thumb now gliding over the back of her hand.

Mack arched her brows in question. Leo took his time answering, and she sensed that he wanted to find the exact right words. "My parents have always been kind and loving and supportive. I never had anything to rebel against because they were always there for me. But when I started racing . . . they double-mortgaged their home and took out loans to pay for everything. They sacrificed so much for me and I never want them to regret it."

"And being impulsive would make them regret investing in you?"

Leo closed his eyes and shook his head. "I was seventeen when I came to karting. You know how it is. Most of the kids I raced against had been driving since kindergarten. I started doing odd jobs, pressure washing and painting and working at a fast-food place to make enough money to buy my own equipment. My parents borrowed money from my grandma to buy my first kart. I still think about that every time I'm too tired to get out of bed. The bare minimum I owe them is my hard work." He reached up and pushed an unruly strand of hair off her forehead. "If I went wild, did impulsive things, did anything that took my focus away from racing, it would feel like spitting in the face of all the sacrifices my family made for me."

"What about your YouTube channel and the dancing competition?"

He held a lock of her hair, twirling it around his finger. "The dancing competition got me a wider audience, and I landed some solid sponsorships after that. My YouTube channel connects me with fans, which keeps the sponsors happy." He shrugged but Mack could tell he didn't feel as casual as he acted. "I really do love the fans, but sponsors mean money, money means repaying my family for all they've done for me."

"See? Shady. You act like you're all calm, a cool guy out here having fun, but it's all calculated."

She said it teasingly, but Leo did not smile in return. "More like strategic. There's so much I want to do for them. I made enough to pay off their mortgages but I'm trying to refill their retirement accounts."

"And what do you get?" Mack tilted her chin up at the garage. "You're working to take care of your family, but what about what you want?"

Leo grinned wickedly. "I want the Indy 500." Mack hummed in agreement, and the air between them vibrated with so much want—of each other, of the win, of someone who understood the want of something bigger than themselves.

His face changed so slightly that Mack would have missed it if they weren't a bare inch apart. She whispered, "What else do you want, Leo Raisman?"

Geezus, the way he looked at her. No one had ever made her feel so wanted.

"Can I trust you, Mack?"

She frowned. "Of course."

"I want more. Janet pulled me up from a junior program and gave me my first shot at IndyCar. I'll always be grateful . . ."

"But," she said for him.

He whispered and Mack didn't know if he was keeping it quiet for himself or because they were in the JJR garage. "But it's time for something new."

"A new team?" The hush of her voice matched his.

He nodded guiltily. "I'm ready for a new challenge. I owe Janet everything, she's a good boss and she's taken me as far as she can . . ." He trailed off but Mack understood what he wasn't saying. JJR was a small team and it was a testament to Leo's talent and Janet's hustle that they'd gotten their one-car team onto the podium multiple times. But the bigger teams had bigger resources, and like everything else in America, bigger resources meant a better chance of winning.

"Is that a possibility?" Mack knew even as she asked the question that it was. Leo Raisman was beloved to both fans and sponsors, and he proved himself on track week after week. Any team would be lucky to have him.

Leo drew an inhale and nodded. "I don't have room for error."

Mack stepped slightly closer into him, until no air remained between them, just space all around them in the vastness of the garage. "Me either," she whispered.

"I know," Leo said softly. His thumb barely ghosted over her neck. "I know."

He took a sizable step back.

Panicked, Mack grabbed the front of his shirt and pulled. She shoved up on her toes and kissed him the way she'd wanted to since they walked into the garage. Leo matched her fervor, his fingers sliding through her tangled hair, his palms cupping her jaw. Her mind knew she was being foolish but her body said he felt so right, so perfect as his rough beard scraped her healing chin and his heat enveloped her body. She pressed down on his shoulders to gain leverage, then jumped and wrapped her legs around him. Leo groaned as he moved his hands to her thighs and pulled her closer.

She had no idea how long they'd been kissing when Leo gently, carefully slowed their pace. Then he eased his hands up her body, softly letting gravity pull her feet back down to the floor. When she was standing, their bodies still tightly aligned, Leo cupped her face again for one last long kiss. Her lips followed him as he pulled away, but Leo tilted his head so that their foreheads touched but their lips couldn't reach, his hands still holding her face.

Mack had never done that before. She'd always followed through, sometimes even as alarm bells went off in her head. She never stopped a thing once she started it. She'd never been with someone levelheaded like Leo, someone who matched her fervor but also tamed it.

She stood breathing heavily, somewhere between embarrassed that she'd thrown herself at him and grateful that Leo stopped them from doing god only knows what in the garage. She glanced up, looking for cameras. She'd told Laurie she knew better now, but making out in the team garage where others could find footage of her and Leo was about as stupid as it got.

Leo ran his thumb over her lip and he was still looking at her mouth when he spoke. "You have to know how much I want to find an empty office." His eyes found hers. "But you told me you didn't want distractions, and I want you to have everything you need to make this race."

Mack studied his face, so serious and sincere even though his pupils were still blown. She wanted him to steamroll over her boundaries, to make bad decisions with her, to act first and think later. She wanted him to be wild and reckless and as self-destructive as she was.

Because he didn't, and because he wasn't, she liked him way too much. It made her furious.

"Why are you so fucking decent?" She'd meant to snap, to throw the words at him as an accusation, but they came out a whisper, swallowed up by the empty garage.

"Not decent," said Leo. "Shady. I'm putting in the hard work and now I'm waiting for the luck to follow."

"Winning Indy?"

Leo hummed in agreement, but it was subdued, like he was holding something back.

INDIANAPOLIS COURIER-JOURNAL

May 14

Indianapolis Motor Speedway: The Greatest Women You Don't Know

The Indianapolis Motor Speedway is full of storied traditions: the chilled milk and wreath of orchids given to the winning driver, the Borg-Warner Trophy, the yard of bricks at the start-finish line. Equally well known are the men who define the track: Carl Fisher, who built the Speedway with millions of paving bricks in 1909; Ray Harroun, the 500-mile race's first winner; Tom Carnegie, the track's longest tenured and most beloved announcer.

Lesser known, but no less important, are the women of the Indianapolis 500. Just in time for Mother's Day, we've compiled an incomplete list of the women who made Indiana's favorite race what it is today.

Maude Yagle: In 1929, Maude entered a car under the name "M. A. Yagle" and became the first and only woman to own the winning Indy 500 car. Women were not allowed on pit lane at the time, so Maude timed her race car from the grandstands.

Alice Greene: As a young copywriter, Ms. Greene coined the iconic term "The Greatest Spectacle in Racing" in 1954. Not long after creating the phrase that would soon define the Indianapolis 500, Greene left the copy room to tend to her nine children. Her son places two checkered flags on her grave every Mother's Day.

Bettie Cadou: Women were not allowed in Gasoline Alley until 1971, when veteran reporter Bettie Cadou sued for the right to earn a "silver badge" allowing her access to all the same areas of the track as her male counterparts. Cadou went on to a prodigious career in journalism.

Janet Guthrie: Janet Guthrie earned many firsts for women in racing—the first woman to qualify for the Indy 500, the first woman to qualify for the Daytona 500, and the first woman to snag a major corporate sponsorship (with Texaco). Guthrie was inducted into the International Women's Sports Hall of Fame in 1980.

Danica Patrick: Patrick was the first woman to lead laps in the Indianapolis 500 (as a rookie) and the first and only woman to win an IndyCar race (Twin Ring Motegi, 2008).

Beth Paretta: In 2021, Paretta formed a mostly-female IndyCar team—from driver to crew to engineers—and remains a strong advocate for women in motorsports worldwide.

Many outstanding women have helped craft the legacy of the iconic Indianapolis 500. Who will be next?

CHAPTER 15

10 days until the Indianapolis 500

Mack received the text ten minutes after she got to the garage the next morning, and she immediately headed for the pedestrian entrance of Gasoline Alley. She'd barely rounded the corner when she saw Wes, Billie, and a bouncing Shaw waving like she'd been gone for two years instead of two weeks.

"Mama! MAMA!"

Mack had Shaw in her arms faster than any car she'd ever driven. Holding her daughter made the anxiety of the last few days melt away, at least for a moment. She looked Shaw over, finding her daughter both exactly the same and yet changed as time took away her childhood second by second.

"I love you, I love you, I love you," Mack murmured into Shaw's soft hair. Not once since her horrible decision to let Shaw stay with Kelley had she spent a night away from her daughter, and even though Mack had craved space and time to herself, she felt like things were clicking back into place now that she held Shaw in her arms again. Shaw grounded her without even trying, the soft embrace of her warm little body and the familiar scent of lotion and chewing gum.

"Mama! Don't smear my face paint!" Mack pulled back enough to see Shaw's cheeks flanked with black-and-white checkered flags. Her blond hair was twisted in a complicated braid that circled her head, and tiny race car earrings dangled from her lobes. Shaw preened at the attention. "Billie helped me look fancy! And she made us all outfits. Look!"

Sure enough, the three of them were all wearing royal blue T-shirts with MACK WILLIAMS #11 emblazoned in bright white font. Wes and Shaw wore matching checkered-flag bandannas around their necks and Billie wore a checkered-flag headband. Wes leaned heavily on his cane, tears bubbling in the creases of his eyes even as he grinned wider than Mack had seen in years. It was a familiar smile, the one that said, *that's my girl.* She'd forgotten that he used to look at her like that night after night when she'd won under the lights, and it nearly broke her. Mack rubbed at her mouth to hide the wobble in her lip. These people had such faith in her and she couldn't even find two-twenty on track.

She pulled her aviators out of her hair and plopped them over her watery eyes. If she started crying now, she might not stop until the entire month of May was over. Undeterred, Wes pulled her in for a bear hug. "You're finally here, Spec. I knew it. I always knew it."

The thick tenor of her own voice made her feel naked. "You look good, Daddy."

Billie rubbed Wes's back in circles, looking at him like he'd just come home from war. "Healthy eating and exercise are miracle drugs. We've been working hard to build up strength to cheer for"—she paused and directed her voice up toward the heavens—"Mack Williams, number eleven!"

Wes beamed at Billie but Mack's cheeks flamed with mortification. What if everyone in the garage overheard and thought she was full of herself when in reality she was so slow she would never make the field? Her breakfast swirled in her stomach and she looked around to see if anyone was looking their way.

"Goddamn! The Indy 500. Sure wish I had a beer to celebrate."

Her dad loved a morning beer, loved a track beer, and his true love in life was probably a beer at the track in the morning, but Mack saw no cooler in sight. "You didn't bring any?"

Wes shook his head. "This keto diet Billie's got me on is no carbs. 'Specially not the boozy ones."

"Not one seizure in two weeks!" Billie beamed. "We're finally on the right track with your diet and exercise, aren't we, baby? No more food from a box and no more moping around the house."

Mack flinched, thinking of her go-to meals. Boxes galore. She knew nothing about keto or supplements or any of the other crap Billie went on and on about. She swallowed and looked behind Wes. "Where's Laurie?"

Wes waved a careless hand. "She said she'd meet us here. Something about work."

Mack frowned. "I only gave you one parking pass."

"Something tells me your sister don't mind pissing away twenty dollars on parking." The Speedway charged a hefty fee for the grass parking lots immediately outside the track, and getting out could take hours on race day. As kids, Laurie and Mack begged Wes to park closer to the track, but he always insisted on parking—for free—over a mile away in a residential neighborhood.

"It was twelve dollars."

Laurie appeared from behind, seemingly materializing out of thin air, wearing a creamy pencil skirt and matching button-down. Laurie's face was inscrutable but Wes put his free hand over his heart. Mack watched as her dad swallowed thickly and held out his arms.

"Hi." Laurie gave her father a full up-and-down perusal before letting herself step into his embrace. To anyone else, Laurie looked cool and calm but Mack could see the faint quiver of her chin over Wes's shoulder.

Her sister visited Haubstadt a trio of times since she left for college: once after Wes was injured and twice on Shaw's birthday, each visit successively shorter and more tense. Four years had passed since her father and sister had been within handshake distance. Shaw, oblivious to the emotional soup, slammed into Laurie, heedless of her face paint and glitter rubbing all over Laurie's clothes. Uncaring, Laurie lifted up

Shaw and held her like a baby koala. Her sister was flaky when it came to her adult family, but she never missed a weekly FaceTime with her niece. Kids were magic like that.

"Shaw-Shaw! Who said you could grow so tall?"

"Hey there, Laurie! I've been dying to meet Wes's brilliant lawyer daughter!" Billie drawled. She pulled Laurie, who was still holding Shaw, into a perfume-laced embrace. How very Billie to hug and coo and gush over someone she just met. She fawned over Laurie's sleek hair and perfect lip liner before pulling a bright blue shirt out of her giant tote bag. "I had to guess on the size but I think it will work. I have extras in the RV if this is too big."

Mack and Laurie spoke at the same time. "RV?"

Wes flashed a shit-eating grin at the same time Shaw began babbling. "Pawpaw and Billie got one of those big houses on wheels! The steering wheel is bigger than a tire and Billie drove it on all the twisty roads while me and Pawpaw sat in the back and played cards. It's got beds and a fridge and a potty and everything!"

Wes pulled Billie into his side and she gave him a quick peck on the cheek. She was so . . . tactile. Mack wanted to wipe away the splotch of bright lipstick that clung to her dad's scruffy cheek.

"Finally got me a good woman and an RV. Me and Billie wanna travel the country. Grand Canyon, Florida, even up where you were in Washington, DC." He nodded at Laurie. "Got a good deal and jumped on it."

A *good deal*? Mack's mind snagged. They had no savings. Wes's health needs had taken most of their collective winnings, and Mack had used the last of her Eldora purse to keep the track afloat during the pandemic. Their track was solvent, but barely. If her dad put a second mortgage on the track, they'd have to work to pay it off until Shaw was drawing social security. "How can you run the track if you're bouncing around the country in a motor home? And what about your doctors' appointments?"

Wes waved his free hand in the air, brushing off her concerns. "Telehealth! I sure wish we'd had something like this when you girls was small. And this rig is fancy as hell. Nothing like the one we had when you girls was kids. I don't have to sleep on the couch no more."

He laughed it off, but Mack remembered how he'd slept on the small kitchen bench that folded into a makeshift bed so she and Laurie could share the one mattress in their small camper. She met her sister's eyes and knew Laurie was remembering it, too. Mack had to physically bite her cheek to keep from asking how he could afford an RV when they were early in the dirt track season and unexpected repairs would inevitably slap them in the face. She knew questioning her dad on finances would lead to a shouting match, and she wasn't going to do that in Gasoline Alley.

"Mama," Shaw tugged at her elbow. "When do we get to meet Leo Raisman? I want him to sign my model car from last year."

A mortifying heat crept up Mack's face and she couldn't bring herself to look in Laurie's direction.

Her sister set Shaw down on the ground. "Your mama needs to get back to the garage now. Practice starts in twenty minutes and she's not even in her gear."

At least one thing hadn't changed in the last sixteen years: Laurie always did know how to bail Mack out of a jam.

Mack glanced over her shoulder and waved one more time as she walked away, both wanting to stay with them and wishing she were at the track alone. As she pulled on her gear in the garage, she tried to push away all thoughts of RVs, Billie's lipstick on her dad's cheek, Shaw, and her father and sister side by side for the first time in years.

From: Daniel.Stormsend@PetDirect.com
To: MWilliams@email.com; Laurie.Williams@StoeppelEvansFirm.com
Subject: RE: Unique Indy 500 Sponsorship Opportunity! [May 14, 2:44 p.m.]

Ms. Williams,

I'm honored that you considered Pet Direct for sponsorship for the Indianapolis 500. We believe our strongest assets are our people, our partnerships, and our furry friends. While we admire your journey, we have a very small marketing budget and cannot provide the assistance you've requested.

We wish you luck as you chase your dreams!

Kindly,
Daniel Stormsend
Chief Marketing Officer
Pet Direct Supply Company LLC
Grand Rapids, Michigan

CHAPTER 16

10 days until the Indianapolis 500

Janet waved her over to the team's timing tent—an elaborate makeshift setup behind the pit wall that housed multiple computer screens with real-time data measurements from Mack's car and even Mack herself. The data would most certainly show Mack's heart racing as she headed toward Janet, who stood with her arms crossed and headphones hanging around her neck, frowning. Whether her disappointment was still over Mack's first day behavior or because she was on day three of horrifyingly slow practice, Mack had no idea.

"You got a sponsor yet?" Janet barked.

Without earplugs, Mack's ears rang with the high-pitched whine of cars at speed and the deep gurgle of engines idling on pit lane. She shook her head. "No, ma'am."

"You're about to lose the one sponsor you have. Hartley is not happy with your performance, or really anything about you. They're mumbling about keeping their money on Leo's car only." Janet held up her hand to hold off any protest. "It's premature, but it's the way money goes in racing. No magic, no money. In your case, no penis plus no magic equals you might as well turn tail and go home."

"I'm working on the pace," Mack protested.

Janet slashed her hand through the air. "Sponsors and media don't want to watch a woman struggle. You've got to give them a good story, or be sexy, or show them you're five times better than anyone else. Right now, you're none of those."

"I'm trying my hardest out there!"

Mack knew she sounded like the same petulant child she swore she wasn't, but dammit she *was* trying. Doubt began to creep inside her heart and helmet. What if she wasn't good enough? She'd been told so often that she was talented, but what if her skills didn't translate, or worse, she'd lost them in the years since she'd stopped racing?

She thought of Wes and Laurie, sitting in the stands and watching her. They were the only people here who really knew what she could do in a car. They'd seen her bring the magic to the track. Were they watching her now, embarrassed for her, cringing as she grasped for something that maybe was no longer there? A brisk wind hit her sweat-coated body and she began to shake. Her hands spasmed and she badly wanted to flex her fingers, but she held still so Janet wouldn't see her weakness. "I'm trying everything. Staying in the turns longer, then shorter. I'm using the tools, I'm trying new lines."

Janet yanked off her sunglasses. Dark circles bagged under her eyes and her thin face narrowed sharply under her cheekbones. "The lone-wolf thing might work on the dirt track but here it takes two dozen people to qualify one car alone. Work with your team and figure out the fucking issue." She dropped the sunglasses back over her eyes. "In the meantime, you've got a sponsor lunch with Hartley tomorrow. Bring the charm, make them like you. Don't fuck it up."

With a flick of her wrist, Mack was dismissed.

Mack stood stupidly outside the timing tent, knowing there was no point arguing with Janet but not wanting the smothering comfort of her family either. She wished she could talk to Leo. She could use an infusion of his laid-back optimism, but she knew they both needed distance to keep their relationship professional.

She was still standing in the same spot when Jimmy appeared at her side. "Let's walk," he said, before turning and heading the opposite direction down pit lane.

Mack glanced at Janet but she was now talking to Lucie. There was nothing to do but to follow Jimmy.

They walked past two dozen pit stalls until they reached the end of pit lane. The first pit stall was empty and Jimmy sat on the white painted concrete and patted the spot next to him. Once her butt hit the concrete, Mack realized how exhausted she was. She wasn't sleeping well and she spent dawn to dusk hunting down sponsorships, at the track, or manhandling the car to the point her joints went brittle and her back throbbed. She wondered if the twenty-year-olds felt this many aches.

"This isn't something you can be great at overnight," Jimmy said.

Mack exhaled. Oh thank Saint Dolly Parton. He got it. "I need more time."

Jimmy shook his head. "No, hear my words. You can't be Scott Dixon overnight. But you *can* be a hell of a lot better than you are right now."

"But I'm—"

"No. *Listen.* You're talented, I can tell. But you're trying to do everything all at once, and to do it alone. No matter what the fans think, racing is a team sport. Surely you know that?"

Mack frowned. "No one else is out there driving the car. The crew can't help me find ten miles per hour."

"That's your problem right there. The team is exactly where you find extra speed."

"But—"

"You a mechanic?"

"Uh, no."

"You a tire specialist?"

"No."

"You understand fuel map data?"

Mack's body rebelled, nausea and sweat and soreness all mixing together. She grasped his point, but she still resisted. "No."

"But I bet you've played around with setups—understeer, oversteer, more or less camber . . . right?"

"We have played around with setup! I'm still going so slow I might as well be driving down Sixteenth Street. *I* need to get back in the car and—"

Jimmy cut her off. "You ever heard of Willy T. Ribbs?"

Mack startled at the change in subject. "The first Black man to qualify for the 500?"

Jimmy's smile lit up his lined face and he patted the wall where they sat. "That's him. I was right here in this spot when he made the field in '91. I remember looking up at the scoring pylon and seeing his number pop up there. It wasn't digital back then, you had to wait for the light bulbs to change. I don't think there was a person of color without tears in their eyes that day. Hell, every decent person was on their feet cheering and hollering at what that man overcame that day." Jimmy's grin faded when he turned to face her. "You know how he got there?"

"Hard work?"

"No one worked harder than Willy but even he couldn't do it on his own. His team never stopped, even when engine after engine blew. They went through five damn engines to make the race. And Willy, he was willing to listen to anyone he trusted." Jimmy gave her a pointed look and she understood that not everyone had a Black man's interest at heart, then or now. "He made the field because he worked *with* his team. He let other people in. He didn't let his ego get in the way of the goal. And let me tell you, that man has ego. But he wanted to make the race more than he wanted to say he did it all by himself."

Mack chewed her lip. She *would* do anything fair and legal to make the race. She couldn't live with herself if she left Indy knowing she'd given anything less than everything. Being here was a gift, a slice of fortune dropped into her lap, and she hadn't known until she arrived how much she'd needed the overhaul. Her life in Haubstadt was safe and secure, but also heavy and stale. She was holding on to this last chance with an iron grip; if she could make this work, make it good, then maybe she could go home and finally be okay with the way her life turned out.

Because if she didn't qualify, if she lost her one shot at Indy, she was terrified she'd let out all the hurt and resentment and devastation that filled up her insides, and that her eruption would smother Shaw. She didn't regret Shaw, but by god, she mourned racing. Driving at Indianapolis made her realize how deep her sorrows had tunneled in and become a bitter core.

Better to make this last chance work and hope it was enough to live on for the rest of her life.

"You aren't the first person to have a hard time here," Jimmy said. "You think it was easy for Janet? Lyn St. James? Willy? People sent them death threats. I've been here a long, long time and they ain't never made it easy on an outsider. But you don't have to make it harder on yourself by pushing away people who want to help you."

Something low and buried in Mack's chest ached. *People who want to help you.* The last ten years had been a slog of unending work and emotional upheaval. Many nights she'd laid in bed and cried into the silence for help, then gotten up in the morning and did what she had to do. She'd been making it work on her own for so long that she didn't even know how to accept help when it stared her in the face.

Her mind flashed to Leo, at how she'd screamed at him on pit lane the first day of practice. She'd asked him to keep their relationship professional, and he'd done exactly that, and she'd thrown his help back in his face.

She shouted to be heard over the cars that streaked down pit lane mere feet from them. "So what do you want me to do?"

Jimmy stood and hooked his thumb in the direction of the team trailer. "We're going to sit down with the data folks and the tire folks, and you're going to talk them through exactly what you're feeling, and exactly when you feel it. Every bump, every blip. We're going to use that information to set up the car from scratch, because what we have sure as shit ain't working. You'll answer every question, and you'll really *listen* to what these folks tell you. Most of these people have been doing this work longer than you've been alive. They want to win as much as you do. Work *with* them and maybe we'll all make the big show."

Mack watched the remaining cars on track whiz by in blurs of bright colors. If she had to set aside her pride, if she had to trust crew members she hardly knew, she'd do it to make the race. She'd do anything.

She looked at Jimmy's weathered face and saw nothing but open assessment, as if he already knew what she'd say. She nodded.

"You know how I knew I picked one messed-up sport?" Jimmy asked as he slapped his knees and rose from the concrete wall. "When I saw that they drink milk to celebrate. Goddamn *milk*."

He said it like a curse but Mack saw the twinkle in his eyes as he walked toward Gasoline Alley.

CHAPTER 17

10 days until the Indianapolis 500

Mack spent most of her pregnancy angry. Furious at herself, enraged at Kelley for not caring, angry at Laurie for being angry with her, and pissed at Wes for being so kind to her. She'd kept that rage close, the fury keeping her from falling completely apart as her world crumbled. First, she'd had to stop racing. Then, she'd lost the respect of her peers, and most of her friends, and finally her whole career. Some days, the anger was the only thing that got her out of bed.

Then Shaw was born and the crying started.

Shaw cried at five in the morning, and at midnight, and all the hours in between. Nothing Mack did calmed her, not the drops on her tongue or calming lotions after baths or oils on her feet or the fancy motorized swing Mack bought on credit. The doctor diagnosed colic and said there was nothing she could do, but what she did not explain was how to survive the endless auditory assault without losing her sanity.

And then Wes wrecked, and Mack and Shaw screamed together.

Even as Wes lay in the hospital hovering between life and death, Shaw screamed from sunup to sundown. Mack's own wails of anguish echoed her daughter's, leaking out like the milk that kept her breasts sticky and wet. Mack had stared down at her infant daughter and her broken dad, sobbing, unable to think anything other than *helpmehelpmehelpme*. Until the day a nurse calmly scooped up Shaw and led Mack into an unoccupied room. "You lay down and sleep as long as you can, okay? I'm Shauna. I've got your baby. You sleep."

Delirious, Mack had crawled onto the sterile hospital bed and passed out, unable to worry about where Shaw was going or with whom. Mack didn't know if she'd slept an hour or an entire day, but she woke to weak sunlight peeking through the thin curtains, her chest hard and achy. She'd found Shaw at the nurse's station, quiet, clean, and contently suckling a bottle in Shauna's arms. Mack was too stupefied to care what was in the bottle.

"Okay?" she'd asked, her voice raw and barely audible.

She'd been asking after Shaw but the nurse gave a sympathetic smile and said, "Same as yesterday. Remember, it could be weeks before the swelling in his brain goes down."

Mack nodded. She wondered if she should hold her arms out for the baby and felt shame that she didn't want to do anything that might make Shaw wake and scream.

"She's not crying."

The nurse smiled down at Shaw. "Some babies just don't want to be babies."

Shauna's words became truth. Around the time Shaw could sit on her own, she started to cry less and laugh more, and by the time she was walking, all traces of that angry baby were gone and a smiling, golden-haired girl toddled in her place. If Mack had gazed into a crystal ball to see the truth of who her daughter would become, she couldn't have believed it on that day.

In the years since, Mack had forgotten to reach out and ask for help, and accept help when it was offered. Outside of the hospital, there weren't many Shaunas to be found. Laurie had been preoccupied with her own life, and Mack was alone, a young single mother with a disabled dad and a precarious business, forced to learn how to change diapers and dressings. She spent a decade powering through on her own, not knowing how to ask for help.

Which made accepting help from the crew infinitely harder.

Instead of going home to shower after the third day of practice, Mack sat on a metal folding chair in the team trailer, still in her reeking coveralls and pinched between a wall of whiteboards and a narrow table. IndyCars were fickle machines and the slightest change could add or subtract substantial speed, and she answered the crew's questions about everything from seat vibrations to the exact sound the car made during gear shifts.

And there were a lot of crew. The eleven car's team of engineers and mechanics crowded around the long conference table, tight enough that Mack's knees touched someone else's, while Janet sat in the middle of the table, one ankle crossed over her opposite knee, taking up enough space for three people. Leo leaned against the corner, shoulder to shoulder with his engineer. Jimmy had called all hands together to figure out the mystery of Mack's lack of speed, and while she didn't make a habit of doubting herself behind the wheel, she worried the problem with the eleven car was *her*.

She'd started the meeting by apologizing, trying to convey sincerity and humility, but after an hour of grilling, Mack's answers grew shorter, sharper. She heard the snappishness of her own voice when she answered a question and then was asked the same thing again in a slightly different way. Over and over, she insisted that she felt a strong understeer, only to be told that she couldn't possibly be feeling anything but oversteer. When she pointed out the places where she did feel oversteer, the engineers told her she was wrong. What was the point of answering their questions if they wouldn't listen to her?

In the hot, crowded room, Mack's mind started to wander. She wanted a shower, and she hadn't even had a second to process an angry text she'd received from Kelley. He never reached out to her first and Mack had been startled to see his name pop up on her phone. He'd seen posts about her on the JJR social media account and demanded to know what she was doing. He didn't ask about Shaw, didn't question the whereabouts of his daughter, but wanted to know why Mack was at

Indy. As an engineer droned on about wind shear, Mack was rereading the text and starting to get pissed off when Janet slapped her hands on the table hard enough to knock Mack's thoughts back into the present, along with someone else's water bottle. "Enough of this shit. We've accomplished zero in here. Time for a walk-n-talk."

Groans echoed around the room as engineers grabbed their laptops and stumbled out of the trailer. Mack jumped at the chance to leave the stuffy room and followed dutifully behind Jimmy.

"What are we doing?"

The older man frowned as he descended the open-weave metal stairs. "When the team is cranky, the boss makes us get up and start walking. We keep working to solve the issue, but we do it while walking. Usually around whatever track we're at." He pointed to his leg. "My hip doesn't like it much, but it does seem to knock the attitude outta these computer nerds."

"I was starting to feel rage-y in there."

"Exactly," Jimmy said. "Harder to be on your high horse when your feet touch the ground."

The track, so loud and crowded an hour ago, was eerily calm. Janet led her team like troops from the trailer to the track, marching like she intended to speed-walk the entire two-and-a-half-mile loop. They all followed in a ragged line, quiet conversations peppering the air as they reached the famous yard of bricks that made up the start-finish line. Jimmy and Lucie walked ahead, heads bowed in intense conversation, but Mack stayed behind the group. She slowed her steps as she passed over the bricks, felt the ridges of the mortar under her toes. It was only earth, clay and lime and water, and yet those three feet meant so much to so many people: history, hard work, heartbreak, holy ground.

"You okay, Rookie?"

Mack hadn't noticed Leo walking out with the rest of the crew, and it surprised her that he'd stayed so long, especially since it had nothing to do with his own qualification. He looked calm and confident, the late-afternoon sun showing off his perpetual tan. Hitting speeds in the two-hundred-thirty-mile mark must be good for the health.

"This feels pointless," she admitted. "It's like they're mad that I'm feeling what I feel in the car."

Leo shook his head. "They don't know you yet. I've been with my team for eight years, and they know the lines I choose, the feel I prefer, even how my body moves in the car. You and your team don't have that yet."

"That's not my fault," she complained. She kept her gaze on the white walls of turn four looming ahead of them. It seemed so close, like they could touch the wall in a moment but in reality they would walk a thousand more steps before reaching it.

"It's not," Leo conceded. "But I promise they want to figure it out as much as you do." Mack stared silently ahead, not convinced. "When you pull into the turn, what is it you need? What do you wish you were getting from the car?"

Her instinct was to snap at him that she'd done nothing but answer that same question for the last hour, but it *was* a slightly different variation. The engineers asked what she felt—in the car, in her hands, in her body—but no one asked what she *wished* she felt in the car. She looked down at the storied asphalt and tried to explain.

"You know that moment when you first start turning the wheel? Like the very millisecond when you first move? It's tight."

Leo considered that for a long moment. "What about the exit?"

Closing her eyes, Mack remembered how the car felt before Jimmy told her to come in for the day. "In the apex of the turn, I'm prepped for the back to swing wide, but on the exit I'm crossing my arms to keep it off the wall."

Jimmy and Lucie had fallen back from the group and were listening carefully to Mack. They shared a long look, the kind that comes from years working together. The four of them walked in silence until Janet eventually stopped.

"We've been keeping the back end tight so she doesn't spin herself around and smack the wall," Jimmy said, his face as expressionless as always. "Maybe that dirt track slide is too ingrained to fight."

Janet was shaking her head before Jimmy finished speaking. "Absolutely not. There's no backup car for the eleven. She crashes, we're done."

Two other engineers spoke up, echoing Janet's concerns. Mack wasn't entirely sure what change they were fighting but she was annoyed anyway. *It won't work* was a bullshit excuse without facts to back it up.

"What we have isn't working, whether it's my lack of experience here or my style of driving. I *know* what I'm feeling from the car, and I can't drive it like that."

One of the younger engineers piped in. "We've made so many tweaks at this point, I still think we should go back to Leo's metrics from last year and start from there. He almost won with that setup."

"That setup was for last year's cold and damp weather. We didn't even try running it this year on the eighteen car," Lucie said.

Janet stood silently with her arms crossed, but her shrewd eyes bounced around the group. "Raisman, you got any bright ideas?"

Leo held out a hand, palm up, in Mack's direction as if to say, *listen to her*. "Let the rookie try a loose setup. We have one more day of practice. Start small and see how she handles it. If it works, loosen it up a bit more."

"And if she slams it into the wall?" Janet asked.

"You wanted someone outside the mainstream. *'Not another karting prick'* you said. You picked her, now you have to trust her to know what she needs," Leo said casually.

I want you to have everything you need to make this race.

Mack couldn't stop her eyes from flitting around the crew, the echo of his words from the other night ringing in her head. What if there was a camera and someone had seen her throw herself at him? She trusted that Leo wouldn't tell anyone about their night together, but what if the crew could pick up on the energy between them? What if they thought Leo was advocating for her because they were sleeping together?

"*She* is right here," Mack snapped. She could fight her own damn battles. "And I'm telling you that I've spent three days doing nothing but trying to keep off the wall. I've done everything you've asked of me on the track and in the garage." Mack didn't even know if she wanted to try a different configuration, or if she just wanted to participate in her own fate. "Let me try a looser car."

Janet's gray eyes stared down the front stretch. As if tuned to the same frequency, the team followed her gaze down the wide lane of asphalt. The scoring pylon stood tall and dark against the fading afternoon light, reminding them all of what was at stake. If Mack didn't get her number somewhere on the thirty-three slots, half of the people standing in turn four would be going home before race day.

Including Mack.

She would go home with nothing but mortification, heartbreak, and a shit ton of debt. She had no idea what kind of operating costs she was racking up with JJR, but when a single steering wheel cost thirty thousand dollars, it couldn't be cheap. The thought of working at the dirt track, and probably a second job, for decades to pay off a failed attempt at Indy made her physically shake. And she still had no idea how Wes had paid for that RV. She hadn't yet let herself think about the financial consequences for Shaw—no car at sixteen, no college, not a single thing Mack wanted to give her—and she sure as shit couldn't think about that right now.

She had no other option; she had to make the race and find a sponsor.

Suddenly, Janet stood up straight and rubbed her hands over her face before resting them in their customary perch on her hips. "If you put this car into the wall, it's over. We don't have the cash and you sure don't either. If it doesn't feel good after a warm-up lap, or if you have an inkling that you might lose it, get on the apron and come in."

She didn't wait to see Mack's reaction; she was already galloping toward the pits, her long legs putting quick distance between herself and everyone else left staring in her wake.

It wasn't until later that night, when Mack was finally showered and wrapped in the soft cotton of Laurie's guest bed, that she let herself really think about Leo's words: *trust her to know what she needs.*

Wes and Shaw loved her, but they also depended on her. Nearly a decade of serving other people's needs, and now she wondered if she herself even knew what she needed. What she wanted.

What she wanted and what she needed felt as far apart as Indiana and Indonesia. What she needed was to find speed so that she could hold on to her one shot at the Indy 500. She needed to take advantage of every second of this opportunity, and then return to her real life. She needed to get this out of her system so she could go home and be a better mother, daughter, business owner.

What she wanted . . . Dammit, she wanted it all. Security for Shaw, safety for her dad. She wanted them to need her a little less, and hated herself for wanting that. And for herself, she wanted a career in racing. Not one desperate grapple, but a life with fast cars and races week after week, a team she'd worked with long enough that they knew her moves before she did. She wanted a life in the driver's seat.

Not for a single second did she let herself picture Leo Raisman sitting next to her, riding shotgun.

@JANETJOYNERRACINGOFFICIAL
May 15

Teammates Leo Raisman and Mack Williams walk the track before the final day of practice.

COMMENTS:

@LEORAISMANSMOM go go go JJR!

@harryhowdidhedoit Did IMS repave the track? Looks smooth as buttah.

@jokrok calling it now, this chick will wreck out one of these dudes

@calebpinkstaff4countycouncil why is he banging this skinny dogface? She's ugly.

@beautyfrominside She's pretty if you're into that natural look. But she needs to use a sun damage serum. **@mackwilliamsracing** I'm a SkinCouncil rep and would love to tell you about our organic, non-GMO, sulfate-free products. Sent you a DM!

CHAPTER 18

9 days until the Indianapolis 500

Across the infield, hospitality kiosks stretched across the concrete, the bright colors of their tents standing out against the gray pavement. Motorsports sponsorship was big business, with most teams relying heavily on funding from corporate entities to support the cost of running a million-dollar car. Mack watched as people in logoed polo shirts scuttled between tents, schmoozing with sponsors, taking photos, and otherwise charming the executives who put money in their pockets. With Laurie's help, she'd purchased simple black trousers, a silky black button-down, and low black heels, and she'd let Laurie give her eyeliner and lip liner and everything in between. Her blond hair was shoved into a painfully tight twist, and she stood outside a royal purple tent emblazoned with Hartley Harvester Manufacturing's well-known logo, hoping she looked professional enough to get more sponsorship dollars.

"Rookie!" From behind her, Leo shouted over the din of whirring golf carts and loud conversations spilling from the hospitality tents. "Ready to unzip the corporate purse?"

She scowled at him, both because she dreaded the coming hour of schmoozing and because he looked so good dressed up in dark trousers and a pale blue button-down that made the dark brown of his eyes richer. It was obnoxious that he could pull off polished and laid back at the same time. He must have been surveying her as she checked him out because he said, low and soft, "You clean up nice, Mack."

She should snap at him to cut it out but couldn't get the words out of her mouth. The way he looked at her—with awe and heat and want—was potent medicine, healing a part of her she hadn't known was hurt. After everything with Kelley, she'd stopped feeling desirable. Everything about her felt hard and weathered, but Leo made her feel like the redbud trees in bloom, new and tender and lovely.

"You too, Leo." She cleared her throat. "Thank you for yesterday, for helping me communicate with Janet and the team. And for all the help you've offered this week. For listening to me. For hearing me. Especially after I've been . . . not nice."

Leo studied her, a half smile on his face, like he'd flipped over his cards in a poker game to find an ace. He leaned in ever so slightly, those intense eyes connected with her own. "I don't scare easily." He stepped back and gestured toward the tent. "C'mon, let's do this."

Mack plastered on her best smile-for-strangers grin and walked inside the tent alongside Leo. He immediately started glad-handing, talking to random Hartley employees as if they were old friends. From across the tent, Janet caught her eye and made a slight gesture toward the opposite side where a cluster of people in royal purple polo shirts sipped twenty-ounce beers. Mack understood the message—Leo would work one side of the tent, Mack the other. Striding up to the group, Mack introduced herself and asked a few inane questions. *How are y'all enjoying the practices so far? What's your favorite place to eat in Indianapolis?* For all her attitude about the event, she was good with strangers. All those years of traveling around the country and then running the track had made her good at chitchat.

A woman wearing head-to-toe purple asked, "How long have you been in IndyCar? I'm sorry, I'm not familiar with your name."

Mack glanced at her watch. "Oh, not even three weeks."

The woman choked on a mouthful of food and her companions laughed nervously. "Wait, seriously?"

Mack smiled with a lightness she didn't feel and recalled her dad's bee-charming ways. Wes Williams had a folksy wit that made reporters and fans adore him. "Seriously. Janet and I wanted to really go for broke in the Rookie of the Year contest."

The circle of purple shirts laughed politely. Another person asked, "What were you doing before IndyCar?"

No point in lying. "My family and I own a small dirt track in southern Indiana. I've been running that and raising my daughter. But I used to—"

"Oh my god, you have a kid?" the woman in all purple blurted. "Isn't that dangerous? Racing these cars and knowing that your child is watching?"

All the hairs on Mack's arms and neck lifted. She made her voice calm even though she wanted to shout. "No more dangerous than all the men out here racing."

"But you're the mom!"

In racing, there were two kinds of collisions: those the driver saw coming and could brace for impact, and the kind that came from the blind side and slammed the car into the wall before the driver even knew she was in trouble. The purple woman's careless words rammed into Mack without warning.

You're the mom.

She was still reeling, the silence in the little cluster of people becoming awkward, when Leo appeared at her side, oblivious to the emotional shunt she'd just experienced. "Fortunately for all of us, breakfast is about to be served, but unfortunately, Mack and I have to sit elsewhere. Trust me, you want Mack to sign your gear later. You thought Sarah Fisher was tough?" He quirked his thumb at Mack. "This woman once won a race with a broken elbow."

Mack mumbled some niceties and followed Leo toward a round table, the sound of the purple-clad woman stuck in her ears.

But you're the mom.

At the head table, Janet sat flanked by three men. One of the men, extremely large from his height to the girth of his belly, held out a hand to Leo. "Raisman! Good to see you running in the top ten." His rheumy eyes flicked to Mack. "And who's this lovely date you've brought?"

Mack was too stunned to speak. Every woman in racing heard insults on any given day of the week—she'd been on the receiving end of countless crude put-downs—but the assumption, at this level of racing, that she was Leo's *date* hurt more than all the others combined.

Leo went into instant action, taking a step back and motioning at Mack as if he were Vanna White and she were the letterboard. "This is Mack Williams, the newest driver for JJR." He overemphasized *driver*. "She's made the podium at several famous tracks. Eldora, Chili Bowl, 24 Hours of Daytona . . ." If the situation wasn't so mortifying, the panic on Leo's face would have made her laugh.

"Oh my, I thought you were Leo's girl. Pardon me." The man extended his palm to Mack. "Hollis Whitfield. Head of marketing."

She was about to lash out with a snarky comeback but Janet caught her eye with an oddly maternal look—*sit down, shut up, do not embarrass me*—followed by a silently mouthed, *Your only sponsor*. Mack pulled her lips inward and bit down hard to stop herself from snapping at Janet, who'd done nothing to correct Hollis's pathetic error, instead letting Leo do her dirty work. Sports money could hobble the strongest people.

Still seething, Mack sat down and spent the next hour making small talk and answering inane questions, trying to be polite even though her insides were boiling. Hollis's whole demeanor changed after Leo's introduction, morphing from Good Ol' Country Boy into Lofty Executive. He rarely spoke to her, focusing his attention on Leo to the point of awkwardness. Ever the peacemaker, Leo tried to pull the conversation around to Mack but her temper got the best of her and she turned in her chair and spoke to the other two marketing people. When plates were cleared and coffee was offered, Mack stood and made a lame excuse to leave.

She stomped out of the tent as well as she could in her heels, heading for the team trailer. She knew without looking that Leo followed her. When she was out of sight of the Hartley tent, she turned. "Don't you dare make excuses for that asshole."

Leo held up both hands, frowning. "Give me some credit. Hollis is barely tolerable on a good day."

"But," she prompted, pulling her hair out of the tortuous pins.

Leo ran his hands through his hair in frustration, loosening the curls from their gelled hold. Hair that good was obnoxious, honestly. "Hartley is our biggest sponsor."

"So it's okay for him to assume I'm your fucking *girlfriend*?"

"No!" Leo looked around them, then gestured back toward the garage. "Let's talk somewhere more private, okay?"

"There's nothing to talk about, Leo," she said, but started walking anyway. Even though she was speed-walking, Leo took one step for every two of hers and it sent her into a fury. She was practically running by the time they hit Gasoline Alley. "Do you see what I mean now? This sport . . . geezus, the shit we have to put up with for daring to be a woman who wants to race. I'm starting this race two laps down just for having a goddamn vagina! You want to think that men like Hollis are nothing unusual but they're the norm. The only woman in the room is a girlfriend, a secretary, a nurse, not the driver or the CEO or the doctor." She whirled to face him. "Do you see? Do you see why—?"

Suddenly aware of the dozens of people in the garage area, she stopped. Her body shook with rage, and she wanted to throw something or hit someone or put the pedal on the floor and drive so fast she nearly lost control.

She wasn't just mad, she was *mortified*.

"I'm sorry for what he said, Mack. It was unacceptable. But you're never going to change a prick like Hollis by running your mouth. But you can prove him wrong"—he pointed toward the track—"out there. I've been there too, where no one believes you belong and the only way you can make them believe is to go faster than everyone else. You have to show them you're too good to be ignored. Show them what you can do *there*." He stabbed his finger in the direction of the track once more for emphasis.

Hollis's comment had embarrassed her, but Leo's words humiliated her. Janet had thrown the same line her way: *You've got to give them a good story, or be sexy, or show them you're five times better than anyone else.* But no matter how Leo looked at her, Mack wasn't the type of woman that could pull off sexy, and her story wasn't one she was willing to share. *But you're the mom.* All she had was her driving skill. In the past she'd relied on her ability to put any car at the front of the finish line, but here at Indy, she could hardly get out of the pit box.

"Fuck you, Leo. You think I'm not trying to be faster than everyone else? You think I don't want this? I want this more than you will ever understand. I *need* this." She paused, not wanting to think of what came a week from now, not wanting to tell him that she needed the memory of racing in the Indy 500 to get her through the next decades of her life. If she wasted this chance, she'd be worse off than ever before, stewing in self-pity and self-loathing, unbearable to herself and her daughter because she'd have no one to blame but herself for ruining her single shot at Indy. "This is all I'm ever going to have, Leo. You'll go on to the next race and the next year and the next 500, but no matter what, I'll go home on Memorial Day."

She hated how her voice broke on the word *home*.

Leo reached for her hand but stopped before actually touching her, as if remembering they stood in the middle of the paddock.

"Then get out there and prove Hollis wrong. Show Janet she made the right choice. More importantly, get in the goddamn car and believe that you belong in the Indy 500."

From: Arya@LovelyLinens.com
To: MWilliams@email.com; Laurie.Williams@StoeppelEvansFirm.com
Subject: RE: Exciting Sponsorship Opportunity! [May 15, 7:56 a.m.]

Thank you for your inquiry into sponsorship methodology at Lovely Linens. While we are intrigued by your request, our marketing dollars are already committed for the calendar year. If you are interested in talking about sponsorship for next year, please give me a call.

Wishing you the best of luck in this year's Indy 500.

Thanks,
AO
Arya R. Ongaleigh
Director of Marketing
Lovely Linens, Inc.
Chattanooga, Tennessee

CHAPTER 19

9 days until the Indianapolis 500

The final day of practice was her last chance to find speed in the car, and as much as it infuriated her to admit, Leo was right. All she could control was what she did on track. The crew had made adjustments, changing the camber and tire balance and triple-checking the bodywork for uneven spots. They'd listened to her and implemented every change they could, and now it was Mack's turn to pull her weight.

She felt the change in the car immediately.

Even on cold tires, it took less effort to turn. Instead of pushing the wheel as hard as possible to the left and still barely managing to make the corner, the car glided through turns one and two. She kept her speeds slower on the first lap, and at the start of the second, Jimmy radioed for her to "give it a whirl." She accelerated on the front stretch and eased into turn one. Midway through, right at the apex of the turn, the back end of the car stepped out toward the exterior wall. Reflexively, Mack countercorrected and caught the car before it noticeably fishtailed. Blood thumped in her head and she could hear her own breathing inside the tight helmet as she exited the turn. Janet and Jimmy surely had seen her lose control, but her radio stayed silent.

When she hit turn two, she anticipated the loose end of the car and kept it steady through the long, sweeping left-hander. She churned lap after lap, focused on finding the right line. After five laps, her hostile manhandling waned into mild uneasiness. In ten laps, uneasiness transformed into a pattern of motion. The other cars around her faded, and for the first time since she stepped into an IndyCar, she didn't feel like she was fighting the car every second.

"What'cha feeling out there?" Jimmy radioed.

"Understeer is gone. Back's a little loose, but it's working."

"That last lap was in the top twenty cars," Jimmy said casually. Even through the radio static, she could hear the grin in his voice.

Time suspended as she hurtled around the track, fine-tuning the balance of the car through the turns and pushing the throttle on the straightaways, finding the razor edge of control. Her focus homed in on each individual millisecond, her only thoughts about her movements and the car's response. In a world full of technology and overstimulation, the singular focus of driving was the ultimate freedom.

A blur of green and black caught her peripheral vision as another car passed her, and she checked her dials to see if she'd lost speed. But then it clicked: *She* was passing the other car.

How had she forgotten how damn fun this was?

This was what she'd missed. The joy and confidence of going fast yet being in complete command of the car. The rest of her life was filled with so many questions, most of them she didn't know how to answer: *Will Shaw forgive me for yelling? What if Dad has a seizure when I'm not at home? How can we keep cash flow through the offseason?* But here in this car, finally, she knew what to do. She felt confidence and pleasure flowing from the steering wheel down into her body, like the car itself was bringing her back to a version of herself that experienced life instead of merely existing.

"Your tires are going to fall off soon," Janet radioed. "Come in."

Mack ducked into the pits, this time managing to at least get all four tires inside the pit box, if not perfectly straight. She killed the engine and a high-pitched ringing in her ears replaced the sound of the engine. She removed the steering wheel and hauled herself onto the lip of the aeroscreen, her chest heaving with adrenaline and effort.

"Well," Janet said, approaching the car. She looked out at the track, and Mack followed her gaze toward the rows of aluminum bleachers dotted with a few remaining fans. The sun was on its downward arc, but these spectators probably arrived as soon as the gates opened and wouldn't leave until the last car was towed to the garages.

"Those last five laps were freeze-the-car fast." Janet's face was implacable as she watched Mack unbuckle her helmet, but Jimmy's lips curled up slightly at the edges.

Mack pulled off her helmet and pushed her sweaty hair off her face. "Fast enough to qualify?"

Jimmy's lips broke into a real grin and his faded eyes lit up. "Fast enough to put you midfield. The type of fast that makes you wish you could freeze the car so it would stay this good."

A second, then two. And then she realized the significance of what he'd said. *Fast enough to put you midfield.* Mack breathed against the hot tears that threatened; she would not be the woman who cried on pit lane. She managed to stop the tears but couldn't dampen her joy, impulsively hugging Jimmy, and then Janet, even though she probably smelled worse than a high school locker room. Janet awkwardly patted Mack on the back and the two quick taps spoke as loudly as a shout. Mack had finally made her new boss proud.

"This is only the start, you get me? When you're out there, you're working to win. That clear?" Mack nodded even though it made her hydration-starved head pound. "And get a sponsor. Get several."

Jimmy shook her hand and Mack's chest felt tight with the honor. As he walked back toward the garage, he muttered, "Rookie likes a loose car. Didn't see that coming."

Mack hoisted herself over the pit wall and high-fived, fist-bumped, and thanked the crew. Whatever they'd changed on the car had turned it into a rocket ship and she was grateful. Jimmy was right that the driver got the glory, but dozens of people built the victory: mechanics who built the cars, engineers who studied telemetry and weather and track conditions, the over-the-wall crew that put the fuel in the car and changed tires. Every single individual on a team contributed to the success or failure of a car, and Mack's win was theirs, too. She saw it on the faces of everyone around her.

Including Leo, who stood behind the wall, smiling like he'd wanted nothing more than to watch her fly. Body still flooded with adrenaline and endorphins, Mack didn't think twice about throwing herself into his arms. For a second too long, Mack savored the feel of solid chest and arms and that intoxicating smell of warm skin and motor oil.

Leo discreetly put space between them, reminding her of her own rule. Teammates only, especially here on pit lane.

"You're almost in the club now. Qualify for the Indy 500 tomorrow, and they can't ever take that away from you."

Her throat closed with unexpected feeling, and she fiddled with the collar of her fire suit to hide the wave of emotion. Soon—too soon—she'd go back to her real life, caring for her family and running the dirt track, but no matter how many bleacher seats she had to repair, or how much popcorn she had to pop, however many school plays and dentist appointments lay in front of her, she could still be Mack Williams, Indy 500 qualifier.

Did Leo understand the gift he gave her?

"A few of us get together the night before qualification starts. It's practically geriatric, no booze, in bed by ten, but it's tradition. Say you'll join us?"

She blinked, surprised by the invitation but more surprised by how badly she wanted to say yes. A night out sounded like exactly what she needed, but Shaw was waiting for her, and Wes and Laurie. And, for Mack, nights out never ended calmly; the night with Leo at Workingman's was one of many nights she'd promised herself to stay calm and ended up in someone else's bed. The only reason they'd stopped themselves in the garage was because Leo had self-control.

She tilted her head back and looked at the sky, needing a moment to sort through all her want-to-do versus should-do calculations.

"Williams! C'mon back to the garage and let's do a quick debrief," Janet called. She didn't wait for anyone before stalking back to Gasoline Alley. Practice was coming to a close for the day, and the sound of multiple engines pulling into pit lane blotted out all other sound. Mack gestured with her thumb toward the garage.

Leo leaned in and cupped a hand near her ear, close enough that his beard tickled her. "I'll text you the info. We'll make it a teammate tradition."

From: Zara.T.Ongaias@EverCold.com
To: MWilliams@email.com; Laurie.Williams@StoeppelEvansFirm.com
Subject: RE: Unique Indy 500 Sponsorship Opportunity! [May 15, 3:29 p.m.]

Ms. Williams,

Thank you for contacting EverCold about Indianapolis 500 sponsorship opportunities. We appreciate your pitch; unfortunately, we do not see motorsport racing as a value-add for our marketing.

Best of luck,
Zara T. Ongaias
Head of Marketing
EverCold Camping Products, LLC
Missoula, Montana

CHAPTER 20

9 days until the Indianapolis 500

Her entire family ambushed Mack as she exited the infield restroom-turned-locker-room, smothering her with hugs even though she reeked of a funky combination of physical exertion, nervousness, and post-practice nausea sweats. Her dad was unfazed.

"My Spec, flying around Indianapolis. I knew it. I knew it would happen yet," Wes croaked as he hugged her.

Emotional, Mack pulled away. This was how she wanted her dad to see her, not the exhausted, cranky bitch she often was at home. He'd never made his love conditional, but dammit if she didn't want to earn his praise anyway. "Shh! I haven't even qualified yet."

"You smell funny." Shaw pinched her nose, doing her duty as a child to keep her mother humble, even as Mack squeezed her tight. Single parenthood was often isolating and thankless, but it all made sense when Shaw squeezed her back.

"I figured you might want a ride home, and Dad and Shaw are dying to show you the RV. According to my niece, it is the height of luxury. Could we escort you to our father's newest home with wheels?" Laurie managed to turn yet another of Billie's homemade T-shirts—a tie-dyed blue-and-white swirl with her name in bold black cursive—into a fashion statement with white jeans and sky-high sandals.

A tram drove them through a long tunnel under the track itself, exiting into the grassy sprawl of a parking lot as the sun kissed the horizon. Each time Mack saw an Indiana sunset, all open skies and waving fields and golden apricot light, she felt it in her bones. Indiana was permanently imprinted in her insides. Even if she'd kept racing, she never would have left the land that made her make sense to herself. She closed her eyes and inhaled the bright floral scent of tulip poplars and dogwoods and the verdant tang of freshly mown grass.

They jerked to a stop at a massive burgundy-and-gold motor coach parked in between dozens of other campers. Wes proudly ushered her inside, and she instantly traveled back twenty years. This motor home was three times the size of the one they'd grown up in, but the concept was so familiar Mack swore she could smell the vinyl seats and Wes's Old Spice cologne. And yet, nothing in this coach felt like Wes. The stainless steel appliances, plush fabric seating, and stone tabletop were a far cry from the orange corduroy and peeling Formica they'd grown up with. A sign proclaiming WELCOME Y'ALL adorned the entryway, and a bouquet of fake white lilies sat on the dining table. Black-and-white buffalo check curtains hung at the windows, and a framed watercolor of a field—with a sunset startlingly similar to the one outside—hung over the small kitchen sink. The entire place smelled like the candle section of Walmart.

Not for the first time, Mack wondered how her dad could afford such a luxury vehicle. She desperately wanted to ask, but she worried the answer would be too terrifying. She'd deal with that after Indy. After she qualified and raced and knew the full extent of what kind of money she owed Janet. If she couldn't find sponsorship, she might be paying back Janet and the RV mortgage for the rest of her life. She'd have to find a second job, maybe a third.

Shaw tugged on Mack's arm as she chattered about all the RV's features, pointing out the dining bench that turned into a sofa, the small bathroom, a row of bunk beds, and large primary bedroom at the back. The hallway was lined with rows of black-and-white photographs in matching frames, and Mack stopped when a familiar image snagged her attention.

A cigarette dangled from a younger Wes's lips while his hands held a large trophy. *Perris, California.* Early on in the heat races, her dad flipped his car, bouncing end over end before landing upside down. Mack was too young to worry much, but Laurie had sobbed until Wes, like a stray cat, crawled out of the mangled chassis without a scratch. He went on to win the main event later that night as the banged-out dents in his car gleamed in the overhead lights. Mack had been full of childlike glee at her dad's victory, but Laurie hadn't spoken to their dad for two days afterward.

Their family history played out in grayscale down the hallway. Wes toasting cans of Miller High Life with his racing buddies after winning the Chili Bowl Nationals, Wes standing on the roof of his car after winning his seventh and final championship. Laurie at thirteen, holding a cardboard microphone at a makeshift podium Wes made for her when she complained about not being able to compete at the school spelling bee. Mack at ten, helmet in hand, the top of her head not even clearing the roll bar of her first quarter midget. Twenty-year-old Mack, sweaty but smiling after a stint at 24 Hours of Daytona. Laurie, peering over the top of *Persuasion.*

At the end of the hallway hung a large portrait of Mack and Laurie at four and eight years old, their arms wrapped tightly around each other. Mack touched a finger to the place where their cheeks smashed together.

"You like it?" Billie asked, startling Mack. Her hands were clasped together, an expectant look on her face. She didn't know if Billie was asking about the RV or the photos.

"It's nice," Mack managed. Where had Billie even found these photographs? It was unsettling that someone she barely knew had seen the still shots of their lives and known exactly how to display their past so that they'd remember the good parts, not the bad.

"It's awesome!" Shaw said as she clambered onto the top bunk, swathed in ruffled blue bedding. "Blankie loves it!" She rubbed her face on her worn fleece blanket, the way she had as a baby, and burst into giggles.

Not for the first time, Mack marveled at the difference between her own childhood and her daughter's. Mack's early years were adventure and chaos, but she'd busted her ass to make her own daughter's life predictable and serene. She'd been so sure that Shaw needed stability, that their life needed to be quiet and calm and uneventful, but looking around the motor coach Mack wondered if she'd steered them from safe into boring. Shaw seemed to be enjoying the adventure.

Mack twisted her hair off her neck, feeling hot and overwhelmed.

"Billie made it all fancy," Wes remarked. "Did all the work herself, too. She could have her own business decorating RVs, couldn't you, baby?"

"This is the only RV I'm interested in, hon." Mack had to glance away from the tender look they shared. "This is our little slice of retirement heaven."

"Retirement?"

Wes startled, then quickly lifted one side of his mouth in a lazy smile. "A man can dream, can't he?"

Billie opened the full-size refrigerator and offered Mack a can of fizzy water but she waved it off. "Hey, this company is a good idea for sponsorship! Who doesn't love flavored fizzy water?"

"Me," Mack retorted. Her body ached and everything about the situation gave her the heebie-jeebies. How could her dad be thinking about retirement when Mack was wondering if she needed to get over her pride and find a job at the local appliance factory to pay for the extravagance of this RV and her few weeks chasing the Indy 500?

"That's not a bad idea, actually." Laurie tapped at her phone. "I'm making a list of specialty beverage companies and emailing tonight."

Ever the older sister, Laurie continued to help Mack with sponsorships despite being swamped at work, and despite their ability to reel in anyone yet. It was Laurie's version of an olive branch, and Mack was trying to accept that Laurie's bossy assistance might be the only piece of her sister she'd ever get. In the two weeks Mack had lived with her sister, Laurie had spent 90 percent of her time at the office, on her computer, or on her phone. When Mack asked about her job, Laurie always responded with the same blunt *It's fine.* Laurie asked Mack endless questions about her time at the track, but it was clear her sister wasn't going to share any of her interior life with Mack.

Shaw tugged on the hem of Billie's cropped T-shirt. "B, can I have a snack?"

Billie handed her a container of hummus and celery from the fridge and plopped down on the padded banquette. Her daughter, consummate Doritos and blue Powerade aficionado, ate hummus now?

A large whiteboard hanging over the table caught her eye. "What's that?"

Wes beamed. "Another one of Billie's ideas. A weekly schedule with all our appointments and activities, right where I can see it. Keeps me from asking Billie a hundred questions."

"I read about it on a blog for caregivers of brain injury patients. Visual cues are so important!" Billie pointed around the room at the light switches and cabinet doors, and Mack saw that each one had a tidy label: Overhead Light. Spices. Plates. Batteries. "We put them up in the bathroom and bedroom, too. The labels help your dad find things independently."

A sickening mix of shame and judgment swirled in Mack's belly. More often than not, it was easier for Mack to hand Wes a fork or turn on the lights herself. Had she held her dad's recovery back? Kept him from being more independent because she was in a rush to get things done?

"We got a shared calendar on our phones, too. Little alarms tell me when to take my meds." He pulled Billie closer with his good arm. "Ain't this woman a goddamn miracle?"

Mack's stomach bucked. The RV felt hot and disorienting and too much like an actual *home.*

Laurie shot Billie a polite but firm look. "I bet Mack is ready to go."

"Oh, right! I'll get us fired up. We'll drop you off but come back here for the night. Paid for the camping spot and all." Billie glided into the oversize driver's seat, buckled herself in, and lowered the steering wheel. Seconds later, they were bumping out of the parking lot and onto the interstate. Outside the window, Indianapolis passed by, its tightly gridded neighborhoods filled with brick and clapboard houses, tidy squares of greening lawns, and rows and rows of sycamores, maples, elms, and aging oaks.

Mack perched on the soft seat next to Shaw, half-heartedly answering Wes's questions about gearing ratio and the in-car tools. Her body was shot after a day of wrestling the car, and being in this RV made her feel extraneous.

The street was quiet when Billie pulled the RV into a no-parking zone and turned on the flashers. The glass and limestone of Laurie's apartment building glowed pale silver in the fading light, and Mack wished she could teleport upstairs and into a hot shower.

"Get some rest," Wes ordered. "Big day tomorrow." She felt her dad's hand, once rough but now soft, on the back of her neck. "Hey," he whispered, as if they were the only two people in the RV. "It's just another day racing, and you know what they say."

In tandem, they said, "A bad day of racing is still better than not racing at all."

From: Binny.Bnai@DitzyCandyCompany.com
To: MWilliams@email.com; Laurie.Williams@StoeppelEvansFirm.com
Subject: RE: Unique Indy 500 Sponsorship Opportunity! [May 15, 11:33 p.m.]

Dear Ms. Williams,

Thank you for contacting the Ditzy Candy Company. At this time, we do not participate in athletic sponsorships.

Sincerely,
Binny Bnai
Marketing Associate
Ditzy Candy Company
America's Go-To Sugar Rush!
Chicago, Illinois

CHAPTER 21

9 days until the Indianapolis 500

"What are you doing?"

Mack paused, mascara wand in hand. She blinked innocently at Laurie's reflection in the guest bathroom mirror. "You're always telling me to wear makeup."

"Not at six p.m. the night before Indy 500 qualifications. Where are you going?"

Mack finger combed her hair off her forehead, determined not to rise to Laurie's bait. She didn't know herself where she was headed, only that Leo sent her coordinates and she needed to burn off her nervous energy. The last thing she needed was to lie in bed and obsess over the various ways tomorrow could go wrong.

"You need to focus. Eat a good dinner and then get good rest. Not . . ." Laurie flicked a glance at Mack's skintight black jeans and thin white tank. "Whatever this is."

"I need to be with other people who understand the pressure of tomorrow." Mack shoved her toothbrush in her mouth and glared at Laurie's reflection.

"People like Leo Raisman?"

Mack spoke around the toothbrush. "What the fuck does that mean?"

With an irritated eye roll, Laurie grabbed a tissue and wiped at the mirror where Mack had sprayed foamy spit. "It means exactly what you think it means. The biggest moment of your life and once again you're going to ruin it by screwing around with some guy."

Mack bristled. Sleeping with Leo had been a mistake, but he wasn't just some guy. She didn't know what they were to each other, but he was nothing like Kelley or the one-night flings she'd once mainlined. He was too good for *some guy*.

"I'm not fucking around with anyone," Mack said honestly.

Laurie skewered her with a look but Mack held her ground. They may have lived apart for the past sixteen years, but Mack knew her sister's tactics. Laurie would wait her out until, pathologically unable to hide from her older sister no matter how much she wanted to, Mack would blab too much and Laurie would judge too much and the inevitable argument would start. She didn't know why she couldn't keep her mouth shut with Laurie, but she was determined to do so now.

Laurie stood and waited placidly. *Shit.*

She faced Laurie head-on. "I'm meeting several drivers for some pre-qual tradition. It's an honor to be invited. Plus, I can't sit here and overthink everything. I need to *not* think."

"And Leo will be there," Laurie said.

"He's my teammate."

"That you aren't sleeping with?"

"Nope," Mack said, pushing past Laurie and toeing on her favorite flip-flops. *Not anymore.*

"My god, at least wear some real shoes," Laurie snapped. She pawed through the mess on the closet floor and handed Mack the white Nikes she never wore because they pinched her toes but couldn't bring herself to throw out because she'd got a good deal in the kids section. She slipped them on, annoyed that the rainbow Swoosh went perfectly with her royal blue jacket.

Laurie ran her hands through Mack's hair, tucking and fluffing until the waves were artfully arranged rather than their usual haphazard mess. Her focus remained on Mack's hair as she said softly, "I get needing distraction but please, please do not make a mess of this like last time."

Mack froze, her momentary appreciation for Laurie's style smothered by shock. The last time Mack had a shot at Indy, she'd had to back out because she was pregnant with Shaw. "Are you calling Shaw a mess?"

"No!" Laurie had the grace to flush. "No, that's not what I'm saying at all." Her hands fell from Mack's hair. She looked both contrite and concerned. "You always do this, Mack. Go wild, do dumb shit, mess around with the wrong people right when you're poised to win the most. You do whatever it is you want without thinking of the consequences."

"Are you fucking kidding me? I think about the consequences of my actions every day! What does this decision mean for Shaw? For Dad? For the dirt track? My whole life is about consequences, Laurie. Which is a hell of a lot more than you can say."

"What are you saying, Mackenzie?"

Her restless nerves popped at the prospect of a fight, and Mack threw out the words she'd been dying to say for years. "I'm saying that you flit around doing whatever you want, not coming home, not caring about anyone but yourself. Not caring about *consequences*."

Laurie's eyes grew round. "I was a first-year associate at a cutthroat firm, working eighty-hour weeks with six figures of student loans when Dad had his accident. You said you were fine, that you could handle everything."

"I could not fucking handle it!" Mack shouted.

They'd argued about their individual choices before, but never so bluntly. They'd bickered as teenagers, fighting over stolen lipsticks (Laurie, from Hooks drugstore) and smuggled joints (Mack, from a mechanic twice her age), but their disagreements over the last ten years seethed with quiet tension and barely hidden resentment. Mack wanted to have it out, to put all the shit between them out in the open so they could examine it, find the rotten pieces where they'd messed up, and excise them. Maybe then they could stop this sickening cycle of cold distance and hot argument. Mack kicked aside her gear bag, carelessly discarded on the floor, and crossed her arms.

"I was left alone with a terrorizing baby that cried all goddamn day and our shattered father. Do you know what a mind fuck it is to change diapers for your baby *and* your dad? You were off sipping lattes and going to a fancy office while I was trying to keep Shaw and Dad alive. I almost . . ." She stopped herself, too close to saying the thing out loud that she'd never told anyone else, not even Wes. "I had no one, and you didn't even fucking care."

Laurie blinked for several silent moments, the quiet crackling in the wake of Mack's shouting. "I didn't know," Laurie said flatly, as if she knew how pathetic her words were.

"Must have been nice." Mack knew she was being mean but *fuck* it felt good to say all the quiet parts out loud.

"That's not what it was like," Laurie said defensively. Inexplicably, she started to pull up the sheets of Mack's bed, tucking the cotton into crisp corners. "I was trying to pay off my loans and make rent and—"

"Dad almost died!"

I almost died. And there it was, the bottom she'd hit that she never wanted to think about again. How she'd been so exhausted and overwhelmed, how Shaw had never stopped crying and wouldn't sleep, how Wes had barely stayed alive, and Mack had thought, *this would all go away if I went away.* She'd considered pills, drugs, even looked up how to buy a gun. She felt sick anytime she remembered that day, and how she'd only chosen to live because she couldn't puzzle out who would care for Shaw and Wes.

And over the years, she'd come to blame Laurie for that day. For leaving her alone with two helpless humans and her own terrifying thoughts. For years, she'd thought, *Laurie would have made it better. Laurie could have fixed everything. Laurie should have kept me from that pain.*

Only now, as she watched her sister tidy the mess on the nightstand, did she understand how incredibly misplaced her anger was, how she'd been so scared of her own almost-choice that she'd turned the blame on Laurie.

But in the end, she'd saved her own damn self, hadn't she?

She was so lost in her own thoughts she didn't hear Laurie at first. "What?"

"I couldn't handle seeing Dad like that." Laurie was crying, a sight as strange as her sister's sparkling white apartment. She sat down on the edge of the freshly made bed. "I couldn't, Mack. I know that's awful. I know." She gasped a racked breath. "Dad and I had a huge argument before I left for Georgetown, and the last thing I said to him was terrible. I was mean and hurtful, and then I saw him in that hospital and all I could think about was that he was going to die believing that I hated him. I'd been so shitty to him, ignoring his calls and refusing to come home on college breaks. When he got better, I was embarrassed. Every month I didn't come home, I got more embarrassed until it was easier to not come home at all."

Mack blinked. "So the reason you didn't come home, the reason you let me fucking *drown* . . . is because you were . . . embarrassed?"

"I was afraid, Mack. You were racing all over the country with Dad but I had to stay and go to high school in Haubstadt. You two left me behind to fend for myself. Half the time I was doing your homework. I hated it. I hated that I was scared to try kissing girls in a town where people say *gay* as an insult, hated that liking Beowulf made me a nerd, hated being the girl that didn't look like the rest of her family. The day I left, I told Wes he was a stupid redneck and I hated him. I said I wished I knew my real dad because my life would have been better."

"Wes is your real dad," Mack said automatically.

"You never got it, how lonely it was for me. I don't look like you and Dad. You two made fun of me when I was scared by your wrecks and made fun of my schoolwork. I was really fucked up about you and Wes and our mom for a really long time. When Wes got hurt and I'd said all those awful things . . . I didn't know how to face him. It became something too big to get past. And the more I didn't come home, the more I felt awful, so I avoided coming home. And you. I was afraid—I *am* afraid—that you hate me."

Laurie wiped her face with the hem of her T-shirt. Mack's perfect sister, who ironed her weekend jeans and wore red lipstick to the gym, was a mess. Thick mascara smeared her cheeks and angry red patches spread over her smooth skin. All these years Mack assumed Laurie thought she was too good for them, that she didn't care about her family.

She sat next to Laurie. "I could never hate you. You could run away for fifty years and you would still be my only sister. I love you."

"I've been in therapy for years. It took me five years to say, 'I fear abandonment so I leave people before they can leave me.' Just ask any of my many ex-girlfriends."

Laurie scrubbed her face with her hands, making the mascara situation worse, and Mack barked out a laugh. She made a circle over her own face.

"There's so much going on."

Laurie glanced from her blackened hands to the clothes and wet towels on the floor of Mack's room and puffed a small laugh. She carefully held her hands away from the white duvet of Mack's bed. "Geezus, Mack, how did we get here?"

"Williamses are stubborn assholes," she said with a shrug, as if that explained everything. Mack grabbed a towel from the floor and handed it to Laurie.

"I guess I still think of you as my wild little sister," Laurie said, wiping her face. "But you're an adult. You've taken care of so much for so long, and I never realized how much you're doing. You know what you need, and if that's a night out with . . . whomever . . . I hope you have a good time. Be safe."

They'd spent so many years shutting each other out. So many years denying and shaming and blaming, but dammit if they weren't still here trying. "I will never"—Mack emphasized the word twice—"never let a man come between me and the Indianapolis 500 again."

Laurie reached out, pulling Mack into the steady circle of her arms. "You don't owe me an explanation. I see it now."

Mack was halfway out the door when she thought to ask, "You never said why you moved to Indy."

Laurie balked and bit down her lip, something she never did. Mack was all fidget and motion, but Laurie was icy reserve. Several breaths passed while she considered her words.

"DC is expensive, the firms are extremely cutthroat, and I'm tired of dating the same type of NGO girls. It was time for a change."

Mack paused, guessing there was more to the answer but Laurie looked exhausted, her face smeared with makeup and tears, and Mack was ready for some lightness after all the dark they'd hashed out. She let Laurie off the hook.

"Lucky for me you did."

INDIANAPOLIS COURIER-JOURNAL
May 15

Indianapolis 500 Qualifying: How, When, Why

The Indy 500 is jam-packed with events and traditions, but it all starts with qualification weekend. Qualification takes place one week before The Greatest Spectacle in Racing. This year, the number of cars attempting to qualify (35) is greater than available spots in the field (33), meaning at least two drivers will be "bumped" from the field. (Why 33? Tradition, baby!)

For the uninitiated, below are some qualification-week terms and timelines:

Pole Position: The fastest car to qualify.

Bubble: A car in 33rd position during qualifying, vulnerable to being eliminated from the final field.

Bump: When a car is pushed out of the race grid because another car qualified with a faster speed. A bumped car may reattempt qualification if time remains; if not, that car is permanently eliminated from the Indy 500.

Friday: Final day of practice, often called Fast Friday. Often a good indicator of how cars will place—or not—the following day.

Saturday: First day of qualifying. Each car runs five total laps per attempt: a single warm-up lap, then four qualification laps. A car's posted speed is the average of the four qualification laps.

Sunday: Also known as "Bump Day." Any driver who failed to qualify on day one can make an attempt. If the "bubble" driver is bumped from the field, the bumped car may take another qualification run. On this day, cars may line up in one of two lanes. A car in the "fast" lane has priority to take to the track, but will lose their previous qualification time. Cars in the slow lane must wait for cars in the fast lane, but keep any prior lap time. When the horn sounds at 6 p.m. on Sunday, each driver is locked into their qualifying position and the Indianapolis 500 field is set.

As a reminder of how competitive and fast these cars are, the actual speed difference between the pole sitter and final qualifier last year was only three seconds.

CHAPTER 22

9 days until the Indianapolis 500

Mack stood outside one of Indianapolis's most renowned establishments, certain Leo had either given her the wrong location or was pulling a rookie prank. He'd said they wouldn't be out late, but this was certainly not a place where patrons popped in for a quick minute. The famous neon sign buzzed as she squinted through the dark windows, looking for Leo. Behind her, a valet discreetly cleared his throat. Before he could tell her to leave, she yanked open the heavy door.

St. Elmo Steak House was a Midwestern institution, known for backroom deals, celebrity appearances, tender steaks, and fine wines. The year Mack attended her first Indy 500, when she was younger even than Shaw, Wes had driven past the famous restaurant on their way home. She and Laurie had begged to go inside to look for sports stars, but Wes had ranted that they could get the entire McDonald's menu for less than the cost of one steak at St. Elmo.

The interior of the restaurant was every bit as plush as she'd ever imagined, the dim lighting making the dark wood and brass-studded leather finishes look even deeper and more luxurious. The tigerwood back bar stretched to the ceiling, flanked by thick columns with carved wood flourishes, and the wall-length mirror reflected hundreds of bottles of expensive booze. Every seat at the bar was occupied and all the tables were packed.

Mack flexed her toes inside her sneakers and rubbed her arms on the polyester of her blazer, certain her cheapness stood out.

"Rookie! You made it!"

At the far end of the bar, tucked near the open-concept kitchen, Jericho, Boomer, and Leo sat in a row, waving her over like she was a good friend they'd been waiting for. Boomer had shaved the scraggly ginger scruff that usually dotted his cheeks, and Leo's long hair was carefully tucked behind his ears. Jericho tapped the empty stool between himself and Leo. They all wore dark suits, all obviously expensive, like a row of Wall Street bankers. "I had to fight off a very unhappy, very important Man in a Suit for this seat, so sit your ass down and give the bartender your order. Nice blazer."

Billie had gifted her the jacket, and Mack refused to admit that she loved the giant silver bedazzled "11" on the back. She slid onto a wide leather barstool. "I thought this was a no-drinking kind of night."

Boomer flipped his gaze between Leo and Jericho. "You didn't tell her?"

Leo shrugged, but his dark eyes glinted with mischief. "The tradition is a surprise for the rookies."

"A tradition that helped me win last year," Jericho boasted, his finger pointing down the bar. He called out loudly, "Right, Craig? We're ready! Bottoms up!"

Mack opened her mouth to protest—she'd been dead serious when she'd told Laurie that she wouldn't let anything get between her and the Indy 500—but Leo waved her off with his snaggletooth smile. "It's not booze. We're clowns but we'd never sabotage the race," he promised.

The soft lighting of the bar highlighted the shine of his dark curls and the warmth of his skin. His beard was neatly trimmed and the suit was a nice touch too, except . . . Mack laughed when she realized the T-shirt under his sports coat boasted My Best Friend Won the Indy 500 and All I Got Was This T-shirt. A glance at Boomer revealed he wore a T-shirt with his blazer and dress pants, except his proclaimed

I Pee in My Seat. Jericho wore a crisp lavender button-down and a shit-eating grin.

"They never should have taken the bet," he boasted. "These numpties agreed to wear a design of my choosing if I won."

She gestured up and down. "You know the lumberjack beard ruins the sharp-dressed-man effect, right?"

"Who needs handsome when you've got the winner's ring, yeah? And my fiancée loves the beard."

"There's no accounting for taste," Boomer rejoined.

"Says the man dating the enemy!"

Boomer rolled his neck from side to side, and Mack could hear the loud crack of his spine over the noise of the bar. It was the worst-kept secret in IndyCar that Boomer was in a long-term relationship with a crewman on another team, but auto racing was yet another sport where too many people kept quiet about their romantic lives in order to remain in good graces with sponsors. It was infuriating, especially considering the only scandal was that Boomer's boyfriend was on a rival team.

"Anyway," Boomer said irritably. He waved a finger between himself and the two others. "These jokers had two 500s under their belt by the time I was a rookie. I was so nervous on the final day of practice that I kept dashing to the porta-pots. My two *friends* here, one of whom is my teammate"—he scowled at Jericho—"decided to help me *relax* the night before quals by bringing me here so I could really roast my guts."

"Right on time," Leo said as a man in a gray sweater approached with a large tray. "Mack, meet Craig Huse, the owner of this fine establishment and purveyor of the finest shrimp cocktail in the world. Craig, it's my pleasure to introduce you to my first-ever teammate and the fastest woman in Indianapolis, Mack Williams."

Craig smiled and leaned forward with a small bow. "It's an honor. I hope your taste in food is more sophisticated than your taste in friends." Despite his teasing, the mutual respect between the restaurateur and the drivers was obvious. He wished them luck and promised he'd be watching from the stands tomorrow before placing a pewter goblet in front of each of them. A handful of plump pink shrimp lined the rim of the cup and chunky red sauce filled the interior. "Godspeed!"

Boomer and Jericho cackled as Craig backed away, grinning and shaking his head. She suspected there was a prank coming but she was distracted by the sheer joy of the camaraderie. The whole thing was ridiculous, the T-shirts and the bragging and the keeping her in the dark, and she loved it. When was the last time she'd hung out with friends, having fun? And when had she ever done that without taking it into chaos?

Leo banged his fist on the polished bar. "Are we doing this or not?"

"Right," Boomer agreed. "It's almost bedtime. On three?"

"What's on three?" she demanded, but the three men ignored her and plucked the shrimp off the side of their silver cups. Boomer braced like he was preparing for a punch and Jericho did some shallow breathing that Mack vaguely remembered learning in a birthing class.

Boomer held the cup of overflowing cocktail sauce. "Drink up, Rookie."

"What?" she shouted a little too loudly.

"DRINK IT!" the three men yelled back even louder. Mack was vaguely aware of other patrons watching them, and for reasons she couldn't explain even to herself, she took the cup from Boomer and downed the sauce.

Other than the odd sensation of drinking a condiment, Mack really didn't see why it was such a thing for these guys but maybe—

Oh shit goddamn holy fucking piss on a power line she was suddenly dying. *Dying.* Her tongue went hot and numb, and the gums above her teeth felt triple their normal size. Salty water spontaneously poured from her eyes and she was pretty certain she had snot running out of her nose and over her lips, but she couldn't feel anything in the general region of her mouth. The inside of her nose felt like she'd inhaled a flamethrower.

"Water!" she gasped, fanning her face with her hands.

"No water!" Leo wheezed.

"Be brave, lads!" Jericho choked out. Boomer sat silently crying, his tears pooling on the shiny wood of the bar. He was smiling, or maybe trying not to vomit. Mack couldn't tell.

"Fuck this is terrible!" She had no idea if she was shouting or whispering.

"Okay, okay it's starting to burn down," Leo rasped. Mack's own mouth still blazed but she no longer felt like death was imminent.

"Well, obviously the rookie lost," Jericho said. Even through the burn of the cocktail sauce, he sounded cocky.

"Of course she lost," Leo said. His voice was returning to normal and he dabbed at his eyes with the napkin. "We didn't tell her the rules."

"How the hell did I lose? *What* did I lose?"

"First to ask for water loses," Boomer informed her. "Rookie always loses. Consider it an initiation."

"You're saying that because you were the first rookie to lose," Jericho taunted.

Mack swiveled her head to take them in, a lightness flooding her body. She didn't care that she'd probably ruined her taste buds for life, or that she'd lost some stupid trick. These people cared enough to initiate her into a tradition. An Indy 500 tradition. "You're all fucking nuts," she said through laughter.

"But now you are, too," Leo said, grinning. His nose was still red but he otherwise looked like he'd never inhaled a full cup of potent horseradish. She was certain her own face was blotchy. "Welcome to the Indy 500, Rookie."

"Extra horseradish this year for extra luck," Craig said, the pride of his work evident in his toothy smile. A round of applause echoed across the bar.

The entire restaurant was staring at them and clapping. Some of the patrons blatantly took photos with their phones.

Jericho lifted a beefy arm and pointed his finger at Mack. "A new rookie!"

Clapping and a few whistles echoed around the pressed-tin ceiling before calming into excited chatter across the storied restaurant. Craig swiped the bar with a towel, bowed gracefully, and disappeared down the length of the bar. Mack could feel the heat in her face—both from the cocktail sauce and the attention—but she didn't hate it. Far from it. She felt giddy, almost like she had a good beer buzz, to be included with the knuckleheads sitting next to her and the atmosphere of excitement bubbling through the entire city. It was impossible not to love everything about Indianapolis in May.

Her joy was tempered by a tiny prick of bittersweet knowledge that next year some other rookie would take her place while she spent the weekend back home.

"Let me guess," Mack said, "loser buys dinner?" Her numb mouth watered at the prospect of a juicy rib eye, if not her wallet. Hopefully she still had enough taste buds left to enjoy a seventy-dollar steak, and enough credit on her card to cover dinner for four.

"Pescatarian." Boomer shrugged as he hit a button on his smartwatch. "And it's officially my wind-down window. G'night, y'all. I hope you sleep well and drive like shit tomorrow!" Without waiting for a response, he threw some cash on the bar, clapped them each on the back, and walked out of the restaurant without a backward glance.

Jericho looked like someone had kicked his puppy. "A weeknight steak isn't part of my trainer's carefully managed, expensively crafted meal plan." He pulled Mack into a surprise embrace. "Cheers, Rookie. Go brush the fire out of your mouth and get some sleep. You're gonna do the damn thing tomorrow." He and Leo clasped hands and slapped each other's backs before Jericho sauntered off, waving to the entire dining room as he left.

"He didn't pay."

"Craig doesn't let us pay, but we leave a tip for the staff. Jericho always cheats. Part of the tradition."

"So I don't owe you dinner?" Mack asked Leo, trying to hide her disappointment as she tossed some bills on the bar. This would be her only Indy 500 experience and she wanted it all—the racing, the traditions, the rookie hazing—including a steak dinner.

Leo shrugged sheepishly and added some bills to the stack of cash. "I'd never make you buy me dinner, Rookie." He gestured toward the door, and they both stood. He cleared his throat in the way people do when they're about to admit something embarrassing. "Rich food is not on the pre-race menu for me."

Mack held in a laugh, more amused by Leo's sudden shyness than his tetchy tummy. She glanced around the restaurant as they walked to the door, wanting to imprint the night on her mind. The leather chairs, the hazy lights, the smell of seared beef and butter. When she told Shaw's children about her one shot at the Indy 500, she would also tell the story of the night she'd burned her face off at Indiana's most legendary restaurant.

They emerged into the dark evening, the air chilly without the late-spring sun, and Mack pulled her arms around herself as she and Leo stood on the sidewalk. A wave of lonely self-pity pushed at her chest; she didn't want to go back to her quiet room at Laurie's. After the wild ups and downs of the day—the awkwardness of the Hartley lunch, finding the pace on track, the sickening coziness of Wes and Billie's RV, the fight with Laurie, and the anticipation of what would come tomorrow—she found herself craving something steady. Sturdy. Something like Leo.

The realization startled her. In the past, she'd coped with stress and anxiety with riotous avoidance, seeking release in booze or men or minor property crimes. But time and experience had tempered her, and while she still had the impulse to run rampant across the city looking for release, she wanted something softer to quiet her mind.

The minute she went to bed, the qualification tunnel would start. She would have one shot not to screw up her one chance. And if she failed, if she went home without qualifying . . . Mack knew, deep down she'd never get over missing this unexpected chance, this opportunity that was hers to lose. She'd grieve the Indy 500 forever if she didn't qualify. She'd go back to Haubstadt a shell of a person, and what if her mind went back to the dark place it had gone after Shaw was born? What if this time Mack couldn't push it away?

"You okay?" Leo asked, snapping her out of her thought spiral. His expression was a mix of kindness and curiosity, and Mack couldn't help being anything but honest.

"Nervous. Excited. A little scared of screwing up. The night before . . . it's hard for me to settle down."

Leo watched her a few moments more, squinting as if he was trying to find the words under her words. She let herself return his gaze. He was handsome in an easy way, none of his features outstanding but all coming together in a unique way, the darkness of his eyes balancing the softness of his mouth and the length of his body offset by lithe muscles. But it wasn't only his physicality that Mack studied. Leo Raisman, for all she'd experienced, was a genuinely good human, and his goodness emanated from him like a warm candle. She couldn't look away from the possibility of him.

Which was why she needed to say goodbye. It was late, they needed rest, and Mack knew she shouldn't delay him just because she felt restless. If she asked to go back to his place, she suspected he'd take her there regardless of the consequences to his sleep or routine, and Mack didn't want to be a person who used other people.

She prepared herself to say good night, but Leo asked, "Wanna go watch a bus race?"

From: Valentina.Petrovskovanivitch@GreenBeauty.com
To: MWilliams@email.com; Laurie.Williams@StoeppelEvansFirm.com
Subject: RE: Unique Indy 500 Sponsorship Opportunity! [May 16, 12:42 p.m.]

Thank you for contacting Green Beauty about sponsorship for your racing event. We limit our sponsorships to influencers with over 50k followers. Please feel free to reach back out if you develop a solid social media following!

Thx,
V
Valentina Petrovskovanivitch
Green Beauty Inc.
New York, New York

CHAPTER 23

9 days until the Indianapolis 500

The Indianapolis Speedrome was a slice of southern Indiana in the middle of the state capital. Haubstadt was dirt and the Speedrome was asphalt, but that was pretty much the end of their differences. Déjà vu swept over Mack as she took in the same rolling aluminum doors over the ticket window, the same cheap red paper tickets used by every carnival in the country, and the same chain-link fence where a sullen teenager waved them through. Mack assessed every element as they passed by: the familiar smell of beer and popcorn, the new LED scoreboard, the grandstands that wrapped almost the entire length of the short track. Leo led them confidently through the crowd, smiling and charming his way across the knees and feet of other spectators until they found a seat in the dead center.

"Did you want anything? Snack or a soft drink?"

Mack pulled a face. "You can probably smell bulk popcorn wafting out of my pores. I haven't been able to eat the stuff for years."

When Leo wrinkled his forehead in confusion, Mack explained the connections between the Speedrome and the Haubstadt track. Leo looked around the Speedrome, a little dazed. "It's crazy that you run a place like this. I can't even imagine the work that goes into making a race happen. How do you balance that with racing?"

"Running a place like this is my job, Leo. Every weekend from April to October. Racing is a temporary thing." She paused, unable to stop her brain from turning to her own track. "With climate change doing what it's doing, we probably should run a longer season. Lately it's sixty degrees even in February."

He looked at her with an indiscernible expression, and Mack turned back toward the track in case what she saw on his face was judgment. She wasn't ashamed of their track or the honest work she did for their family. But what if Leo saw it differently? What if racing and tracks were like that old saying: "Those who can't do, teach?" *Those who can't race, run a track.* She liked the version of herself Leo reflected back, and she didn't want to see herself diminished in his eyes.

The first cars edged onto the track before Mack noticed the odd orientation of the track's white striping. When she asked Leo about it, he tilted his head toward her to explain, all laundry soap and warmth, and she struggled to care about anything other than Leo's leg pressed up against her own. Mack could see the stray copper threads in his otherwise dark beard, and in a flash she recalled the way his beard felt against her skin, the texture and weight of his body on hers. Goddamn, how she wanted to take him home and defuse the stress and jitters swirling in her body. To use his body to make her body forget.

Except Leo was more than a stress screw. Going back to Leo's house would be unfair to both of them. He was a lot like Shaw, she realized; kind and easy. She'd always been attracted to arrogant, insolent, wild bad boys, but sitting with Leo in a crowd of strangers, Mack understood the appeal of the guy next door. Leo was like coming home after a hard day of work. He deserved better than being used for stress relief. And she deserved to give her own attention completely to the Indy 500.

"It's a figure-eight race," he said evenly, unaware of her racing thoughts. "The Speedrome was the first track to host these kind of races. They're mostly modified stocks, but tonight is a special feature."

"You said buses?" Mack asked, but the heat race started and there was little point shouting at each other while the first cars took the green flag. They watched and cheered and gasped and groaned as twenty cars raced in a swirling figure eight, narrowly missing each other and occasionally clipping bumpers. It was loud and chaotic and wildly entertaining. She'd heard about this style of racing but never seen it in person. She involuntarily considered adding it to her track lineup, evaluating recruitment and purse costs, additions to the garages, advertising.

Mack rubbed her temples as the wild racing continued. She didn't want to think about home but the initial joy of the night was fading fast. Tomorrow, she would buckle into an IndyCar but no matter how well she did, she'd be back at her own track come Memorial Day.

Why did one Indy 500 no longer feel like enough?

Several heats raced, and then the track fell silent while the crowd waited for the special feature. Mack and Leo chitchatted about everything and nothing, from the engine specs of the modified stocks to their projections for who could take the pole tomorrow. Mack shouldn't have been surprised, but was, when Leo asked, "So how'd you come to own a dirt track?"

"Oh. My dad inherited the track, and after his accident, someone had to run it." She paused as the announcer revved the crowd up for the bus race, wondering why she felt like telling Leo the thing she had always been too ashamed to say out loud. He waited patiently. "Honestly, even if he hadn't been injured, I don't know how long Wes would have run the track." She thought about Wes's excitement over the new RV. "He's not good at staying in one place. Growing up, we lived in a pull-behind RV more than we ever lived in a house."

Leo's dark eyes reflected the grandstand light as they widened. He scratched a hand through his hair, and Mack noticed a small scar that cut into his hairline, a perfectly vertical stripe of shiny white. She wanted to know the story behind that scar, and all the others on his body. She wanted to know everything about Leo Raisman.

"My parents still live in the same house where I was born. It's comforting, I guess, that kind of stability, but I bet your childhood was a lot more fun."

"I mean, that's what most people want, right? Stability and comfort." Mack thought of Shaw. She was trying to give Shaw the steadiness and routine a child deserved. The kind of childhood her sister had wanted.

Leo arched a brow, his gaze as intense as a laser beam, and Mack could picture him with that same look as he zipped through laps at the track. "But not you?"

They were interrupted by a loud cheer all around them, and Mack and Leo stood in anticipation as the spectators rose. Yellow school buses rumbled onto the small oval track, dribbling out from the garages one at a time in a haze of crunching gears and squealing brakes.

A woman behind Mack screamed, "Fuck yeah!" and the crowd around them roared. Mack rolled her bottom lip over her teeth with both index fingers and whistled, getting into the electric vibe of the Friday night crowd. It wasn't the same rush as booze or sex or driving way too fast, but she felt a surprisingly solid artificial high. She let the energy of the crowd infuse her.

The bus race itself—a dozen buses, some spray-painted and others still bearing the name of the county where they'd been in service, plodding through the figure eight—was disturbingly thrilling for something so slow. The lumbering vehicles barely hit a top speed of forty, but each time they passed through the middle crossing of the track, the crowd gasped. Once, when a decommissioned Dubois County bus clipped the back bumper of another, causing the front vehicle to lose its brakes and the trailing bus to teeter on the terrifying cusp of tipping over, Mack screamed in the same shrill note Shaw hit when she saw a kitten. It was peculiarly exhilarating waiting for a slow-motion disaster.

They were still laughing about the inanity of racing school buses as they walked back to Leo's car, a sleek silver Porsche Boxster convertible. Mack had admired the car on their drive to the Speedrome, but they'd been in the middle of a conversation about Boomer's situation. Now, she whistled low. "Laid back Leo Raisman coming in with another sick ride. 2012?"

Leo flashed a cocky grin. "2011 Boxster Spyder 987.2."

"I don't know enough about Porsche to know the difference, but your face tells me I'm about to get a lesson."

Leo explained why the Boxster S 987 was a car nerd's pick—dual-clutch manual transmission, hydraulic steering, over three hundred horsepower in a lightweight frame—while they drove west toward downtown. Hoosier spring was in full bloom, and the smell of dogwood and clover swirled through the open air of the car as they turned onto Washington Avenue. It was the perfect night to be out, the air fresh and cool, like the night Janet first appeared in Mack's life. In two weeks, she'd traveled from a small short track in Haubstadt to one in Indianapolis. A part of her heart would always love the small little ovals that dotted the country, the same way she'd always love Indiana. Neither was flashy or demanding of attention, but they were solid, accessible, and rarely pretended to be anything they were not.

A lot like Leo Raisman.

"I can tell," Leo said. She jumped, unsure how much she'd spoken out loud. "You love the short tracks. It's a great feeling to go to work and love what you do."

"I didn't say that," she snapped. Leo flicked a confused glance at her. She huffed and pointed the air vents away from herself. Leo had turned the heat on low, but Mack wanted to feel the briskness of the air. "I love short tracks. I'll always defend them. But . . ." She chewed her lip, afraid to admit some things even to herself, but the night air and Leo Raisman made her feel like confessing. "Do you think you can love something and hate it at the same time?"

Instantly embarrassed, she rubbed an eye, forgetting she'd put on mascara. She checked her face in the side mirror and swiped at the black streak under her eye. They were in an industrial area now, a vestige of Indianapolis's manufacturing roots that still bordered downtown.

"I think you can love an idea but hate the actual work," Leo said slowly. "That's what happened to my mom. She went to law school in the eighties, thinking it would be badass to be a woman in the boys' club, but she hated practicing law."

Mack latched onto the subject change. "My sister is a lawyer and I'm not sure she loves it either. How does your lawyer mom feel about you driving fast cars for a living?"

"Oh, she hated it at first." Leo laughed. "She hated the whole idea of racing at all, and then she really hated the demands of the karting circuit. My dad's an ER doctor—" He cut his eyes to her. "Do not even say it. Jewish kid, doctor-lawyer parents, I've heard all the jokes." Mack raised her hands in submission and Leo continued. "My dad couldn't travel much so my mom drove me all over California for the races. I think she saw how much I loved racing, and even though she didn't love it, she saw that I did. They've always been really great parents that way. If I was interested in something, they were interested, too."

Mack thought of Shaw, how she loved school, loved learning new things, loved dancing and gymnastics and softball, and never complained about homework. She tried to celebrate Shaw's interests, even if she didn't share them. Didn't she? Parenting was a constant internal performance review and Mack always came up short in her own evaluation.

She could still hear the woman at lunch earlier today. *But you're the mom.*

They'd reached downtown now, the bright lights and sounds drifting into the car as Leo's warm voice drifted out. Briefly, he caught her gaze. "I wonder if it might be hard for someone who loves racing to watch other people do it week after week."

Mack held his look, her insides buzzing with the joy and agony of someone else understanding her situation so perfectly. Embarrassed, she motioned at the windshield. "Watch the road. I thought you were a professional."

He verified Laurie's address, turning right up Delaware to avoid the chaos of Monument Circle. They'd passed the old City Market before Mack said, "Could you tell your mom was unhappy? When she was a lawyer?"

Leo turned onto Michigan, weaving through the one-way streets of downtown to loop back to Laurie's building on North Meridian. If he thought it was an odd question, he didn't show it. "I knew she hated her job, but she never let me think her frustration was my fault." He paused, thoughtful. "Maybe that's why she was so supportive of racing. She didn't want to watch me make the same mistakes. And she figured it out. She's always loved to write so now she's the communications director at a huge law firm."

He parked near Laurie's building and killed the engine.

"The problem is that I've never wanted to do anything except drive fast cars in circles," Mack whispered into the silence left by the Porsche's V-6 engine. "I don't want to balance the books or deal with shitty contractors. I don't want to spend one whole day of my week mowing and weed-whacking and pressure washing metal bleachers. I hate running a business and I'm pretty sure I'm bad at it, which makes me hate it more. I just want to *drive.*" She swiped at her nose, forcing herself to calm. She would not cry in front of Leo. "And don't you dare fucking say something stupid like, *There's always next year*. I don't have a next year. I can't even get a sponsor for this year. My inbox is full of 'no' and 'we're sorry.'"

Leo palmed the gearshift, phantom shifting through the pattern. They'd parked in the shadow of Laurie's building and his face was obscured by the darkness, no expression visible. She'd told him not to say anything but his silence annoyed her as much as any trite words he might have said. He made it disconcertingly easy to say the things she usually crammed into the back of her mind, and even though the darkness made the night air feel colder, Mack's body felt hot with embarrassment. His silence made her want to pull him across the console and kiss him stupid, so she reached for the door handle and was halfway out of the car before Leo called out to her.

"I'm sorry, Mack. I really am."

She closed the car door and shuffled her feet on the curb. She wanted more from him, wanted him to say something that would keep the magic of this night going. But what else could he say? It didn't matter how she did here in Indy, she'd still be back in Haubstadt after Memorial Day.

"Thanks for including me tonight."

Suddenly, he was out of the car and next to her on the curb, closer than a teammate should be. His posture was easy, his bearing laid back. His dark eyes searched her own, and she thought he would kiss her again. She wanted him to, but he simply laid a finger to the freckle on her left cheek.

"If tomorrow is your only shot at Indy"—he overemphasized the *if*—"I don't have to tell you to make it count. But in case you don't already know, you've got a teammate, a *friend*, and an entire crew of people who want this as much as you do." He spoke softly, slowly. She flicked her gaze toward the street, needing a momentary break from his gentle intensity. Needing to stop herself from breaking her own boundaries when he was respecting them so well.

"I'll be cheering for you tomorrow, Rookie. And on race day. And for a long time after that."

She leaned toward Leo, willing to step over the line she'd drawn herself, but Leo shook his head and stepped back, saving her from herself. She watched as he got in the car and drove away, wishing she could have all the things she wanted. If only life was that easy.

CHAPTER 24

8 days until the Indianapolis 500

Frenetic energy buzzed through Gasoline Alley on qualification day. Teams scurried with purpose and the echoes of whirring tire jacks, clanging wrenches, and shouted instructions bounced in the air throughout the long rows of garages. Soon cars would take to the track, and by five o'clock fates would be sealed: Some teams would spend tonight drinking champagne and celebrating, while others would work until dawn looking for more speed.

"Williams, you ready?" Janet emerged from the back of the garage in her traditional white button-down shirt, aviators, and a scowl across her weathered features. She pushed the glasses up her forehead. "Don't be a bitch baby out there, but for god's sake, do not put this machine into the wall. We don't have the cash to fix damages."

As far as pep talks went, Mack had worse. Wes once told her *Don't lose and don't die* and she'd managed to win the whole damn thing in Kansas City.

"Fast, but not furious. Got it."

"No funny shit. We're sending Leo first. Could be several hours before we get you out there."

Mack peered over Janet's shoulder, where her car sat ready to be pulled onto pit lane. It was freshly painted and painfully devoid of decals other than a small Hartley logo on the sidepod. One garage over, so many logos plastered Leo's car that the paint scheme was barely discernible. With Laurie's help she'd mailed over two hundred packets, sent twice as many emails, cold-called anyone with a phone number, and struggled through a few painful Zooms, all of which ended with the same result: No.

"About the sponsorship . . ."

Janet sighed, hands resting on her narrow hips. "I knew it wouldn't be easy but I thought we could get a few folks on board."

"I've been trying—"

"You think Sarah Fisher had an easy time getting sponsorships before she led laps here? This isn't just about you, Williams. It's about women in motorsports, and how men in C-suites don't think we can earn back their investment. There may be more women in this paddock than when I was here in the nineties, but there sure as shit ain't the money to match." Janet pulled her sunglasses back down over her eyes. "If you're not getting death or rape threats, I guess they think that's improvement." She blew out a long stream of breath. "Go walk around. Get some air, wave at fans, see if anyone will interview you."

Knowing she was dismissed, Mack left the garage. As she walked around the paddock, she thought about Janet's words. She was definitely an anomaly as a female driver but she didn't feel threatened or unsafe. Women had given their blood, sweat, tears, and dignity for Mack to stand here today and she wouldn't waste the chance.

She rounded the corner of the Gasoline Alley exit and ran chest-first into Wyatt Venter, the large and gregarious owner of Ampersand Autosport. Ten years ago, when she'd called Wyatt and explained why she had to back out of the IndyCar test drive he'd offered, he'd been polite and told her to call him after she'd had the baby and they'd work something out. She hadn't spoken to him since.

"Whoa! Mack Williams!" He took a step back and held out his hand.

"Hi, Wyatt."

He'd gained fifty pounds and lost a head full of hair in the years since she'd last seen him. "I was only a little surprised to see you on the entrant list. Couldn't stay away, huh?"

Mack shrugged. How could she explain that she'd never wanted to stay away? He'd been gracious when she'd bowed out, but it still felt like a burned bridge. She'd naively expected him to keep pursuing her after Shaw was born, and it had taken her way too long to accept that the world didn't work like that for women. She was angry with him, not for anything he'd done personally, but because he'd let her down just as much as she had disappointed him. "Something like that."

"Well, it's good to see you back out there." His smile was warm but he looked over her shoulder distractedly.

"Thanks," Mack said lamely.

He clapped her on the shoulder as he said apologetically, "Gotta run, but good luck!"

She closed her eyes as the chaos of Gasoline Alley swirled around her. If things had gone differently, would she still work for Wyatt Venter? Would she be walking down the paddock with years of experience under her belt, knowing intimately how to race at this unique track? Would she have earned pole position, signed a huge contract, maybe even won the whole damn thing? The what-ifs swamped her and she closed her eyes against everything that could have been.

"Mack!"

Her eyes popped open to see her family striding toward her, pit passes dangling from their necks. Billie, in tight white jeans, black-and-white-checked heeled sneakers, and yet another homemade MACK WILLIAMS #11 T-shirt carefully knotted to show off her small waist, had mastered the art of track chic: a tiny bit tacky, a lot bit festive. Laurie walked next to Wes, who kept pace with his cane, but neither was smiling.

"Where's Shaw?" Mack asked, something foul tingling in her gut. She'd barely finished the question when she noticed a familiar figure partly obscured by the crowd of people milling around the garage. For a moment, she wondered if she was hallucinating, or if the heat was affecting her vision. Maybe she was coming down with something, a fever or vertigo. But the crowd cleared, and she knew she wasn't imagining it.

There was Shaw, holding the hand of Kelley Caruthers.

Mack's brain stuttered, unable to digest what she saw.

He walked through the paddock with the same loose-limbed confidence she once found so attractive, a cocky grin lifting one corner of his mouth as he took in the sights of Gasoline Alley. When they'd been together, Kelley wore Wrangler jeans from Rural King and free promo T-shirts; Mack had liked his sartorial ignorance and his fuck-you attitude had driven her lust into hyperdrive. But now he wore tight jeans, designer sneakers, and a leather jacket that looked so new it didn't even have creases at the elbows yet. Thin silver bracelets tinkled on his wrists and his short dark hair was swept back with shiny gel, like a knock-off Reynaldo.

"Mama! Look what Daddy brought me!"

Shaw held up a small plastic replica of a 1000cc bike, complete with a tiny rider wearing Kelley's hallmark lime green helmet. Her daughter held the toy as if he'd given her a rare and precious piece of art. Idols were easier to love when you didn't know them. Shaw didn't seem to remember what happened when she was three, and Mack hoped it stayed that way. She would carry the memory for both of them.

"What are you doing here?" Mack loathed her own high-pitched tone.

Kelley did what Kelley wanted to do, whenever Kelley wanted to do it, and this type of unannounced visit was his signature style. When Shaw was first born, Mack had clung to his sporadic involvement, hoping against all reason that he'd grow into an involved father. And that one fateful time, when she'd been desperate and overwhelmed, she'd jumped on his random offer to take Shaw to Spain for two weeks. She'd thought it would be good bonding time for Shaw and Kelley. Ignorantly, she'd even daydreamed that her daughter would grow up splitting her time between two countries, becoming well traveled and cultured, maybe even bilingual. Kelley might even come to appreciate the sacrifices she made for their daughter. She knew he wouldn't love her—she understood that by then—but maybe he'd see how they could be a family. At the time, she was twenty-three while Kelley was thirty-three, and she'd been relieved to have help from someone who seemed more adult than she felt.

Instead, Kelley left Shaw in the care of a random girlfriend, which Mack learned about when the girlfriend called her and told her to come pick up her crying brat. By the time Mack maxed out a credit card and landed in Barcelona, she found Shaw covered in red sores on her bottom and holding her arm. Kelley refused to see anything wrong with the situation, blaming Shaw for crying too much and not yet being potty-trained. Young, furious, terrified for her daughter, Mack waited to take Shaw to the doctor until they were back in the States. She'd wanted to get Shaw as far away from Kelley as possible. She would never forget sitting in the emergency room as a doctor showed her the X-ray of her daughter's dislocated shoulder, and then the next day when the Department of Child Services knocked at her door.

They'd followed her for months, showing up at random hours, talking to the neighbors but barely talking to Mack at all, scrutinizing every inch of their home, and worst of all, calling Kelley.

She could still hear his enraged voice on the phone: *If you ever put me through this kind of attention again, I will make your life hell. I will get custody of Shaw and move her to Spain and you'll never see her again. You will tell those DCS people that she fell and that's the end of it. I have money, I have lawyers, and I will bury you in court until you're broke and alone. I can make Shaw disappear and there's nothing you can do about it.*

It was the only time Mack had called Laurie and begged for help. Laurie helped Mack navigate DCS, and after six months of state supervision, they'd finally closed Mack's case. Her sister wanted Mack to file for a formal custody agreement, but Mack refused. She knew Kelley was serious about taking Shaw away, not because he wanted her, but because he hated losing. She'd been on her best behavior ever since, never doing anything to attract the attention of teachers, coaches, other parents, and especially not Kelley. Mack was a bland, perfect mom in public and tried her damnedest to be the same at home. She'd finally understood then that Kelley didn't want Shaw, didn't want a family, and certainly didn't want Mack. He wanted to have the upper hand.

Kelley smiled like he'd pulled off a movie-worthy surprise, like when the hero arrives just in time for the heroine's big moment in a rom-com. "When I heard you were running at Indy"—he widened his eyes theatrically as he gestured around them—"I thought my daughter might need some time with her dad while you're . . ." He waved his hands. "Whatever this is."

The noise and movement of qualification day swirled around them but Mack felt like a furious, frightened rabbit, terrified to move. On the exterior, she remained still as stone, but inside her mouth flooded with bitter saliva.

Oblivious to the adult tension, Shaw began prattling. "Daddy saw Pawpaw's big house on wheels!"

Kelley arched a perfectly waxed and trimmed eyebrow, and despite the years apart, Mack recognized the shrewd look on his face. For someone who'd grown up on a hog farm in southern Missouri, Kelley wore snobbery well. "Shaw tells me she's living in . . . a bus?"

"It's a luxury RV. All the drivers do it for race week." Ugh, she hated that anxiety made her defensive. She crossed her arms and tucked her hands under her elbows.

"Shouldn't she be in school?"

Mack's eyes popped wide like a cartoon character about to plunge over a cliff. Fear churned in her body next to pure, unfiltered rage. She struggled to calm herself. "There's only two weeks left in the school year and it's mostly field days and parties. She's ahead of everyone in her class and her teacher had no problem with her absence. I left multiple voicemails. And emails. And texted your assistant telling you everything. Every. Last. Detail."

Kelley shrugged but his smooth forehead didn't move. "I didn't get the messages. You should have contacted me before leaving our daughter with your father. He's . . . you know." Kelley tapped his temple.

"Sounds like a you problem," Laurie snapped. Mack grabbed her sister's wrist but Laurie kept on. "Our dad, who has approximately seven more championships than you ever will, has a traumatic brain injury, one that doesn't affect his hearing or vision."

Wes waved in a wide arc. "Hey there, fucker."

Mack glared at Wes and shook her head, even though she wanted to blacken Kelley's eyes herself.

"What?" Wes asked in mock innocence. "Sorry. I can't always control myself. I'm—" Wes pointed his index finger at his temple.

Billie chose that moment to cut in, her mountain drawl extra thick. "We didn't really get introduced before your little ambush. You must be Shaw's sperm donor. I can't see the resemblance but context clues, you know? I'm Billie Summit, Wes's girlfriend."

"Ah." Kelley limply shook Billie's hand while keeping his eyes on Mack. *I can make Shaw disappear and there's nothing you can do about it.* "My daughter is under the supervision of one of your dad's many girlfriends?"

"Oh, you joker! The pot knows the kettle, am I right?" Billie winked, her hot-pink smile Bama Rush ready. "You know, Wes was there the very second Shaw's beautiful soul came into this world and has been there for every birthday and milestone. But if you want to feign parental concern, do you want to hear about my bachelor's degree in nursing? Or how I put myself through college as a live-in nanny for five kids? How about the six years I cared for my husband during his cancer battle, or the dozens of children we fostered before that? Maybe you'd like to know I run an afterschool homework club and provide nutritional counseling for parents using EBT?"

Mack and Laurie exchanged a wide-eyed look.

"Billie makes the best food," Shaw added nervously. "I like the sweet potato fries and chocolate chia pudding." Billie winked at Shaw and for once the affection between her dad's girlfriend and her daughter didn't make Mack feel like screaming.

"As charming as this unwanted reunion is," Laurie said coolly, "Mack needs to prepare for qualifications." She waved a careless hand in Kelley's direction. "Feel free to do . . . whatever it is you came to do, but I've promised my niece a frozen lemonade."

Laurie gave Mack a pointed look, one that said she would protect Shaw with her entire being.

Mack was so floored by Kelley's surprise appearance that she'd temporarily forgotten it was qualification day. If she wanted to make the race, she had to trust Laurie, Wes, and Billie to keep Shaw in their sights, safe from whatever Kelley was scheming. She would not let his sudden arrival throw her off, no matter how rattled she was. And she was goddamn *rattled.* She already had a million reasons to hate Kelley, she did not need a million and one. Pulling Shaw into a tight embrace, Mack whispered to Laurie not to let Shaw out of her grip, then finally said goodbye to her family.

She didn't say a word to Kelley, but she'd hardly taken a step when he called out, "I'll come with you."

He was the last person she wanted to be around before qualifications, but if he was with her, he couldn't take Shaw away, or hurt her. She shrugged like she didn't care and headed back toward the garage.

He didn't even say goodbye to Shaw.

@RACINGNEWS
May 16

A follower spotted a quartet of IndyCar drivers at St. Elmo last night! According to a source, Jericho Blair, Boomer Compton, and Leo Raisman have a yearly tradition of meeting at our city's finest institution the night before qualifications. This year they were joined by rookie Mack Williams.

COMMENTS:

@eyerisbleu: seems irresponsible to be drinking the night before quals. Dumb bitch

@paulaandterrywatson @eyerisbleu I can't believe she talked those good men into a bar

@pinkbottle: this slut is out at a bar when she has a kid at home

@bombbber: no idea who this girl is but she's not nearly as hot as Danica.

@racetagram: OMG! These 4 are together a lot lately. One of my followers sent a pic of them outside Body Work gym too. #TrackPack

@ilaRee52: @racetagram love the hashtag! #trackpack

@charls78: @sportsillustrated get this hottie on the swimsuit edition

@terribleanium: @charls78 nah she ain't got no titties

CHAPTER 25

8 days until the Indianapolis 500

"So. You finally made it to the Indy 500."

Mack did not answer. She fast-walked out of Gasoline Alley, no idea where she was going but desperate to get away, both from Kelley and from anyone who might see them together.

"What is your problem?" he asked, easily keeping pace with her as she marched through the paddock. "I came here to check up on Shaw, to make sure she's getting what she needs. That's in my rights as her father."

"If you're here to see Shaw, you should actually spend time with her instead of harassing me." She didn't want him near her daughter, but she knew it was the right thing to say, and that Laurie would never leave Kelley alone with Shaw.

"Harassing?" Kelley made a face. "I'm trying to help you, Mack. I'm worried about you." Kelley grabbed her elbow, and she shook him off with a sharp snap.

"Don't. Touch. Me."

He removed his hand but gave her a look of stomach-curdling pity. "You're embarrassing yourself, Mack. Why are you even here?"

Why am I here? She was furious that his words echoed her own concerns. She'd found pace yesterday at practice, but her ability to make the Indy 500 remained a giant question mark.

"Fuck you," she said, forgetting to be calm and mature. The shock of his appearance was wearing off, replaced by white-hot rage. How had she ever found this man attractive? And why was she stupid enough to link her life with his forever by having a child with him? She doubled her pace. "My work has absolutely nothing to do with you."

He caught up to her quickly, his long legs eating the pavement twice as fast as her own.

"Your work?" he mocked. "Your *work* is selling overpriced beer to rednecks. This is . . ." He gestured around them, shaking his head. "I don't know what this is, Mack, but it makes me wonder about your mental state. You haven't raced for years and you think you can win the Indy 500?" He barked a laugh. "You're making a joke of yourself, trying to race but partying like you're a teenager. I'm worried about you."

Panic mixed with her anger. "What are you talking about?"

"It's all over social media. You're staying out all night, fooling around with Leo Raisman, screaming at people."

She knew she shouldn't rise to the bait but she couldn't stop herself. "Of course I spend time with Leo. He's my teammate."

Kelley squinted at her. "You're sleeping with him while our daughter is living in a van."

"It's not like that!"

Kelley shrugged. "I don't care who you whore yourself out to. I told you, I'm worried about Shaw. It isn't good for her to see you make such a spectacle of yourself. This"—he waved his hands around, encompassing the track—"this whole ridiculous thing is not good for her."

"Oh, and you're a paragon of parenthood?" Mack hissed. She was losing control of the situation fast, her panic and rage and anxiety swirling together. Her vision began to narrow. "What do you want? Be a fucking adult and admit what you're doing here."

I will get custody of Shaw and move her to Spain and you'll never see her again.

She wanted to hear him say it out loud. She'd lived so long with the specter of losing Shaw that she needed to hear him say the words.

But before he could give her any satisfaction, someone called his name. The manager of one of the large racing teams held out a hand and they greeted each other with dude-to-dude back slapping. As if they hadn't been in the middle of a conversation, Kelley turned and started chatting with the manager. Mack watched as one conversation rolled into another, with drivers and fans and crew all coming over to say hello to the bad boy of motorcycle racing. In the hierarchy of motorsports, MotoGP racers were like fighter jet pilots: a lot of excitement, a little unhinged. With each new back slap, Kelley rehashed his monster wreck, describing how tough he was during recovery, how he felt better than ever now.

Mack left Kelley to preen under the attention and plunged through the pandemonium of the busy paddock, no idea where she was going or where she was supposed to be. Her mind seethed with the things Kelley had said. Was she really embarrassing herself by trying to make the Indy 500? What the hell was on social media about her and Leo?

She was lost in her own mind when someone called out her name.

Mack turned and saw a well-known reporter holding a microphone and wearing a Motosport logoed polo, a cameraman hovering close behind her. Hana Park had won a European women's-only racing series twice, and despite promises from Formula One that the program would lead to more opportunities for women in F1, she got no offers. She'd done a few stints in Australia and Japan before transitioning into an astute and well-liked reporter for the premier North American racing channel.

"Mack, do you have a moment to speak with *Motosport*?"

Mack looked over her shoulder to see that Kelley was fully occupied. She'd yet to have an on-camera interview, and not only would it get her good attention, it would throw Kelley's words right back in his face. She wasn't a laughingstock; she was here to race. "Of course."

While the camera guy adjusted the shot, Mack straightened her shirt, making sure the JJR logo was visible, and tried to forget Kelley.

Hana positioned Mack so that the track was at her back and smoothed down a lock of Mack's flyaway hair before giving a countdown signal.

"I'm here at Indianapolis Motor Speedway, where teams are making last-minute preparations for qualification day. With me is rookie Mack Williams, the only woman vying to make this year's field." She turned toward Mack. "Mack, you're new to IndyCar. Tell us what it's like to run this track for the first time."

Mack mined her brain for the PR training she'd done at JJR's office, grateful for the softball question. Most IndyCar reporters took it easy on drivers but Hana was known to throw occasional punches. "Hi, Hana. It's wild and humbling to drive at this place. Indy means so much. I've been watching this race since I was—oof."

"Mama! I met Leo Raisman!"

Shaw slammed into her side and Mack looked up to see Laurie wearing an expression of unbridled horror. Aware that the camera was rolling and there was nothing else to do, Mack laughed and gestured at her daughter. "Well, I've been coming here since I was my daughter's age."

Hana's eyes lit up. "And this is your daughter?"

Mack looked right into the camera and told the truth. "Yes. I can't tell you what it means to me to have my family here today. It's a dream come true."

Just as Hana started to ask another question, Kelley sauntered into the frame and stood on the other side of Shaw. Hana stopped midsentence as her eyes bounced between Mack and Kelley and the spot where Kelley rested a proprietary hand on Shaw's shoulder.

Hana blinked rapidly but recovered quickly. "Oh my! Folks, joining us is MotoGP star Kelley Caruthers!"

Mack willed her face to stay blank but she suspected it was turning pink anyway. She was a little flustered by Shaw's presence, but she was utterly humiliated by Kelley's. He might as well have pissed on her and Shaw to mark his territory.

"Hey there, Hana." Kelley soaked up the attention like a dry chamois towel, standing ever so slightly in front of Mack and Shaw. Another inch and he'd topple his own daughter.

"Kelley, it's great to see you back racing after that monster wreck!"

"It's great to be back, Hana," he said smoothly. "My entire focus for the past year has been on recovery and training. Motorcycle racing is my only reason for living. Nothing else matters."

Hana blinked, seemingly unsure how to respond. Mack could feel the tension in Shaw's body, the way she held her arms tight to her sides.

"You should come across the pond and cover two-wheel racing. More exciting." Kelley winked and smiled like a goddamn toothpaste commercial, even as his hand still rested on Shaw's shoulder.

Unbidden, Mack thought of Leo, his genuine smile and comfort with not being the center of attention. Nothing like Kelley's slick, sleazy arrogance.

Hana recovered and gestured around. "But even you couldn't stay away from the excitement of Indianapolis in May!"

Suddenly, Kelley pushed past Mack and Shaw. "Hey, man!" He clasped hands with a figure in a black polo shirt, and when they pulled away, Mack saw Mario Andretti. If there was such thing as track royalty, Mario was king.

"Hey hey, Motorcycle Boy!"

Mack could tell by the angle of the camera that she was completely out of the shot now as the cameraman tracked Kelley and Mario's reunion. "You see this guy?" Kelley hooted. "My old buddy Mario is here!"

Ever affable, Mario clapped Kelley on the shoulder. "Heard you're racing again. It's hard to stay away, eh?"

"I'll be dead before they take me off the bike." Kelley grinned, not at Mario, but directly at the camera. Next to her, Shaw flinched. Mack reached for her daughter's hand and squeezed tightly, wishing she could dick-punch her child's father on national TV.

Hana touched her earpiece, then flicked her hand and the cameraman lowered the bulky equipment. "Riley Motors is doing a last-minute engine switch and we need to report on it. I'm sorry, Mack."

Mack smiled but it felt fake even to her. She felt as nauseated as she had after the first day of practice, as if she were under g-forces instead of locked into a power struggle with her ex. Today was supposed to be the biggest day of her life, the day she achieved her biggest dream, and instead she was sinking deeper and deeper into an emotional quagmire.

"Can I get a redo later? Maybe after your qualification run?" Hana looked pointedly at Kelley. "We'll do it over the wall. Solo."

What else was there to say? Mack nodded. "Yeah. Thanks, Hana."

Hana leaned in, her voice low. "Go show the boys how it's done. I'll be rooting for you this month." She wound the microphone cord around her wrist and nodded behind Mack. "Hey, Leo. One-on-one interview later? Maybe a JJR teammate interview?"

Mack whirled around to see Leo standing behind her. His eyes flicked from Mack to Shaw to Kelley, a look of revulsion on his face.

From: SethPopolous@RiverRunGrocery.com
To: MWilliams@email.com; Laurie.Williams@StoeppelEvansFirm.com
Subject: RE: Unique Indy 500 Sponsorship Opportunity! [May 16, 3:31 p.m.]

Dear Ms. Williams,

Thank you for contacting River Run Grocery Stores about sponsorship opportunities. Unfortunately, we are already committed to our yearly marketing budget and have no room to accommodate your request.

We wish you the best of luck in your endeavors.

Sincerely,
Seth Popolous
Director of Marketing
River Run Grocery Stores
Full of Food, Fun, & Family Values™
Davenport, Iowa

CHAPTER 26

8 days until the Indianapolis 500

Mack held her elbows, arms crossed defensively as she and Leo walked past the Pagoda. Leo hardly said a word to her, other than to inform her that Janet wanted them both at the team trailer. She'd said goodbye to her family, ignoring Kelley, and followed Leo toward the makeshift JJR office. She stayed equally quiet, not wanting the conversation to come, the one that would likely ruin their friendship and certainly kill any attraction he had for her. But instead of turning left toward the rows and rows of haulers, Leo turned right.

"Aren't we supposed to—"

"Let's go somewhere quieter first," Leo said. He pointed toward the infield museum, and while Mack didn't see how the wide-open area would provide any privacy, she followed him anyway. She had a feeling she'd follow him too far for her own good, if she gave in and let herself.

"Leo, I'm sorry."

His dark brows drew down in a quizzical look. "Why are you apologizing?"

Mack blinked. "Because . . . I didn't tell you I have a daughter."

He was quiet a moment. "I figured you'd tell me when you were ready." He cleared his throat and the tips of his ears turned boyishly red. The sun glinted on his black hair, a handful of copper threads highlighted by the bright sky. For a stupid moment, Mack wondered what might have happened if they'd met when they were younger, before he'd earned those lines by his mouth. "I read it. On social media."

"It's on social media that I have a kid?"

Leo's face turned a shade of scarlet she'd never seen on him. "You were right. People are crazy online."

Fucking social media. She could only imagine what else people had said about her. She wanted Leo to see her how he had that first day, brave and bold and as a driver he respected. Now, she could only imagine what he thought about her.

"I don't know why I didn't tell you about her. I didn't try to hide her from you." Mack stared down at her own feet as they walked. "I wanted to be . . . just me."

Even as she said the words, she knew they weren't accurate. They weren't complete. Because motherhood was inextricably part of who Mack was now. *Shaw*—getting to love her and be loved by her, to watch her grow and live and blossom—was an essential piece of Mack.

"I'm glad I got to meet her," Leo said, leading them around to the grounds in front of the museum. "Apparently I'm her favorite driver."

"Don't get cocky," Mack warned. "She's ten. She likes the star pattern on your car." Leo pointed to the giant fountain bordering the museum, and they sat on the concrete lip containing the pool of water. The sound of the bubbling water drowned out the din of the paddock. "Shaw's a great kid. Sweet and laid back and funny. It sounds lazy, but she's an easy kid."

"She told me that she wasn't sure if she wanted to be a horse rancher or run a butterfly garden."

"Last month it was an astronaut. She's so curious. She likes school and loves to read. She's smart like my sister." It felt good to talk about Shaw, to share this piece of herself. She gave herself a moment to enjoy telling Leo about her daughter, to enjoy his smile as he learned about Shaw. But it was qualification day, and soon enough it would be race day, and then they would move on from each other. She glanced at Leo, not wanting to say what she knew she had to say. "She's the other reason why we can't . . ." She flicked a finger back and forth between them.

Leo frowned. "I like kids. My godsons would have you know that I'm the greatest Uncle Leo they've ever had. I told you, I don't scare easily."

"Leo," she pleaded.

"Does Kelley Caruthers have anything to do with it?"

"No," she said adamantly.

"But he's . . ."

"Shaw's father."

Leo stared down at his hands, and Mack watched him clasp and unclasp his long fingers. She pictured those graceful hands in his signature white driving gloves, strong and sure, confidently steering toward victory. Before she'd ever met him, when she'd only seen him on the screen of her TV, she'd noticed his hands. She wanted to grab them in her own and feel his warm calluses again. Behind them, the fountain burbled placidly, unaware of the tumult of anxiety and regret bubbling through her chest.

"Believe me when I tell you that Kelley Caruthers is nothing to me but a giant pain in the ass." She inhaled, knowing what was best but not liking it. "I love Shaw to the ends of the earth, but getting involved with Kelley ruined my career." Mack licked her lips. "You told me to prove what I'm worth out on track, but I can win this whole damn thing and still the only thing people will talk about is if there is an *us*."

Leo shook his head. "It shouldn't be like that."

"It is like that, Leo! Denying it makes you part of the problem. You said there were posts about me. Be honest, are there posts about me and you?"

He wouldn't meet her eyes. "We're teammates."

"Leo," she demanded.

He dropped his head back. "Yeah. There are pictures. At St. Elmo, at the bus race, on the track walk. Someone even came up with a stupid name for us. *Rilliams.*"

She flinched. This was exactly why she didn't look at social media. People were terrible and terribly stupid. "Can you even imagine what they'll say after that goddamn interview? Now I'll be the paddock slut."

"Don't say that. People online are grotesque." She heard the bitterness in his voice, knew he was holding back from telling her the worst of it. Frustration and hurt marred his gentle face. "It's not just a hookup for me. I *like* you, Mack. What about after the race? When the spotlight dies down? We could try . . ."

Mack shook her head. "I live in rural Indiana and you travel nine months out of the year. I've never introduced Shaw to a man and I won't start now."

The way Leo looked at her made her want to scream and cry at the same time. As if he wanted to argue but respected her enough not to.

Leo Raisman was all the things she'd never respected herself enough to want.

Would she have appreciated him if they'd met earlier? She thought of herself at eighteen, wondered if she would have slowed down enough to sift through the dirt and see the shining gem of Leo Raisman. Or could she only understand now that he was the best of what a man could be because she'd permanently tied herself to a man who was the opposite? What if she'd met Leo instead of Kelley? What if they'd driven the same circuit for years, or they weren't teammates, or if she wasn't tied to Haubstadt? What would have, could have happened between them then?

So many what-ifs. But what was real was where they were now.

He watched the fountain and Mack watched him, wanting to absorb his loveliness, his goodness for a moment longer. She couldn't stop herself from touching his dimple. "I wish things were different," she whispered.

"Me too," Leo said softly.

"Williams! Raisman! Where the hell have you two been? It's go time!"

They both jumped up from the fountain, looking blatantly guilty. Janet's mirrored aviators hid her expression but her mouth hung open just enough that Mack knew she'd seen them. Mack squeezed her eyes against the instant smart of tears.

Leo had the wits to ask, "I thought we were going out midpack?"

How could his voice sound so calm and normal? Mack fought the urge to put her fist in her mouth.

"Plan changed! Jimmy and Lucie are worried we'll need a second run to get the placements we want. We're doing the eleven first."

Mack's eyes popped open in fear. She was going out for qualification now?

Janet's posture was stiff, hands on her hips and chin jutted slightly. She stepped forward until she stood inches in front of them. Her voice, normally so sharp, was slightly louder than the burbling fountain. She pointed at Leo. "You, I swear to god if there's any Me Too shit going on I will fry your balls in hot oil while they are still attached to your body and then cut you from this team immediately. Fucking *men*." Mack opened her mouth to defend Leo but Janet was having none of it. She moved her finger to Mack's face. "And you. I shouldn't have to explain to you that you are embarrassing yourself and embarrassing *me*. I've worked my ass off to get respect at this track and if you have tarnished my good name I will make your life so fucking miserable you won't even be able to get a ride in a carnival bumper car." She made a growling noise that demonstrated her disappointment better than any words. "Get your asses to the garage. Now. I'm going to watch you like you're the stupid children you are."

They fell into line behind Janet, and Mack refused to look at Leo. Would she never, ever learn her lesson?

CHAPTER 27

8 days until the Indianapolis 500

In the garage, Mack scrambled to get her gear out of the storage locker and tried to keep her heart rate down even as her mind swirled with panic. In the bathroom, she pulled on her layers without taking the time to make sure all her seams were smooth and wadded her hair into a crappy braid. Hot nausea bubbled in her gut, and Mack pushed her hands against her stomach to stop it.

Outside, Jimmy wound his finger in the universal sign for *let's go* and Mack jogged toward pit lane, awkwardly pulling her balaclava one-handed over her face while holding her gloves and helmet. She tried to get her mind right as she hustled to pit lane, but all she could think about was Janet's face when she'd shown up at the fountain. Janet knew her history with Kelley and Mack could only imagine what her boss was thinking now. Probably that all those social media posts were true.

A flash of shiny lacquer caught the sunlight, and adrenaline flooded Mack's body at the sight of her car being towed toward the most famous track in American racing. There was no time to find her family. No time to hug Wes, hear Laurie's voice, no time to promise Shaw that she'd be safe.

This was her one shot at making the Indy 500 and she was thinking about everything but the herculean task ahead. Janet was right. She had to get her shit together *now*.

She focused on the mechanics of what she needed to do to physically get ready: A quick lick of her earbuds before shoving them into place. One final crack of her neck. Helmet on, straps tightened under her chin. HANS device around her neck, gromets snapped to her helmet. One leg on the sidepod, one leg over the aeroscreen and into the car. Buckles snapped in place and pulled tight. Gloves on, each seam smoothed to lay perfectly flat. Steering wheel snapped in place.

Her hands shook against the wheel.

No, no. She had to get calm. Had to focus.

Jimmy appeared to her right and she looked up at him from her low seat near the ground. "No lift, Rookie. Run your line."

Before Mack could thank him, he was gone.

Through her earbuds, Janet reminded her to go flat out, but above all, protect the chassis. Did she hear condescension in Janet's voice or was it the radio static? She gripped the wheel tightly, settling her fingers in the grooves, and a crew member pulled the starter. The whole world roared at her back.

The cockpit pressed in on Mack and her helmet felt too tight.

Unwanted thoughts assaulted her as she waited to be released from her pit box. Her adrenal system was too active, her heart rate way too high already. She'd let herself get distracted with Leo's and Laurie's confessions and Kelley's sneer and that stupid RV, and now she was about to take to the track so rattled that sweat puddled under her eyes and in the crease of her neck. A geyser of bile pushed up Mack's throat.

Distractions were costly, even deadly. She had to focus, if not for herself, then for Shaw.

Above her, she could see spectators in the grandstands, tiny dots of color watching every move on the track. She imagined Shaw up there, watching and waiting. Wes wasn't always careful with his phone, and what if Shaw googled and saw the things people were saying about Mack online? What if Shaw was hiding how much it had hurt her when Mack up and left for Indianapolis? What if Kelley was with her right now, poisoning her against Mack, encouraging her to move with him across the ocean? What if Shaw was already gone?

"And now, driving for Janet Joyner Racing, rookie Mackenzie Williams!"

Mack released the clutch and accelerated out of the pit box. Her mind was still not settled, not clicked in the way it should be, but the only thing she could do was throttle up.

She rounded the first two turns and headed down the backstretch, warming up the rubber tires so they added extra grip on the track surface. The asphalt stretched out before her and Mack tried to feel awe and overwhelming gratitude that she was in this car, about to take the green flag at Indy. She knew she should feel the magnitude of this moment, should feel the power and joy of her first qualification run for the Indy 500.

What she actually felt was numb panic, like her mind lagged two laps behind her body.

As she rounded the last turn of her warm-up lap, she willed herself to get it together, to remember this moment, to cherish it. Today was the meal that had to nourish her forever.

She felt the uneven rumble of the bricks beneath her tires, saw the flash of green fabric in her peripheral vision, and heard Jimmy mark the start of her run through the radio. As if he could sense her nerves, Jimmy radioed, "Stay on it. Stay in it."

Mack gripped the wheel tighter, letting the pressure ground her. She muscled her way through the first lap, holding as flat as she could in every turn but knowing the speed wasn't there. Was Kelley watching her, thinking that she was a fool to try for the Indy 500 after all these years? Why did she care what he thought? Was she now the butt of all the female race car driver jokes, fans laughing over her looks, her body, her relationship with Leo?

Where was Shaw right now?

She dove into the second qualification lap and willed herself to neither downshift nor lift off the accelerator. The back end gave a slight wiggle as she steered left, but she caught it at the last millisecond and held her line through the long turn, then kept it flat through the short chute before turning into two.

"228.181," Jimmy radioed in her ear.

Not good enough.

What if all anyone saw was a driver who didn't really deserve to be here? Hartley, the main sponsor, certainly thought that. No other sponsor had seen enough in her to back her. The other drivers were kind to her, but she had no idea what they thought or said about her in private. What if they all thought she'd slept her way into this opportunity? Did Boomer and Jericho know about Leo, had they seen the posts?

Shaw. Shaw. Shaw.

Down the backstretch, Mack stuck the throttle to the floor and watched the numbers on her accelerometer tick up. The rear end kicked and bucked through turns three and four, but she held on. Her arms screamed with tension as she manhandled the steering rack.

"Starting lap three. Lap two, 228.399," Jimmy radioed.

But you're the mom.

Mack doubled down, tried to settle her mind into the very bones of the car itself. Each lap took less than forty seconds to complete but each fraction of a second expanded, each movement exacerbated as finally, finally her mind dialed in as she held the car on the knife edge of control. Her arms went numb as she rounded the final pass through the short chute and into turn two for her final lap. Just as she began to steer into the sharp left-hander, the world began to spin a moment before she heard a loud *pop*. Vibrant, violent bands of color chased before her eyes and she barely registered the white wall closing in on her before the colors sharply ended and the world went dark.

INDIANAPOLIS COURIER-JOURNAL

May 16

A Sprint to the Scene: The AMR Safety Team Won't Settle For Anything Less Than Perfection

IndyCar's safety team has a reputation for being the best in the business, arriving at accident sites mere seconds after a crash. Anything other than a virtually simultaneous response is seen as a failure, says team boss Dante Sabourian.

The AMR Safety Team has traveled from race to race with IndyCar since 1996, the first dedicated safety team for any racing series. Often called "The Gold Standard of Motorsports Safety," the AMR Safety Team includes over forty doctors, nurses, paramedics, EMTs, and firefighters, all of whom participate in frequent training for IndyCar-specific incidents. The team has their own fleet of trucks and tools, many of which are custom made for safely extracting drivers after an accident.

"Everyone on the team knows driver extrication is a ticking clock, so we practice over and over until we can do it in under two minutes," says Sabourian.

Approximately eighteen safety team members are present at each race, spread out in three separate response units across the track. Because the AMR Safety Team travels to each race, team members are familiar with the individual drivers.

"We never, ever want to see someone hurt because these are our friends and colleagues," remarks Sabourian. "That means we will bust our butts to respond to our friends quickly and get them to safety as fast as possible."

CHAPTER 28

8 days until the Indianapolis 500

"Mack, are you okay?"

"Repeat, are you okay?"

"MACK!"

Empty silence surrounded Mack. Her body was both floating and compressed, like she was asleep under a weighted blanket. Shapes and colors clouded her vision, creating an opaque veil. She tried to think but her mind only swirled in and out of sensations—the eerie, hollow silence, the pressure on her chest, the fog in her mind. Finally, a sound registered but she couldn't place the low, dull roar around her. Then another sound: *crunch, pound, clang, crunch, pound, clang,* followed by a metallic slam. Behind them all, an odd whine needled in the deepest core of her ears, causing cringing pain inside her head.

What happened?

Her brain blared a warning signal, and Mack slowly realized she felt a paralytic tightness in her chest. She couldn't breathe. She tried to gasp but her lungs felt concave and empty. Desperate for air, she smacked her lips like a fish, caught on a hook and desperate for the comfort of the water.

The veil before her eyes lifted and a large man in a bright orange suit appeared inches from her face. His voice was loud and solid, but unhurried and smooth.

"Mack Williams, can you hear me?"

Frantic for a breath, she waved her hands in front of her face. The movement caused a jarring pain in her hand and shoulder but it felt unimportant next to her desperate need for oxygen. Tiny wisps of air seeped through her mouth and into her chest, but they brought no relief.

"She's moving, eyes are open."

Her surroundings faded for a moment as a loud whooshing sound filled her ears and cold, crisp oxygen filled her chest. She made loud, embarrassing, gasping sounds but she couldn't remember why she should care.

The large man lightly tapped her helmet. "Got the wind knocked out of you, huh? Do you feel pain in any other area?"

Mack blinked up at the large man. His eyes matched the dark shade of his skin and he looked familiar, but not someone she immediately recognized. He asked her a question, but what was it?

"Focus on my voice. Do you feel any pain?"

She looked around, gaining awareness of the tight seat belt straps against her chest and the steering wheel in front of her. Her hands in gloves, her face constricted by a helmet.

She was in a race car.

An IndyCar.

An IndyCar that was facing the wrong direction on the track.

Shit shit shit. She'd done the thing Janet warned her not to do. She'd wrecked the car.

She blinked and felt grit against her eyes. Her brain remembered the man in front of her, Dante Sabourian, the head of the safety team. He'd conducted the drivers' safety meeting yesterday.

"What happened?"

Dante lightly tapped her helmet again. "Stay with me. Do you feel your toes?"

Slowly, Mack wiggled her feet and felt a rush of relief when her toes scraped the top of her shoes. The movement jarred her brain into connection with her body, and she began to flex and stretch, suddenly feeling sensations everywhere. Most of them hurt. "I can feel everything. Nothing hurts too bad, except maybe my hand is a little sore."

Dante nodded and held a thumbs-up toward the rest of the safety team. Another safety worker unbuckled her harness, removed her steering wheel, and helped her sit on the side of the aeroscreen. From her perch, Mack watched the fleet of orange suits scatter around the track, picking up pieces of her car both big and small. Her eyes followed the skid marks left by her tires to where they terminated in a fresh, dark smear of rubber on the wide white wall. While she'd impacted in turn two, the force of the hit threw her into the backstretch before her car finally came to rest on the inside of the track, several hundred feet from where she'd hit. Slowly, she unbuckled her helmet and pulled it off.

She turned her head in time to catch a replay of her accident on the infield jumbotron. Despite her foggy head, she keenly registered a small puff from the back left side of her car. Seeing the smoke reminded her of the pop she'd heard right as she'd started to spin, and the entire incident flooded her mind in crystalline memory. The back end stepping out, the popping sound, the spin, the wall. She didn't remember hitting the wall, but she remembered trying to pull her hands back from the steering wheel, not wanting to break a bone in the quick snap as the front axle crumpled. Her sore hand told her she hadn't entirely succeeded.

"I cut a tire," she said to no one.

Dante gently touched her arm to guide her toward the waiting ambulance.

"I'm fine," she protested. No way was she going to a hospital. She needed to get back to the garage and convince Janet that she'd lost a tire.

"Everyone who busts the wall gets a free ride to the infield clinic. Indy Uber."

His deep voice made it clear he would brook zero arguments so Mack got in the vehicle. As it pulled away, she watched the remaining safety crew sweep the shattered remnants of her car into neat little piles.

~

Mack exited the infield track hospital to a dizzying array of cameras, microphones, and people. She'd passed the concussion protocol but the swirl of sensory input from the sea of people and phones and lights overloaded her shot nerves.

A small figure darted through the crowd, straight toward her, and Mack lifted a sobbing Shaw up into her arms.

"Mommy, we saw you crash on the big TV! You didn't get out of the car!"

Shaw's messy sobs flooded Mack's ears and her arm screamed in pain as she hastily turned away from the reporters and walked back inside the medical center so they could have privacy. The din of voices muffled as the door closed behind her, and Mack sat down on a gurney and set Shaw on her lap. Mack gently touched her daughter's forehead with her own, lining up their noses the way she had when Shaw was a toddler and still wanted ugga-muggas. Up close, Shaw's lashes shimmered with clusters of tears.

"Mommy!" she wailed over and over as she squeezed Mack's neck. "Mommy!"

Mack held her daughter and let her weep until she stopped making sounds, dry heaves racking her body as she continued to cry long past the point of making tears. It had been years since Shaw last crawled into Mack's lap, and Mack ignored the throb that pulsed in her hand. If Shaw needed to be held and comforted, Mack would do it as long as her daughter let her. Minutes passed as she rubbed Shaw's back in slow, soothing circles. Shaw was on the cusp of a change, still silly but sometimes quiet and contemplative. Soon, she'd care more about what her friends wore than what mermaids ate for dinner, and Mack preemptively grieved the end of Shaw's childhood. She'd always be Shaw, always have that essential lightness that defined her, but puberty would change her in ways Mack could not know. It would change *them.*

A hand settled on her shoulder, and she glanced over Shaw's head to see Wes and Billie. Laurie was not with them. She'd always hated it when Mack and Wes wrecked, but before she'd always rushed to make sure they were safe.

"You okay?" Wes asked softly, and Mack nodded, Shaw's hair tickling her face. The deep grooves around Wes's eyes pulled tight with strain as he scanned her up and down. Mack and Wes had been through this many times before, one of them checking on the other after an accident, the familial part of them scared and shaken while the professional driver assessed.

As she stroked Shaw's hair, Mack remembered the times she'd watched her dad climb out of a battered race car. Only rarely was she truly afraid; mostly, she'd felt a blind faith that her father would be okay because he was Wes Williams, the man who could survive anything. She'd always been grateful she wasn't at the track the night of his accident, that she hadn't been there waiting for him to climb out of his car, feeling the swirling dread when he did not.

But you're the mom.

She wasn't only the mom, she was the only parent Shaw could count on. Mack wished she could feel the pain of the crash twenty times more instead of the pain of hearing her daughter cry.

Mack met Wes's eyes and he shrugged a shoulder almost imperceptibly, and she understood him as clearly as if he'd spoken: *That's the cost of playing the game.* Drivers never spoke of the ultimate consequences of their profession, but they made ironclad wills, took questionable sponsorships to pad bank accounts for spouses and children, wrote secret letters to be opened in the event of disaster. Every driver made a choice—undeniably selfish, arguably unforgivable—every time they drove out of pit lane. Even when Kelley broke his body into pieces, Mack hadn't begrudged him his profession. It was his most redeeming quality.

Mack was okay with the risk. She'd grown up with it. Made peace with it. But she'd never considered what it would feel like for Shaw to watch her mother wreck. Mack was hardened to racing injuries, but Shaw was soft, unfamiliar with her mom showing any weakness, let alone physical injury. She'd accepted the risk for herself, but Shaw hadn't been given a choice. Unconsciously, she pulled her daughter in tighter, causing a pain in her right arm so intense that she momentarily saw spots.

Once the adrenaline left her body it would hurt even worse, but she couldn't think about that now. Just like she couldn't think about facing Janet or finding out what would come tomorrow. Would she have a car to qualify? Janet said she didn't have the money to rebuild the car—was she serious? What if Janet decided Mack wasn't worth a second chance?

Shaw had quieted, and Mack gently nudged her chin up. "I am one hundred percent fine, okay? I know it looked scary, but I am right here in front of you. I'm safe. You're safe. It's okay."

"You're supposed to lift your visor to tell people you're okay. That's what Pawpaw told me." Her voice sounded soft and childish, and for a moment Mack could see toddler Shaw, chubby cheeked and freckled, crying over a dropped Popsicle. Tears clung to her lashes, the little blond wisps stuck together in clumps.

"I know, love, and I'm so sorry. I was a little surprised and I forgot." Mack cringed for the fear her family must have felt for the few moments before she caught her breath, but she wasn't about to tell them that she'd forgotten to lift her visor because she'd had the wind knocked out of her.

"You can't forget," Shaw scolded. Mack pressed her lips together to hide a smile. She'd take a sassy Shaw over a sad Shaw every day of the week.

"I won't ever do that again."

"But you could crash again. That's what Daddy said, that you were gonna wreck and get yourself killed because you don't know what you're doing."

For the second time that day, Mack couldn't draw air into her lungs. Angry, she clenched her hands, hissing at a sharp stab of pain at the base of her right hand. The doctor had wanted to x-ray but Mack had refused. The medical team wouldn't let her go back on track if it was broken.

"Racing has accidents but these cars are very, very safe. I only wrecked because a tire blew, not because I don't know what I'm doing. I promise you this, Shaw Westly Williams, I will always come back to you. It's been you and me from the beginning. I will never, ever leave you."

Mack knew it was a white lie—all parents eventually leave their children, if they are lucky enough to die first—but what parent didn't say the same? Parents who went on business trips, or vacations with friends, or out to the store to buy milk assured their kids they would come home, too. Accidents and loss were part of life, and parenting sometimes meant telling your child things that you couldn't know for sure but hoped like hell were true.

"Are you going to get back in that car?" Shaw asked quietly.

Mack couldn't look at Wes. She didn't want him to know that her chance at Indy may already be over. She didn't want Shaw to know that she wanted back in the car more than she wanted to go home and play it safe.

"I don't know, honey. I have to go find out."

@RACINGNEWS
May 16

Rookie @mackwilliamsraces crashes on the exit of turn 2 at Indianapolis Motor Speedway on Saturday, May 16th.

COMMENTS:

@f1f1f1f1 that's a gnarly hit. Hope she's ok. The speeds in indycar are mega.

@donniedaytona these girls come to the track and have no idea what they're doing

@alexa1999 @donniedaytona k you go out there and do it since u r such an expert

@leftymclefterson here come the feminazis

@cafecito why do they let these girls on the track. Unsafe!

@lakelifelover4 my cousin works at the track care center and said she broke her hand but refused treatment

@donniedaytona Probably didn't want a bandage on her manicure

@alexa1999 @donniedaytona 1954 called, it wants its misogyny back

CHAPTER 29

8 days until the Indianapolis 500

When she left the infield care center, the world around Mack accelerated as fast as the spin that put her into the wall. A baker's dozen of reporters were still waiting for an interview, and she gave a concise account: She was pushing the car to the limit, she heard a noise, she hit the wall. The irony of getting her first, and possibly last, prime network interview slid into her belly, heavy and sour.

After she gave her statements, every single correspondent—from the veteran network reporter to the blogger using voice record on their phone—apologized to Mack and promised to delete any footage of Shaw. It was kind but unusual, and Mack turned and saw Billie at her shoulder, glaring at the reporters with a stern *fuck around and find out* look. She pointed two long metallic-blue fingernails at her eyes, then turned and pointed the fingers specifically to the reporters with cameras. One journalist even showed Billie how he'd deleted the footage from his phone, and Mack gave Billie another mental thank-you.

Slowly, she made her way to Gasoline Alley. She'd asked her family to wait at the RV until she had clear news from Janet; the conversation to come wasn't something she wanted anyone else to witness. Her chest ached, her hand and wrist throbbed, and her entire body felt like she'd been through the rock tumbler she'd given Shaw for her seventh birthday, but she couldn't focus on her physical discomfort now.

From the doorway, Mack got her first view of the splintered parts of her car spread across the JJR garage floor. Mack knew it was a hard hit—she felt it ringing in her body even now—but the extent of the damage was shocking. Fiberglass and metal littered the floor, and what was left of the machine was hardly recognizable as a car. The left-side wheels were both missing, the nose cone completely sheared off, the sidepod crushed, and the rear wing dangled by a metallic thread. If the bodywork was this damaged, Mack imagined the corresponding components underneath suffered catastrophic damage. She'd felt the impact but seeing the carnage in person was sobering.

Crew members methodically laid out pieces of bodywork on several tarps, separating salvageable parts from garbage. They'd worked endless hours to prepare a qualification-worthy car for her, and if there was a worse scenario, Mack couldn't imagine it. She'd not only missed her chance to qualify today, she'd smashed the team's hopes for tomorrow.

As she approached the fractured car, two crew members noticed her and stopped their work. Then another turned and stared, and another, and another, until everyone in the garage was watching her. She didn't know if they wanted penance or a platform, so she spoke first. "You guys worked so hard to put together a hell of a machine and I'm truly sorry for ruining it."

She wanted to say more, but words would not put the car back together.

"Mack. You're okay?" Leo was in his coveralls, earpieces dangling from the zipper, helmet in hand. In the next garage over, she could see his team rolling his car to pit lane.

"Shouldn't you be getting ready to go out?"

Her voice sounded cold even to her own ears. But the crew was right there, and Mack couldn't help but wonder if they'd seen the social media posts, if they also thought she'd joined the team because of Leo's influence, if they were judging her as much as people were online.

"That was a scary hit." He rubbed a palm over his beard and exhaled, and the look of tender relief on his face made Mack wish she could touch him. She clenched her fists to keep from reaching out and an eye-watering stab of pain zipped up her arm. "You're okay? Not hurt anywhere?"

Mack shook her head, dangerously close to crying and not because of her wrist. Why did she want all these things she couldn't have? IndyCar, Leo, freedom from Kelley.

"What can I do to help you for tomorrow?" Leo asked.

"There won't be a tomorrow," Janet snapped from the back of the garage. Her frizzy hair stood straight on end as she put her hands on her hips and pinned Mack with a look of utter disappointment.

Mack inwardly crumpled, the physical pain forgotten. She'd expected this response but some latent, pathetic optimism convinced her she might get a Hail Mary.

"Janet, I'm sorry."

"Don't tell it to me!" Janet shouted. She swept her arms toward the crew, who were doing a bang-up job of ignoring the scene in front of them.

"But I think—"

"I don't give a flying fuck what you think!" Janet scrubbed her hands over her face and then pressed all ten fingers against her forehead. "I gave you one instruction: Do not. Wreck. The car. And what did you do?" Janet gestured at the debris around them. "I thought you would take this chance and give it every part of your being, that you would give a million percent to this race." She glared at Mack, a look filled with frustration but also something more. Something that made Mack think of a bruise. "I thought you got it. That you knew the Indy 500 is everything. The only thing."

With those words, Mack knew for good there would not be another qualification attempt. Even before she'd wrecked the car, she'd damaged any respect she'd earned from Janet by touching Leo at the fountain, and Janet wasn't the type to forgive.

Mack's IndyCar run was done.

She should keep her mouth shut and slink away, but she kept seeing the small snippet of the replay on the jumbotron. If she fucked up, she'd own it. But if she could earn back even a small amount of Janet's trust and respect, she had to try. The Indy 500 wasn't the only reason she wanted to stay. She wanted to stay with Janet and the team.

"I think the left tire went down. I had the speed, and then the back end flipped on me."

"We could check the replay," Leo offered, too quickly.

Janet stood rigidly, staring at the floor. "The goddamn tire was fine. It was a stupid rookie mistake and I'm the dumbass who let you run a car that loose."

Was it? She'd been on the very edge of her ability to control the car when she heard that *pop*. Maybe she'd simply lost the back end. But she could see the last few seconds of the accident replay on the giant infield TV screen. She knew what she'd seen: Her, flat out in the turn, and then a small blip of movement on the left tire.

"And you," Janet hissed at Leo. "We will talk after you go out there and qualify in the top ten or else your time on this team is severely limited." Leo kept his gaze forward as Janet walked away, but Mack could see the lines of tension around his mouth.

The look on Leo's face, the fear and frustration compounded with the stress and anxiety of the day, the pain in her hand, and Mack couldn't stop it. She burst into tears.

Not little streamers at the corners of her eyes, but loud, ugly, racking sobs that echoed through the garage. She'd ruined her own reputation, for good this time, and possibly hurt Leo's career. Shaw was hurting and Mack couldn't fathom the financial consequences of her brief time at Indianapolis. Who knew what Kelley would do, and Laurie had disappeared again. She hadn't even come to the medical tent to check on Mack.

Not only had she not made the race, she'd hurt almost everyone she cared about in the pursuit of nothing. Ashamed, she covered her face and ran toward the exit.

"Mack, wait!" Leo called. He reached for her hand but stopped before he touched her, and the way he held his hand back made her cry harder.

"Shit, Mack. Mack." He pulled her into his arms and she gasped as her right hand bumped into his chest. She wrapped her other arm around his back and pulled him in close, giving up on protecting her reputation. She was going home now and she wanted this one final feel of Leo. She melted into the steadiness of his embrace and let herself have this one thing, for one moment.

"I'm sorry," Leo whispered.

"Stop," Mack sobbed. He smelled like laundry soap and motor oil, even in his coveralls. "I don't need you to try to fix this. I started this whole thing. I can't seem to stop myself from being impulsive and making bad choices."

Leo flinched and pulled back. "This isn't an impulse. I want to see you again. I can come to you on our off weekends and fly you and Shaw out for some races—"

"Leo, stop," Mack demanded for a second time. "It's over. It's all over for me. I'm going home, and Janet's not wrong. You need to focus on getting out there and qualifying."

"You don't want to try?"

My god, she did. She wanted to know all of him. But Shaw and Wes and the dirt track needed all of her now that she'd ruined her shot at the Indy 500. She'd promised herself that after the race, she'd go home and rededicate herself to her family and the family business.

"I can't."

Leo watched her, his dark eyes searching hers for the truth of her words. She must have faked it well, because he gave a single nod.

"Do one thing, then. Not for me, but for yourself." Leo smoothed his thumb over her brow. "Don't quit. Try again next year. Run some karting races, get back on the dirt track. Don't slink away like you did something wrong."

She pulled away from him. "I'm not slinking away, Leo. I got fired!"

Leo shoved a frustrated hand in his hair. "I meant don't quit on *you*. You get to choose your life, Mack. Not Janet or some pissant online or your dad or Kelley Caruthers. Don't let other people make your choices.

If you want to race, race. Find any ride you can and drive the wheels off it. Don't give up racing."

Mack blinked in fury. What did he know about quitting? Leo didn't have a child's school schedule or a father's medical bills to consider. He didn't get called *track bunny* or *whore*. Leo didn't know shit about quitting because he'd never had to find out.

"You know *nothing* about my life, Leo."

Leo's mouth tightened but he held her gaze. They stood there, too long, but Mack couldn't walk away. She wanted him to yell at her, to tell her where to shove it, to say horrible things so that she could walk away and forget about him.

But he was Leo Raisman, ever steady and kind, so of course he did not. Carefully, he closed the gap between them and Mack stared at his dimple.

"I see you out there on the track, keeping pace with drivers who've been doing this for years." There was an intensity in Leo's warm gaze that made it impossible to look away. He leaned in an inch. "You feel it, don't you? When you're out on the track, you feel it. That's where you're meant to be. Walk away from me, Mack. I'll figure out how to live with that. But don't walk away from yourself."

Mack let herself study his face one last time, let herself pull in one last breath of fresh laundry and grease. Then she turned and walked away without saying goodbye.

She'd never see him again anyway.

To: MWilliams@email.com
From: Kelley@KelleyCaruthersRacing.com
Subject: [No subject] [May 16, 4:13 p.m.]

I think it's the right time for Shaw to come to Spain. Seeing you crash like that was not good for her. She needs someone focused on her needs. I'm dating someone new and she would be cool with Shaw. I'll have my lawyer send over paperwork to make it official.

CHAPTER 30

8 days until the Indianapolis 500

"With a speed of 232.111, Leo Raisman is locked into the Fast Twelve! Tomorrow, he'll compete for the pole position along with eleven other drivers, including . . ."

Mack tuned out the rest of the announcement over the PA and leaned against the side of the RV, trying to stanch her tears before going inside. She was happy for Leo. He deserved nothing less than the success he was having this year. She wanted the best for him. But she couldn't stop wanting success for herself, too. Tomorrow, he would compete for the pole position while Mack would be back in Haubstadt sorting through whatever paperwork mess Wes had left for her.

She took several deep breaths, not wanting Wes and Shaw to see the depth of her heartbreak. She was in no mood for people, but the RV was her ride home.

Home. If only she could muster up some excitement over that word.

Mack pulled her phone out of her bra, hoping her sister had at least texted. No messages from Laurie, but one terrifying email from Kelley. She scanned it quickly, then read it again and again, the words calling back her depleted adrenaline.

She'd been terrified ever since that day DCS had showed up at her home that this moment would come.

She was going to lose Shaw.

She dropped her phone and put her head between her legs as her endocrine system pushed sweat through every pore in her body. She could smell her own fear. A strange, loud wail came out of her body and she shoved her fist in her mouth to stop it.

She couldn't do this right now. Kelley and his email could wait until she was home, where she could think and breathe and figure her shit out. Indianapolis had been a worthless interlude, and now she needed to go home and face her life, her real life, head-on. Still in her sweaty coveralls and driving boots, standing in the itchy grass outside her father's RV, she couldn't think.

She yanked open the door and stomped up the steps. "Let's go. Now."

Wes and Shaw sat at the dining table playing War. Mack swore it was the same banged-up deck of cards she and Laurie played with as kids, with the two mismatched cards they'd stolen from a mechanic in Illinois. Her breath stuttered at the sight of her daughter.

"Mama!" Shaw flung herself into Mack's arms before she'd finished stepping up into the vehicle, and Mack pulled her in tightly, even when the contact jarred her hurt hand. How could she keep her daughter safe if she was an ocean away? Shaw pointed to her hand of cards. "I'm winning," she announced proudly.

"Of course you are," Mack said, refusing to let go of Shaw's light and warmth. How could she live without this?

Billie poked her head out of the bedroom as Mack finally released Shaw. Of all the shit today, Billie's current outfit might be the biggest shocker and that was really saying something considering she'd recently face-planted into a concrete wall at two hundred miles per hour. Billie wore a knee-length satin nightgown, cheetah print with hot-pink lace trim, under a long black cardigan. Fuchsia fuzzy slippers swallowed her feet and her hair was still perfectly curled in an intricate updo. The corners of her eyes crinkled when Mack's eyes finally traveled back up to Billie's face. "Best part of RV life is that you can drive in your jammies!

Now sit down and I'll get you over to Laurie's. I bet you want a shower something fierce."

"I want to go home," Mack said again, her voice cracking on the final word. She opened the refrigerator, then closed it. "To Haubstadt. Now."

Billie shot a look at Wes and something passed between them that made Mack feel sick. She could not deal with their lovey-dovey shit right now.

"Why don't you sit down for a minute, hon. I got a natural electrolyte drink for you to try. Do you want orange or passion fruit?"

She did not want to be coddled or comforted or taken care of, she did not need the mother-she'd-never-had act, and she sure as shit did not want a gross hippie drink. All she wanted was a ride home. Mack thumped her good hand on the refrigerator door, trying but unable to contain the emotional hodgepodge burning through her insides. "I don't want your fucking drink, I want to go home," she said through clenched teeth.

"Swear jar!" Shaw said with all the seriousness of a child hearing curse words.

Wes laid down his cards and flicked another look at Billie.

"Shaw, honey," Billie said. "Pawpaw's a sore loser. How 'bout some TV time in Pawpaw and Billie's room? There's that new mermaid movie."

Cards scattered as her daughter happily skipped to the back bedroom, Billie following behind her. Mack fought the urge to make Shaw return just so she could see her and know that she was, for now, still here. She sat down gingerly in the warm spot left by her daughter and tried not to cry as she unzipped her coveralls, tied the sleeves around her waist, and peeled off her undershirt. She'd left her gear bag in her rush to escape the garage, and she mourned the loss of the blue helmet Janet had made for her, even though it would have joined her old helmet on the shelf to gather dust.

"You feeling okay? Sure you didn't get your bell rung?" Wes asked, studying her closely.

"Fine." In the silence of Shaw's departure, Mack realized the RV was too empty. "Where's Laurie? And Kelley?"

Wes sneered. "Who knows where Fuck Face went. He took off not long after your wreck. Didn't even say goodbye to Shaw." How very like Kelley to forget his actual daughter in his rush to sue her for custody. She bit down on her lip to keep another one of those pitiful wails from coming out. She didn't want to talk to Wes about Kelley; saying it out loud would make it real. "Your sister had an emergency at work or something."

There was no reason for Laurie to have stayed, except Mack wished she had. They'd spent enough time together in the past few weeks for Mack to remember the way her smart, sharp, big sister used to help her laugh the pain away. Maybe Laurie was looking forward to having her apartment back to herself, was excited to be away from the drama Mack dragged along with her wherever she went.

She couldn't think in this HomeGoods on wheels. Suddenly she wanted the familiar comfort of the dingy little house in Haubstadt.

She looked up to see Billie reentering the living space. "Can we go now?" Her voice was raspy and hollow. "I need . . . I want to go home."

"Sure," Billie said, sharing another one of those pointed looks with Wes. "We'll get you to Laurie's, hon."

"Not Laurie's. Home. Haubstadt."

Billie widened her eyes and pursed her lips at Wes in the universal gesture for *say something or I will say it.* Mack wished she had the energy to say something snarky, but her mind was on Shaw, lying in bed and watching a movie about mermaids. Would Kelley even know that she hated her hair in a ponytail? Or that she only ate yogurt if it was layered just so with cereal? That she still needed to hold someone's hand to fall asleep? Would she be sad and scared in Spain? Would she forget Mack? Would she be safe?

Mack could still see the sores of her diaper rash, the sickening way her little arm had dangled from the socket. The way the DCS woman had looked at her with revulsion, convinced poor, young, uneducated Mack had hurt her child.

Wes cleared his throat and shifted nervously in his seat, pulling Mack back to the present. Billie perched on the edge of the recliner across from the dining bench. "Okay, sit down. Oh right, you are. Shit. Okay. Well, um, okay, I gotta tell you something."

She knew that tone in Wes's voice. It was his *this is going to be bad news* voice. He used that tone when Laurie refused to come home for her first college break, and when he learned he needed a third corrective surgery on his left knee.

"We, um, well, we can't take you home to Haubstadt 'cause I'm selling the house."

A second passed, then another, then another before the words registered.

Mack was right back in the car smacking the wall head-on. She had to be, because this feeling was equally abrupt. Her mind froze, unable to process basics. Her eyes couldn't register Billie reaching over to squeeze Wes's hand, or Wes's worried expression. She didn't hear the tinny sound of Shaw's movie from the back of the vehicle or feel the air-conditioning blasting from the vent over her head. She was distilled down to her elements—the sound of her own breath sawing in her ears, her skin dotted with goose bumps, her eyes clouded with brimming tears.

"You're what?"

"Me and Billie are gonna live in the RV. Now that you're here in Indianapolis, ain't no point keeping the house."

The words slowly leached into her mind until their full impact assaulted her. The frozenness in her body boiled over, rupturing with unbearable heat.

"I'm here in Indianapolis now?" Billie flinched at the volume of her voice, and Mack delighted in the pain she'd caused. She gestured out the window in the direction of the track. "Did you not see what happened?

I just wrecked myself out of Indianapolis! I had one chance and I blew it to pieces. I never had a reason to *stay*, Dad."

Wes waved his good hand carelessly. "Accidents happen. You'll get another shot at Indy, and you've got Laurie here now—"

"I don't have Laurie! She took off as soon as I crashed out. I don't have anything but you and Shaw and now you're selling our fucking *home*." She may not even have Shaw, not if Kelley got his way. Her mind tumbled, each thought like a piece of paper in a fire, igniting and burning before she could catch it. How would she make a case for custody if she didn't have a home? Where would she live? Would she stay in Haubstadt? Or move somewhere with more options for housing and schools for Shaw? She'd need a newer car for reliable transportation if she lived farther from the track.

The track. If Wes was traveling around the country . . .

"What about the track?"

Wes scooted forward in his seat and gave Mack a look so full of apology that she knew what was coming before he spoke. "I'm selling the track, too."

She shook her head vehemently, physically rejecting his words. The movement made her dizzy and she clenched her teeth against the hot bile sliding up her throat. "No. No. You can't sell the track."

"Running a track was never my dream. My parents loved the track but I don't have big love for it. You know that. I never had a head for business."

Mack almost blurted all the ugly things that popped into her mind, things that would wound Wes and hurt her to say: Shaw wasn't the only reason Mack stopped racing, Wes had a shit head for business and if she hadn't stayed to manage the track it would have gone under a long time ago, he'd willingly let her take on more and more of the work until she was doing it all and he was merely the poster boy. Love and duty soured into a resentment she'd denied for years.

Even in her anger, she couldn't hurt him. He'd raised her, championed her, loved her when there was no one else to do it. Caring for him had kept her alive that first year after Shaw was born. Wes was unconventional, a little rough and messy, but he loved hard and wasn't embarrassed to show or say it.

She loved him fiercely, but hated him in that moment.

Thirty years of codependency and Wes knew what she was thinking. "You been doin' all the work, Mack. I know that. And if you'd get your head out of your ass, you'd admit that you hate it, too. You run that track like you're serving a life sentence. Hell, you live your life like you're in prison, afraid to step out of line."

"No I don't," she said automatically.

"I ain't stupid and you don't hide it as well as you think you do. You're not any better at running a business than I am." Mack glared at her dad and he raised his hands in a *don't shoot* gesture. "Okay, better'n me, but still it ain't for you. You were made to drive fast and take chances, Spec. You quit on yourself and I'm goddamn *tired* of watching it."

The echo of Leo's words was a kick to her gut. She didn't need one, much less two men telling her to do more with her life.

"This from the man who told me to throw him in a ditch and keep driving?"

"I was in a bad spot after my wreck but I didn't have much choice left. You've always had a choice, Spec. Stop being so scared and small."

"Are you okay, honey?" Billie interrupted in an effort to defuse their tempers. "It's a lot of information, and change can be scary. Your dad has been chewing on this for a long time."

"As long as you've been living in my house? Was this your idea? Did you convince my dad to sell our entire life?"

Fury and betrayal burned in her chest, hot and wild. Mack welcomed the comforting familiarity of rage.

"You watch your damn mouth!"

"I want to know! Was it her fucking idea to trade our house and our family business for this . . . this . . . country castle?"

Billie waved Wes off, unbothered by their yelling. "It was our idea together. Honey, you've taken such good care of your daddy. You got him through a terrible, awful thing. He's where he is today because of you, but you don't have to do that anymore. You deserve to live your life for you. And your dad, he deserves to live his life however he wants." She slipped her hand in Wes's. "You and your daddy deserve to have a father-daughter relationship, not a patient and caretaker, not business partners."

"You have no fucking idea what my dad needs," Mack spat.

"Listen," Wes said, his voice irritatingly calm now. "I could live thirty more years or thirty more days. I want to travel again, to see oceans and mountains and I want to see them with Billie. No one in this family wants that damn track."

Wes made a casual waving gesture with his hand as if this were all a hilarious joke. How could he tell her that he'd *sold her whole damn life* with that goofy smile on his face? She'd never get another shot with any IndyCar team. She had a GED and no work history or vocational skills outside of racing. She didn't take vacations or have hobbies, didn't go out for dinner with friends, or date, or spend money on herself. She lived for Shaw and Wes and the dirt track, and now she was losing them all.

If she lost those, she had nothing.

A second wave of terror hit her: If she had no track, no job, no source of income to return to, how would she ever repay Janet? She had no savings, no money of her own, and Kelley would use that against her in a custody battle.

I have money, I have lawyers, and I will bury you in court until you're broke and alone.

"You didn't even think to ask me if I might want to keep living in my own home? My job? Did not even ask me before you spent money I've busted my ass to earn?" Mack hated that she felt tears returning to the corners of her eyes, and she brushed them aside. Her anger smoldered into angst. "What the hell am I supposed to do now?"

Wes pointed a finger right at the center of her chest where it was sore from the seat belt. She hated that she noticed his finger shaking with light palsy. "Get out there and live a big damn life!"

"I have a kid," Mack snapped. "I can't pick up and move around the country like a maniac."

Wes shrugged off her immature dig. "Shaw's gonna be fine. You're the one I'm worried about, Spec."

Mack hated the concern on Billie's face, loathed the pity on Wes's. She hated that they were suddenly a team and she was the outsider. She hated that she had no plan and no control over the future. She hated Kelley's email that threatened to take Shaw away. She hated that they were sitting in the parking lot of the Speedway, where she'd failed spectacularly. She hated that she had no idea how to pay Janet back. She hated the words reverberating over and over in her mind.

You have nothing, nothing, nothing.

From: Tydarius.Moore@EOSCo.com
To: MWilliams@email.com; Laurie.Williams@StoeppelEvansFirm.com
Subject: RE: Unique Indy 500 Sponsorship Opportunity! [May 16, 5:59 p.m.]

Ms. Williams,

Thank you for considering Evergreen Outdoor Supply Co. for your sponsorship request. Unfortunately, motorsports racing does not align with our company statement of values.

We wish you the best of luck in your future.

TyDarius Moore
VP of Marketing
Evergreen Outdoor Supply Co.
Bend, Oregon
2019 Winner: Greta Thunberg “Green Standard” Award
2016–2021 Winner: Best Chain Outdoor Outfitter, *Outdoors Magazine*

CHAPTER 31

8 days until the Indianapolis 500

Mack ran across the parking lot, weaving between the motor homes and campers that dotted the wide expanse of grass. She had no plan, only knew that she couldn't stay in that bullshit motor home for one more second. She didn't think about leaving Shaw, didn't think about where she would go, didn't realize she was heading back toward the track. The spring air did nothing to cool her scorching skin. Her sports bra was soaked with sweat and she wished she could take off her fire suit but she had nothing on underneath but underwear, and even in her panic she knew she shouldn't run around half naked near campers grilling up hamburgers and hot dogs for dinner.

The PA system blared as another driver started his qualification run, and the signal flags that lined the back of the grandstands flapped in a light breeze. It was the perfect weather for racing: warm but mild, not too windy, crystalline blue skies. It should have been the perfect day for *her* to qualify. Instead, she'd demolished her last shot at a lifelong dream and her dad had come in with a secondary hit and eliminated her home and job. Kelley finished her off.

When she reached the crushed cinder path that led into the track, she stopped fighting her gag reflex and vomited on the road. A fog of terror and pain enveloped her mind and she couldn't think of where to go or how to get there. Her hand throbbed and she used it to press down on her thighs, wanting the clarity of the pain. She'd left her phone in the RV and had no way to call a rideshare, and even if she could do that, where would she go?

She was hunched over, hands on knees, debating the merits of walking the five miles downtown to get her stuff from Laurie's, when a golf cart stopped next to her. Probably some asshole who thought she was drunk. She waved them off.

"Mack?"

She must be in worse shape than she thought, because it made no sense that Leo Raisman—freshly showered and looking like a snack in vintage Ray-Bans, a black JJR polo and black jeans—would be on this dusty path after he'd qualified in the top five for the race. She'd crashed out, lost her dignity, her home, her job, and maybe her daughter, and now she was vomiting outside Indianapolis Motor Speedway while Leo Raisman, top qualifier and guy she liked way too much, watched. Today's blows seemed to have no end.

For once, she wanted someone else to figure out how to fix things, and Leo Raisman was the type of person who could probably fix anything. But she'd treated him horribly and damaged his standing with Janet. She forced herself to stand, not wanting to bring any more drama to him than she already had.

Her stomach lurched and she spat on the grass. She was not okay. She worried she'd never be okay again.

For the second time that day, Mack burst into tears in front of Leo.

Leo hopped out of the golf cart and put his arm around her. "We'll go somewhere quiet. C'mon."

She didn't even have the self-respect to push him away. It felt so damn good to let someone else take her weight for a moment. He was sturdy and clean and everything she was not. He guided her toward the golf cart and she sat down heavily, already mourning the loss of his touch.

"Where were you going?" Where the hell *was* she going? She had no idea. Her sobs increased. Leo frowned. "Did Caruthers do something?"

She didn't want to dump her baggage on Leo. He'd been kind to her, he'd made her remember that she was a woman as well as a mom, and he deserved so much more than the chaos she'd brought. She wanted to tell him that, but instead she blurted, "I don't have a car."

Leo nodded as if that was the logical next thing for her to say. "Do you need a car?"

Yes.

A car.

A car would get her the hell out of here. She nodded through her tears.

They rode quietly through the long, low tunnel beneath the track, under the short chute between turns three and four, and into the infield. Leo turned toward the rows of luxury motor coaches where many drivers lived during the final week of May and parked alongside a shiny silver RV. Mack rubbed her snotty face with the sleeves of her coveralls as Leo popped in and out of the bus, returning with a set of keys and a bottle of water. She swished water through her mouth as she followed him to the backside of the coach, where a dark blue 1969 Pontiac GTO Judge sat glistening in the late afternoon sun.

"Whoa," Mack rasped, her tears momentarily paused.

Leo beamed as he ran a hand lovingly over the car's hood. "On my thirteenth birthday, my uncle brought me a rusted pile of what used to be a car. We restored it piece by piece and I drove it for the first time on my sixteenth birthday. I know you'll take good care of it."

He tossed her the keys, and she gasped when her attempt to catch them sent a throbbing ache up her right arm. She ignored Leo's curious look as she plucked them off the ground with her left hand.

Impulsively, she dove into his arms. "Thank you, Leo."

He pulled her close and Mack let herself enjoy the feeling of his warm palms on her back. "Keep the car as long as you need. One condition," he said, releasing her enough to look her in the eye. "Take good care of yourself, too."

She hugged him again before sliding into the dark blue leather upholstery and turning the key.

CHAPTER 32

8 days until the Indianapolis 500

The Judge had a full tank of gas and a 400 Ram Air IV under the hood, and Mack had nowhere to be. She drove aimlessly, turning onto Sixteenth Street and then south onto Main, through the small incorporated town of Speedway, Indiana, weaving through one neighborhood after another. She had to shift with her left hand, but it didn't stop her from driving south with no plan other than finding roads where she could let the car fly. Eventually suburban housing developments turned into two-lane roads bordered by fields and barns, and Mack shifted into fifth and put the pedal on the floor. The thunder of the GTO Judge's three hundred and sixty horsepower filled her ears as the wind blew her hair back into her face.

The road settled her, pulling all the messy parts of her into tight focus.

She drove until she became another component of the vehicle, the line between machine and woman unclear. Using her left hand to steer and bracing her right palm against the gearshift, she braked late into curves, floored the throttle on the straight lines, felt her stomach flip as she got air on a small hill. The Judge barreled down the narrow roads with confidence, and the corners of Mack's mouth tugged up when she pulled off a drift on a tight right-hand turn. Driving fast was distraction and dopamine, pushing away the events of the day until all she thought about was when to shift and when to steer. Like going to bed and knowing the sun would rise in the morning, pushing the clutch and pressing the pedal always brought Mack to herself.

She sped across central Indiana until the sun fully set and the horizon filled with pale peach light. Long, dark shadows from sycamore trees crisscrossed with the waning sunlight, creating disorienting shadows across the narrow road. She took a curve too fast, corrected, then overcorrected, the front end of the car careening from the opposite lane to the ditch at the side of the road. With a lot of luck and a little skill, she caught the pavement and straightened the Judge up in the right lane.

She slowed, not even going the speed limit. Her hand throbbed from gripping the wheel too tightly during the slide. Her heart pounded against her sore ribs and she greedily pulled cool night air into her lungs.

Then reality came crashing down, turning the Judge from her supernatural getaway vehicle to the pathetic avoidance of her failures. She promised to never leave her daughter, promised her safety and stability, and then took off with one whisper of the Indy 500. She'd taken the once-in-a-lifetime chance Janet had given her and acted like a moody teenager, raging at the crew and sleeping with her teammate. Then she'd crashed her IndyCar chance while Shaw watched, then argued loudly with Wes before slamming out of the RV without saying goodbye. She'd used Leo when it made her feel good, then almost put his beloved car in a ditch. She could have hurt someone else, or herself, driving like a reckless maniac.

She created chaos, then left without any explanation or warning.

Like Kelley.

Her hands shook on the wheel as Mack pointed the Judge back toward the Speedway, carefully winding back up the same dark roads she'd just flown down. She was messy, but she didn't run from her problems.

Mack came to Indianapolis to retrieve some part of herself she'd thought she'd lost, and instead lost everything she'd built for her daughter. She had to go back and make things right with Shaw, then figure out what was next.

She'd driven farther out of the city than she realized, and thirty minutes passed before she hit the lights of the suburbs, and another thirty before she turned right onto Sixteenth Street. The track loomed large in front of her, impossible to miss at this section where the back of the grandstands bordered the road. As she stared up at the giant letters above the roadway proclaiming Racing Capital of the World, a swatch of light caught her eye. The exterior tunnel entrance to the track was open, no gate blocking the entrance.

The Judge rumbled into the quiet infield, and Mack felt like a trespasser even though she'd driven this track only a few hours ago. On Gasoline Alley, lights leaked out of a few garage stalls as crews fine-tuned their cars, relying on caffeine and hope to get them into the race. Mack wondered what her team would be doing if she hadn't slammed her car into turn two. Would they be out at a bar, celebrating her qualification? Or would they be here, looking for every millisecond of speed to get her in the field tomorrow? She'd felt the pace coming on at the end of her stint, sure that she was gaining enough ground to make the field, until that *pop*. She looked away from the bands of light.

To her right, she could make out the fountain where she'd sat with Leo, putting both of their reputations at risk and landing them on the other side of Janet's good opinion. What had she been thinking, touching Leo out in the open like that where god and everybody could see? She hadn't been thinking of her reputation, or his, or what Shaw might see, or anything at all other than what she wanted in that moment.

Reckless.

The Indy 500 had been a symbol of hope and dreams for most of her life, but now it felt haunted by her mistakes.

Easing the Judge into the parking space behind Leo's trailer, Mack hoped the loud rumble of the engine wouldn't wake him. She left the keys under the mat, making a mental note to send him a Venmo for a car wash and hoping he didn't ask questions about the muddy wheels.

She'd planned to go straight to Shaw, but a quick glance at her watch showed it was long past her daughter's bedtime, so Mack turned toward the track instead. Might as well take one last look at the Speedway and let Shaw sleep until morning.

Her soft-soled boots were quiet on the pavement as she passed the towering Pagoda and arching grandstands. She walked through a break in the fence, and then she was standing on the same pit lane she'd left only hours ago. The concrete wall felt cool and rough on her hands as she hefted herself over into the pit boxes, and the smell of burnt tires lingered faintly in the air. She walked parallel, tracking through double streaks of rubber, trailing one hand along the inside of the wall. After qualifications, each driver's name would be painted on the wall of their pit box, and Mack blinked her eyes to clear the mirage of her name written in blocky black letters on the stark white surface.

Crickets squeaked over the distant drone of traffic and moonlight reflected off the aluminum grandstands behind her, casting a pale glow onto the asphalt of the track. In a week, over three hundred thousand fans would fill the track, but tonight it was eerily empty. Mack walked to the wall that divided pit lane from the track, lifting her legs over one set of barriers, then another, before her feet touched the front stretch of the track.

What would it have felt like to drive past these stands full of cheering people on race day? To hear them, see them, experience the spectacle of the Indy 500 with them?

When she reached the yard of bricks, that infamous three-foot swatch of the original track surface, she came to her knees and gingerly placed her hands on the textured blocks. She remembered the vibration of the car as she sped over this strip, the brief *zoop* of the tires as they hit the roughness. She rubbed the bricks, breath catching as she imagined the emotion of driving over this sacred piece of pavement as the green flag waved. She'd been so close. So very close.

A decade ago, she thought she'd lost any chance at the Indy 500. Janet had given her that hope back, and the second loss of it hurt worse than the first. Back then, she hadn't really known what she lost. But now, she knew it was more than a race she'd squandered: She'd lost the support of a team, the regard of people she respected, participation in something bigger than herself. But more than anything, she'd lost the last chance to prove to herself that her earlier success wasn't all a fluke.

The Indy 500 was her chance to redeem herself, to herself. And she'd failed.

Mack rolled to her back, lying directly on the row of bricks—a pathetic imitation of Dan Wheldon, a beloved driver gone way too soon, who famously celebrated his win by rolling around on the yard of bricks. The rough texture of the pavement on her back was a pleasure-pain, cold and coarse and full of longing.

Was Wes right? Was Mack living her life like a prison sentence? She knew she was lucky—Wes was healthier than ever, Shaw was bright and solid, Mack had a roof over her head and work that paid the bills—but why could that never be enough for her? Why did she feel like she needed this place, this experience, *this race* to complete her?

The ground was cool but Mack's face heated with shame. Here in the dark silence, she could admit that Wes was right about one thing: Her deepest self had exhaled in relief when Wes told her he was selling the dirt track. She did not want to run a small business. He'd hurt her by going behind her back, but he'd released her, too. She sat up and hugged her knees tight into her chest. The dark sky was starless, the blinking lights hidden by clouds and light pollution. Above her, the bird's nest hung thirty feet high, the signal flags neatly rolled and tucked away.

If she was released from the dirt track, what would fill that space? Shaw, of course, always. She'd build new stability for Shaw, and if Kelley wanted to fight her for custody, he'd better come with a dozen lawyers and a crowbar because Mack would fight clean, dirty, and everything in between to give Shaw the life she deserved. She'd move the damn galaxy to keep her daughter safe.

But what if the life her daughter deserved wasn't the life Mack was giving her? What if Wes was right about that, too? Had she made Shaw's life too predictable and too small? Mack had closed out anyone from her former career who'd bothered to stay in touch. She didn't have local friends, didn't hang out with the other school moms, never dated and only did the hookup apps. In closing herself off, had Mack accidentally closed off Shaw?

Mack pushed away Leo because she wanted to protect both Shaw and her reputation. Her reputation was garbage now, but still she couldn't imagine opening Shaw up to heartbreak and exposure if Mack pursued something with Leo and it didn't work out. Mack could hardly imagine opening herself to it. But she pictured Leo handing over the keys to the car he'd built with his own hands, putting his faith in her after she'd shut him out repeatedly. Was she right to push him away from herself and, possibly, eventually, Shaw? She'd put Leo firmly in the category of things she could not have, but what about what Mack deserved? After so many years of deprivation and denial, after being released from the family business and Wes's caretaking, what could she allow herself to have?

Surrounded on both sides by grandstands, she remembered how, as little girls, she and Laurie begged Wes to buy seats in this section so they could see the start-finish line, but her dad insisted they sit in turn three. He swore they were the best seats in the arena, with sight lines coming out of turn two, down the entire backstretch, all of turn three, the short chute, and a solid sight line of turn four. They grew to love the seats, learning firsthand to sit where they could see most of the racing, not only who won or lost.

Racing. Winning. Losing.

Even the best drivers in history lost more races than they ever won, yet they continued to get in the car and floor the throttle anyway. Every driver's ultimate goal was winning, but no one would race—and take on the risks—if they didn't enjoy what happened in between the start and finish. Before her first race, Wes had gotten down on his knees, pulled her hands into his own, and said, "Spec, you can't choose everything that happens to you in a race, but you can choose to never, ever quit. *That's* what racing really is. It's not always the best driver who wins the race, but the driver who refuses to give up." The words looped in her head, drawled in Wes's slow Hoosier accent, as if he were sitting next to her on the bricks.

Mack looked out at the grandstands and watched them disappear around the turns. Over the years, she'd let the dream of the Indy 500 become bigger than any other element in her life except for Shaw. She'd wanted to race here above everything else, and when that dream disappeared, she let all of racing disappear, too. She'd been afraid Kelley would take Shaw away, and she'd let that fear keep her quiet and small. Laurie had hurt her, big and blindsiding, and Mack had never let her back into her confidence. She'd taken every one of her responsibilities and heartbreaks—Shaw, Kelley, Wes, Laurie, the dirt track—and treated them as impenetrable roadblocks.

Mack had been so focused on the finish line of her life, so focused on the one win she would never have, that she'd forgotten to run the rest of the damn race. Hell, she'd stopped pulling up to the starting line.

She'd thought she'd had no choice, but she hadn't even let herself consider options until that night Janet showed up and forced her hand. Until Laurie let her move in without a single question. Until Leo encouraged Mack to be herself, then told her that her ugly, unruly parts didn't make her unworthy.

Now she was surrounded by choices: where to live, what to do with her life, how to create new relationships with her family. How to get in the car and *race*.

Maybe Leo was right: She'd lost the Indy 500 today, but it didn't have to be the end of racing. Of her second chance. Of anything.

She got to choose the direction of her life.

She'd always protect Shaw above all else, but maybe Mack could do more than just protect. Maybe she could buckle Shaw in tight, stop looking in her rearview mirror, and drive the damn car forward toward something instead of staying parked in place.

There was a lot of race left to run, and Mack refused to give up on herself any longer.

With one last glance at the Speedway, she jogged back to Leo's trailer. She couldn't figure out her entire life tonight, but she could steer toward one thing she knew she wanted. Leo answered her knock, hair sleep-mussed but his eyes warm and welcoming. He stood several steps above her, and Mack tilted her head up to study him.

"I don't know where this leads," she whispered.

"We don't have to have a map," Leo said softly, stepping down until he stood barefoot in the grass next to her.

They could do such damage. He could hurt her, or Mack could hurt him more than she already had. They could crash out. But they'd never know if they didn't start the engine and see where the road led. Slowly, Mack stepped forward until they were close enough to feel each other's body heat. Leo waited patiently, his breaths audible but his body still. She stood on her tiptoes and kissed him, gently at first and then firm and fast, trying to say everything she couldn't say with words. With her body, she told him what she needed, what she wanted, until he grabbed her by the waist and lifted her up the stairs of the RV.

CHAPTER 33

1 week until the Indianapolis 500

The morning sky was overcast, too dark for Mack to see who was incessantly pounding on the RV door at such a cruelly early hour. She fumbled for the lock and when she finally yanked the door open, Laurie took a step back.

"What the hell are you wearing?"

Mack looked down at her body, ensconced in a neon pink-and-orange zebra-stripe pajama set with pink feathers on the cuffs. Billie hadn't said a word last night when Mack showed up at two a.m. in one of Leo's T-shirts, and she'd stayed silent as she turned the sofa into a bed and handed Mack a pair of clean pajamas. She'd treated Billie with suspicion and rudeness, and sometimes Billie deserved it with her weird kelp noodles and scented body glitter, but she'd done nothing worse than love on the Williams family with generosity and joy. As she'd left a glass of water and two Advil on the table by Mack's bed, Mack had decided she'd try to get to know her dad's girlfriend.

"Why aren't you answering your phone?" Laurie demanded. "I tried you twenty times last night and I called and texted another twenty times this morning. Dad didn't answer either."

Mack motioned for Laurie to lower her voice as she glanced behind her at the RV's interior. "My phone died," she lied. She wasn't about to tell Laurie about running away, driving Leo's GTO, and then ending up at his motor coach.

"You can't walk away from your phone, Mack!"

Mack stepped barefoot into the dewy grass and pulled Laurie away from the door. She'd close it but was afraid to lock herself out in these ridiculous pajamas. "Shh! It's the ass crack of dawn and—"

"Didn't you check your messages at all? It's eight thirty! Get dressed!"

"Do you want my crap out of your apartment so bad that you'll wake everyone in this parking lot?"

Laurie let out a squeal of frustration. She pulled out her own cell, tapped the screen, and found the text thread she shared with Mack. "I've been trying to tell you that your car was repaired overnight. You've got to get to the garage and get ready to qualify. *Now.*"

Mack flinched. "What the hell are you talking about? There's no money—"

"I got the money! You've got one shot this afternoon to make the field. *Get! Dressed!*"

Mack stood perfectly still as the wet grass soaked into the satin fabric of her borrowed pajama pants. It couldn't be true. She'd seen the shattered pieces of the car, knew it was impossible to fix overnight, recalled every one of Janet's words. Mack stared at her feet, watching the damp climb her legs, small capillaries of water ruining clothes that weren't hers.

"Aunt Laurie!" Shaw barreled through the door Mack had left cracked open, and Laurie took a step back to absorb the impact of Shaw's tiny body hurtling off the steps.

"That true?" Wes appeared at the top of the RV steps and Billie peered out over his shoulder. "You paid Janet so Mack could qualify?"

Laurie spoke over her niece's head. "I didn't pay her anything. I'll explain later." She turned to Mack. "But you have to get to Gasoline Alley *now.*"

Mack shook her head. "No, it's over."

Wes waved the hand not leaning on his cane manically. "Someone tell me what in the hell is going on!"

"Swear jar, Pawpaw!"

Laurie yelled loud enough to make Shaw cover her ears. "Why is no one moving?"

Billie gently beckoned Mack toward the doorway. "C'mon, honey, let's find you some clean clothes and go see what all the fuss is about. Sometimes, it's easier to do the thing and ask questions later. You want a quick banana and some peanut butter toast?"

Maybe Mack did have a concussion and this was some kind of bruised-brain dream. The wreck was real, her aching body and throbbing hand confirmed that truth. But her cool, reserved sister showing up in the morning, shouting like a maniac? Waking up in an RV wearing her dad's girlfriend's satin pajamas? A second chance to qualify? It was easier to believe she had a brain injury than hope that she truly had one more chance at the Indy 500.

Numbly, Mack gathered her dirty gear from yesterday and accepted a slice of toast from Billie. She moved on autopilot, not willing to think about what she was actually doing, until she noticed Shaw watching her from the corner of the couch. She rubbed the tag of her blankie in the nervous way she had as a toddler.

"You okay, little love?" When Shaw didn't answer, Mack sat down next to her. "You wanna talk about it?"

Glossy tears spilled down Shaw's cheeks. "I don't want to go!"

Had Kelley said something to Shaw about moving overseas? "Go where?" she asked carefully.

"I don't want to go to the track. I don't want you to wreck and get hurt!"

Mack exhaled and pulled Shaw into her side, careful not to put pressure on her hand. "Oh love, I know the wreck looked scary but the car is made to break apart like that. I didn't even get hurt."

"Yes you did!" Shaw pointed accusingly at the hand Mack held carefully away from her body. "I heard you say a swear word when you bumped it. And Pawpaw got broken too, and Daddy left and I don't want you to go!"

Shaw was full-on sobbing now, liquid streaming from her eyes and nose. Mack shifted and pulled Shaw into her lap even though she was almost too big for it. She'd read that parents often don't remember the last time they held their child a certain way—the last time a baby rested on a hip, the last time a toddler rode piggyback, the last time a child sat on a mother's lap—but Mack felt it in her bones that this was the last time Shaw would lean into her just like this. At ten, Shaw wasn't a baby anymore, and Mack couldn't keep hiding all the hard parts of the world from her.

"You're right. There is a risk in racing. But Pawpaw got hurt a long time ago when things weren't as safe as they are now, and Daddy's wreck was very, very rare. There is so much technology today to keep drivers safe. But even then, you're right. There is risk." She paused, knowing she had to be honest. "So much of life is a risk, Shaw. Climbing the monkey bars or riding bikes with your friends or driving race cars or swimming in the ocean, all those things could hurt you. The things we love most usually have danger, but we do them anyway because the joy of doing them is worth the risk."

Shaw considered that for a moment. "I want to swim in the ocean."

"I know, love. And we're going to do that, I promise." She'd make it work if it took her last penny. "And it might seem a bit scary when you're standing in front of all that open space, but once you feel that cold, salty water, it will be worth it."

"Promise you won't ever leave me? You won't leave like Dad does?"

Mack waited until the thickness had cleared from her throat before speaking. "I promise I will never choose to leave you. Someday, you may want to go out on your own adventures, but I will always, always be right there waiting for you when you want to come back to me."

They sat quietly, ignoring time and urgency, as Mack smoothed Shaw's soft waves with her uninjured hand the same way she had since Shaw was an infant, focusing on the soothing, repetitive motion. Not nearly enough time had passed when Shaw sat up and wiped her face. "I like watching you race against all those boys."

Mack grinned, not knowing she'd needed to hear those exact words from this exact person. "I like doing it. Are you going to be okay if Mama goes to the track and tries to beat all the boys again? Today, and maybe other times?"

Shaw nodded and hugged Mack again, and her heart filled and broke at the huge, easy faith children put in their parents.

Minutes later, Mack held Shaw's hand as they walked toward the garages, followed by Billie and Wes, with Laurie marching next to her carrying a giant white paper bag.

"Finding a primary sponsor has been a nightmare, not because of you but because the men who hold corporate marketing wallets are arrogant asses. If you want to beat the tycoons at their own game, you have to think like a wealthy person. The rich get richer by investing. I've been looking for people—women, specifically—to invest in your career. Angel investors, but *you* are the product. There are some back-end ramifications—interests to be paid—but I protected you, don't worry. I'd been working my connections but yesterday pushed us into a now-or-never situation. I asked Janet what number she needed and managed to raise enough to pull it off. The crew worked through the night and Janet said they'd have it done by the time qualifications opened up. Blah blah blah, technical stuff that made no sense to me, so you'll have to ask her about that. But there's a car, it's waiting for you, and if anyone can figure out how to make it go fast, you can."

Mack jerked to a stop. She thought of the light leaking from the garages last night. Had that been her JJR team? Laurie took a few more steps before she realized she'd lost Mack. She turned, breathing heavily from talking as she walked at a furious pace. Mack noticed for the first time that her perfectly put-together sister wore leggings and a rumpled T-shirt.

"You . . . invested . . . in me?"

"Not me exclusively. A group of investors, including me, provided funds toward your career, like repairs on the car right now and some extra support cash, and in return, you'll owe us a small percentage of your future earnings. It's a gamble. If you don't qualify, we get nothing. But when you do"—she looked pointedly at Mack—"we'll get a return on investment." For the first time that morning, Laurie looked nervous, even a little timid, as she glanced at Mack. "I promised that even if you don't have a career in IndyCar, you have strong prospects in other future races. That you'd have winnings, Indy or otherwise."

Mack studied Laurie, unsure what to say. Still unsure that she was headed back to the track for another shot at making the Indy 500. "How long have you been working on this?"

"I've been making calls, taking meetings, working to find any cash at all since you told me you were coming to Indy. I've pitched sororities, women's funds, book clubs." Mack thought of all those hours Laurie spent on her phone and computer, and how she'd disappeared yesterday. Mack had assumed it was all legal work, but Laurie had been working for her, too. "Turns out, lots of women are willing to support another woman trying to make it in a man's field. The Women's Bar Association was particularly keen to help. It's high time I used my law degree for good."

Liquid welled in Mack's eyes. She'd shut Laurie out, punished her for years without allowing any explanation, and yet Laurie had spent her time and resources on Mack. Her sister had faith in her long after she'd stopped believing in herself. Mack shook her head, knowing she couldn't speak without breaking into sobs.

Her sister waved a hand as if it was all inconsequential and motioned for Mack to keep walking. "I did it for you, obviously, but it felt good to do something more than making rich people more money. I don't know . . . maybe I can keep working with angel investors for causes I believe in. For you and for other women in sports. We can do a second push to fundraise for a sprint car, if that's what you choose." She glanced at Wes, who was laser focused on the conversation as Billie, in four-inch platform pumps, guided him across the uneven grass. "You know Dad will help us make some calls, find some old connections to get you into races."

"Laurie, hon," Billie cut in, pointing to the track with a bejeweled nail. "Let's focus on what Mack needs for today, mmm? There's lots of time to talk about what comes after, but Mack needs to focus on the here and now."

Of all the things Laurie had said, the ones Mack heard loudest were simple: *we* and *us*.

Above them, a flock of purple martins swirled, individual birds turning and swooping in one mass. Mack's thoughts were like those birds, lifting and swinging from side to side and moving forward at a pace that made her dizzy. Sponsorship. Another shot at Indy. Other races. Shaw holding on to her hand for dear life. She'd been prepared to say goodbye to it all and now she was getting a chance to resurrect a life she'd hardly dared to dream of. Maybe even create a better one.

Mack was going to get another chance, and for the first time in years, she didn't feel alone.

She was getting another shot at the Indy 500.

At living.

@ ENGINESTARTERS
May 17

We are pleased to announce Engine Starters, an alliance of angel investors dedicated to advancing women in sports. We are Indianapolis based but plan to grow into a national network of women supporting women across various disciplines.

Our first venture is with @MackWilliamsRacing, the only woman competing for a place in the Indianapolis 500 this year. If she qualifies, Mack will be only the tenth woman to start the world's most famous race.

Too often, women are excluded from motorsports opportunities, not from lack of talent, but from lack of funding. 90% of sponsorship dollars in racing goes to men. By pooling investments of individual donors, we hope to overturn some of the financial barriers faced by women in racing.

We are proud to be part of Mack's chase for the checkered flag!

[Comments disabled]

CHAPTER 34

1 week until the Indianapolis 500

Mack hovered in the entry to the garage, balancing a tower of white donut boxes in her arms. Laurie had the good sense to purchase Long's donuts for the crew, a mea culpa in the form of sugar and yeast. She stood unnoticed for a moment, watching the team work on the machine she'd shattered yesterday. Everything looked shiny and new, even if it was . . . a bit patchwork. Pre-wreck, Mack's car had been classic JJR red, white, and blue, but this car was a mishmash of mismatched carbon fiber. Lines and logos cut off at odd intervals and some pieces lacked any vinyl paint. The crew worked quietly and efficiently, but Mack noticed several rub their eyes, blink rapidly, or shake out their hands. Along with the usual funk of new rubber tires and grease, the odor of burnt coffee permeated the garage.

Trepidation and embarrassment squeezed in her chest. "Who wants Long's donuts?"

Metal tools clanged and parts were abandoned, and she was rushed by crew-turned-zombies, arms outstretched for apple fritters and sugary glaze. A potbellied mechanic named Homer—he loved his cartoon doppelgänger—grunted his appreciation after a bite. "Someone must'a tipped you off. Leo brought Dunkin' once and he still ain't lived it down. Nothing like a Long's."

Leo had no reason to be in her garage, but Mack looked for him anyway. She'd gone to him last night thinking their professional relationship was over. Would he judge her for telling him they couldn't have anything while they were colleagues, sleeping with him, and then winding up on his team again?

"I'm not sure donuts make up for the night y'all had." Mack cleared her throat to make sure her voice didn't wobble. "I'm so sorry."

Another crew member, Carlo, shrugged. "Eh. It's the job. We can sleep tonight after you've made the big show." At least that's what Mack thought he said. Hard to tell between his mouth full of donut and his thick Italian accent.

"Your brain can't be too scrambled if you remembered donuts," Jimmy said from his post at the computer bank. "Better be a chocolate Long John in there for me. Plain, no cream?" Mack handed him a donut, unable to gauge Jimmy's mood. He pointed to the car. "Rebuilt the machine the best we could, but . . . well, you can see it's a hodgepodge. These knuckleheads are calling it the Frankencar. It's set up the same as yesterday but we'll be relying on your feedback from the few laps you'll get before qualifying."

"I will do everything in my power to get this car into the field," Mack vowed. She hoped he didn't notice the crack in her voice.

Jimmy lifted his lips in a half smile. "Don't take it too hard, kiddo. Wrecking is racing. Glad you brought reinforcements." He lifted the donut in cheers.

"Excellent choice of donut, Rookie," Janet said from behind her. Mack squared her shoulders and faced the boss, hoping her face showed the humility she felt. She recalled Janet's disappointment when she'd caught her with Leo, and again after the wreck. Mack didn't want to assume Janet still wanted her in the car just because Laurie found a way to funnel repair money to the team. If she wasn't wanted here, she wouldn't impose herself.

She also didn't want to say that in front of the entire team.

As if sensing her hesitation, Janet waved toward the garage door. “Let these people do their work. Come to my office.”

As they walked to the JJR semitrailer-turned-office, Janet pointed at her tape-wrapped hand. “What’s going on there?”

“Nothing.” Mack reflexively pulled her hand to her chest. Janet raised her eyebrows, as if she wanted to say more, but ultimately she didn’t push.

Outfitted with bright LED lights, whiteboard walls covered in mathematical formulas, a long conference table, and frigid air-conditioning, the trailer felt more like a suburban office park than a transport vehicle. Janet rounded a desk cluttered with two laptops and sheathes of data reports and plopped into a cracked vinyl chair. In the bright lights, she looked worn out and burdened by worries. Her usual white shirt was wrinkled and her hair, always frizzy, seemed tangled beyond repair. “You were right about the tire going down. The left rear had clear signs of a puncture. Debris, probably. No way you could have saved the spin.”

The popping sound.

Indignation flashed through Mack’s body, followed by relief. She *knew* what she heard, and she opened her mouth to remind Janet that she’d heard a pop, but the boss held up a hand. “I should have listened to you about the tire. I am sorry for my temper. It’s not my best quality, but you know a little something about that, yeah?” Her mouth lifted as she pushed away some of the papers on the desk to make room for her elbows. She looked directly at Mack as she leaned forward. “Two things can be true at the same time. I’m sorry and I was pissed off. Losing a car means losing a team, and it’s only because of the extra sponsorship your sister pulled in that all those people over there”—she waved a hand in the direction of Gasoline Alley—“have jobs today and a shot at some prize money next week. When I formed JJR, I promised myself I’d never forget that real people, with real bills and real lives, depend on me.”

Mack had been so absorbed with her own loss that she hadn’t considered the dozens of other people who lost their job yesterday.

For too long, she'd been up her own ass, bogged down in her own pain. Her face warmed with a mixture of relief and shame. "I'm sorry, too. I haven't been my best self on this team." She cleared her throat, decided to call herself out before Janet could. "With the yelling and the crying, and . . . with Leo. I've been unprofessional and I'm sorry."

Janet laced her hands behind her head and propped a foot on top of her opposite knee. Her face was implacable. "Is that going to be a problem?"

Mack chewed her lip. She couldn't predict what would happen moving forward, but she had faith that she and Leo could separate their personal relationship from their team relationship. "Absolutely not. I'm here to run the Indy 500 and I promise that is my focus."

"Be careful there. Love and racing don't often mix." Janet spoke with a softness Mack had never heard from her boss. "And if he so much as blinks in a way that makes you uncomfortable, you come to me." Janet sat up straight and cleared her throat. "Moving forward. You saw the car. It's full of borrowed components. We have no idea what the Frankencar will do out there, and you'll only have a handful of laps to feel it out before your qualification run starts."

"Borrowed components?"

Janet cracked her knuckles. "Even with the influx of cash from your sister's friends there are certain parts we can't get on short notice. We got some generous donations from Ampersand, and . . ." She pursed her lips. "Against my vehement protestations, Leo gave up his backup components. That's why the eleven looks like a fucked-up quilt."

"If Leo wrecks . . ."

"Then he's screwed to high heaven. We'll have to scramble to find more components for race day."

Leo had given up a level of security, his safety net, for her. She knew he wanted to win the Indy 500 more than anything; they'd talked about his near-miss last year and she'd seen the frustration and hurt in his face. If he wrecked during qualification today, if he had an issue during the actual race, he could lose his chance because he'd given it to her.

No one outside her family had ever believed in her that much. Except, she realized as she watched Janet studying her, maybe the woman sitting in front of her now.

"You didn't have to let me come back," Mack hedged. "Even with Laurie's money."

"I did not," Janet agreed. "I never wanted you gone, Williams. I run a shoestring budget. JJR truly didn't have the money for repairs to the eleven car until your sister came through. Even when you piss me off, I want you on the team. You . . ." Janet's ears were suspiciously pink. "You remind me of myself, once upon a time. More heart than sense."

Mack's face had to match Janet's, pink with pleasure. "I haven't done much to earn your faith, but I will. Thank you."

"Don't thank me, get out there and put the car in the show."

Mack gave a firm nod, then stood. She was almost to the door when she asked impulsively, "Do you regret retiring early?"

Janet shook her head, unbothered. "I didn't retire so much as I stopped kicking a concrete wall. I licked my wounds for a bit, then found a better way to stay in the game."

"But do you wish you'd done it on the track yourself?"

"Of course I do," Janet snapped. "Chip Ganassi is one of the most successful owners in this paddock and you don't think he wishes every year it was his name on the Borg-Warner Trophy instead of his drivers? It was a different time when I raced. There were challenges that had nothing to do with the cars or tracks. Maybe I gave up too soon." She shrugged. "Looking back won't help me go forward. I wanted to stay in racing, and this was the best way for me to do that. Stewing in regrets won't help me win an Indy 500."

It was the opposite of how Mack approached her racing career. For years, she'd focused on what she'd done wrong, what she didn't have, what she'd given up, instead of thinking of how she could have it, but differently. She had stewed for a decade, never thinking of how to take her failures and turn them into a future.

"There are a dozen ways to win a race, Williams. You just have to find the right lane."

Janet slapped her hands on the desk and stood. "Okay, enough emotional shit. Get out there and make the grid."

"Any advice?" Mack asked.

"Yeah. Don't get bumped."

CHAPTER 35

1 week until the Indianapolis 500

As Mack accelerated through her warm-up lap, she focused on every sound, vibration, and sensation, trying to get a read on the car. By the time she took the green flag for her qualification laps, all she knew was that the car was loose and she had no choice but to mash the throttle and hope she didn't wreck a second time. On the radio, Jimmy and Janet were silent.

For ten miles, she white-knuckled the finicky car around the turns and pushed the throttle on the straights. Distantly, she felt a sharp ache in her hand and the heavy thump of her own heart but she ignored both. She didn't think, didn't talk, didn't even look at her own speed. She did nothing but drive on the edge of control.

She could barely remember a single second of the four laps, but when Mack took the checkered flag to end her run, she knew the answer in her body before Jimmy called over the radio.

"230.040."

There were still two hours left in qualifying, her position was precarious, pain radiated up her arm, but Mack was in the Indy 500.

Her body felt effervescent, all pain momentarily forgotten, lifted away by the knowledge that she'd done the thing she'd set out to do all those years ago.

Back in the pits, the crew hugged and slapped her back as if they'd already won, and Mack took a moment to celebrate with the people who'd made the impossible happen. She wished she could tell her twenty-year-old self—the one who'd torn down the posters of her idols, Dario Franchitti and Tony Kanaan and Sarah Fisher, not caring that she ripped straight through the signatures—about this moment. Mack's heart broke for that young, angry version of herself, and she wished she could go back and tell that heartbroken girl that it would happen, but not the way she'd planned. Not linear, not clean or pretty or easy or fast, but she would get there. She'd *made* it there. And, somehow, being here today felt even better than if she'd traveled in a straight line.

But there were still drivers to qualify, and one absolute truth of the Indianapolis 500 was that the range of fates here were as big as the track itself. A beloved favorite could get bumped out of the race before it even began, like James Hinchcliffe in 2018, or an unexpected rookie could win it all, like Alexander Rossi in 2016. There were still drivers on track and all she could do for now was watch and wait.

Back in the quiet of the garage, she chugged water and wiped her face. She hissed through her teeth as she gingerly pulled the sweaty tape off her hand. The ache from this morning had turned into a fiery burn after gripping the wheel for her qual run. If she had to do it again, she wasn't sure she could even touch the wheel, much less grip it.

"Congrats, Rookie."

She turned at Leo's voice, yanking the last of the tape and jarring her hand. The garage wasn't exactly private but she couldn't stop herself from walking over and standing too close to him. He'd been with his own team all morning and she hadn't had a chance to thank him for the loaner parts. She sighed in relief when he pulled her in close, squeezing her so tightly her spine cracked.

"Thank you, Leo. Thank you." She couldn't stop the wobble in her voice. She'd gone from the woman who didn't cry at the track to the one who teared up at every damn turn. She pulled away and swiped at her eyes.

"Why are you thanking me? You went out there and put down the laps."

"For the components. I wouldn't have had a car to qualify without them. If you wreck . . ."

"Teammates, Rookie. You'd do the same for me."

Would she? Her first instinct was hell no, she'd do whatever she needed to protect herself in a race. But Leo seemed to expect everyone else to have his same level of goodness, the same kind generosity, and somehow that expectation turned into a reflection. His easy, compassionate nature encouraged everyone around him to do the same. She watched him rake a curl of hair off his face and realized what she felt for him wasn't only attraction, it was a tenderness she'd never experienced.

He pointed at the hand she held gingerly against her chest. "What's going on there?"

"Nothing," she said automatically. Between the strain of correcting the Judge's almost-spin last night and the tight grip for qualifying today, the pain was increasing by the minute. He arched a brow and lowered his voice. "You were babying it last night, too."

Heat exploded up her neck and she focused on rewrapping her palm and wrist. Last night, they laid in the giant bed of Leo's RV and Mack told him everything—Kelley's email, Wes selling the track—while he held her tight and listened patiently. She'd never shared so much of her insides with anyone. It was embarrassing, and it was freeing. Her body warmed remembering how he could so easily inspire both comfort and desire in her. But the loud, hot garage wasn't the place to think about that, so she licked her lips and shook her head. "I hope my time holds. I feel stupid, being so excited about thirty-second place."

"Stupid? For making the Indy 500? C'mon, Mack." He leveled her with a knowing look. "Don't pretend like thirty-second isn't incredible when the alternative is staying home next Sunday."

Leo wasn't concerned with playing it cool or mysterious, and it was possibly her favorite thing about him. "I'm still shaking. I'm worried it's not real and I'm dreaming."

"It's real. You did it."

Mack was dangerously close to kissing Leo right there in front of the crew, but her family came running into the garage at that moment, Laurie squealing like a child and pulling Mack into her arms.

After Mack's first win—a quarter midget race when she was eleven—Laurie had cheered louder than any Colts fan on a Sunday night, and that was nothing compared to the tears and wild joy her sister gave her now. Mack had to hold back her own emotions as she squeezed Laurie. They weren't perfect, they weren't how they used to be, but they were together and they were trying, and maybe that's what love and family really meant.

"Mama, why does your car look all funny? Is it still broken?" Shaw's face looked uncharacteristically serious.

"Oh no, honey. The replacement parts came from other cars so they don't all match. But the car's as good as new."

Shaw barreled into her, and Mack kept an arm around her daughter as she hugged Wes, who was openly weeping. Her dad held her face in his hands as he rambled on and on, telling her all the ways he always knew she'd succeed, sobs muffling his words. Billie produced a black-and-white bandanna to wipe at his face, and Mack saw tears in her eyes as well.

Mack choked down the emotion in her chest. "We're okay?"

Wes touched her cheek. "We will always be okay, Mackenzie Mae. I'm sorry I didn't talk to you before. I see now that I should have. I thought . . ." He frowned. "Maybe you needed a push."

The hurt wasn't gone, but in the light of day, Mack admitted there was a kernel of truth to Wes's logic.

"And the money . . . I didn't take anything from the track. I promise. Billie bought the RV and we're gonna use money from the sale to live on. But half of it is yours, Mack. I ain't forgot that."

She squeezed her eyes shut. No crying. Not here, not now. She opened her watery eyes to look at Wes, and they didn't need to say anything more. She knew and he knew that they'd always do right by each other. Even if they didn't do it perfectly, they'd never stop taking care of each other.

Over Shaw's head, Mack saw Leo trying to slip out of the garage, but she called him over before he could disappear. She made a round of introductions and Leo shook hands with everyone, including Shaw, who wiggled out of Mack's arms to tell Leo exactly which pieces of racing paraphernalia she wanted him to sign. Leo gave Shaw his full attention, carefully listening without making promises he couldn't keep. Wes gently redirected Shaw when she began to ramble, and then introduced himself to Leo. Mack bit her cheeks to keep from laughing as Leo bumbled through his earnest excitement at meeting her father. It was a hero worship she'd witnessed dozens of times and Wes ate it up.

But it was Bump Day at Indianapolis, and the bubble was bound to burst.

A collective gasp came from the back of the garage where crew members gathered at a row of computers and televisions. Mack squinted but couldn't read the text on the screen. Janet cursed.

"M. J. Martin beat your time. Roethlisberger got bumped from the race."

The warmth she'd felt a minute ago instantly turned to a chill. "What does that mean?"

Jimmy appeared beside Janet, a deep crag between his brows. "It means Roethlisberger will scramble to get out there and bump *you*."

No no no. Mack shook with the instant flash of panic that flooded her body. She'd done it, she'd made the field, and even though she knew this could happen she felt like someone had stolen a prized possession from her hands. How many times could she lose the Indy 500?

She closed her eyes and chewed her lip. "What do I do?"

Jimmy frowned. "Sit and wait."

The impotency of the situation made her growl. At least yesterday she'd been the one to slam herself into a wall. She didn't want her dreams made or crushed by sitting on her ass. She'd let her life amble by her for nearly a decade, and now she wanted to run toward it.

"That's it? We sit here and let time determine my fate?" Mack noticed the crew pretending not to listen and she thought of the time and effort they put in last night and in the early hours of morning. "Our fate," she corrected.

Janet stood with her hands braced on her head. "We always knew we could end up here."

"Or . . ." Jimmy said, pursing his lips.

"Or what?"

Janet was already shaking her head as Jimmy said, "Time's a ticking." He glanced at his watch. "But you might have enough time to go out and put down quicker laps than Roethlisberger. If you get out first, put down faster laps, you can keep your spot in the show."

Janet put her hands on her hips. "No. It's too risky."

"I didn't say it wasn't a risk," Jimmy said, as casual as if they were deciding between two different restaurants. "Going back out is no riskier than sitting here. They're both a gamble."

"Is that what you think we should do?" Mack asked. She tried to flex her right hand, inhaling sharply when the slightest movement sent searing pain from her pinkie to her elbow.

The older man raised his eyebrows impassively. "Dammed if you do, dammed if you don't. Guess it depends if you'd rather wait and see what happens or try to go do something about it."

Do something, her brain screamed. Her hand throbbed in protest.

"If she uses the priority lane, she loses the spot she has!" Janet barked.

Leo looked at the large clock on the wall. "If Mack goes back out, she has to use the slow lane and hope Roethlisberger doesn't jack around out there. If we're out in ten minutes . . . it could work."

Jimmy clicked his teeth. It was nearly impossible to get the car towed out and her gear on in ten minutes. "Yep."

Janet checked her watch as if the time calculation would magically change, then sighed heavily. She studied Mack, and the undisguised hope and fear Mack saw on her face made her feel like Janet wanted her to make the field not just for the team, but because she wanted it for Mack herself. "Your choice, Rookie. But slow lane only. Don't throw away the shot you already have."

Wes taught Mack that when there was no clear answer, her gut would never steer her wrong, and as she stood in the garage with Jimmy and Janet and the crew all watching her, her instinct shouted that she didn't want to let life happen to her anymore. She wanted to take every chance, even if it meant risking failure. Wes told her to live big, and there was nothing bigger than not wasting a second more of this second chance.

"Pull it onto pit lane. We're going out."

Mack had her helmet in one hand and was trying to zip her fire suit with her aching hand before she registered the sound of crying. Shaw stood at Billie's side, weeping into her hands while Billie rubbed her back and whispered soothing words. Mack kneeled down in front of her daughter.

"What's this, Shaw?"

"Sccccaaa . . . monster . . . nooo waaann go."

Janet called from the other side of the garage, and Mack held up her index finger.

"She's scared," Billie said softly. "She's afraid you'll wreck again since the car is made up of so many different pieces. She called it the monster car."

Mack squeezed her daughter tighter but her eyes strayed outside the garage where the crew towed her car toward pit lane. She had to leave now if she had a chance of getting in a run before time ran out, but Shaw's pain pulled at her resolve.

"I promise you, Shaw, I will be okay and I will come back to you. Always. Always."

A hand tapped her shoulder, and Leo lifted his brows in a request for permission. "Hey, Shaw, have you ever really seen inside an IndyCar? There are hundreds of components to keep drivers safe. Your mama needs her car right now, but my car is in the next garage over, and I could use help making sure everything is ready to go. I need someone to try on my helmet, too. Would you want to do that?"

Shaw looked skeptically at Leo, and then to Mack, visibly torn between her fear and her interest in her favorite IndyCar driver. Mack felt similarly torn between her desire to stay with Shaw and get onto the track. Sometimes parenting meant trusting the inner resilience of your child, and the adults that filled your shoes for a moment.

"Maybe your, uh . . . your Billie would stay here in the garage with us, and you can check out my car, and we'll listen to your mom's run on the radio. That way you don't have to watch. Even though she's going to be super safe and come right back here, sometimes it feels better to listen. Would you like that?"

Shaw nodded slowly, and Mack gently encouraged her toward Leo's garage space. Billie winked. "Go. She'll be fine, but you won't be if you don't get out there and give it everything you got. Show her that moms get to chase their dreams, too."

CHAPTER 36

1 week until the Indianapolis 500

"What speed do we have to hit?" Mack pulled on her balaclava as she and Jimmy speed-walked behind the car as the crew towed it back to pit lane. Her family and Janet followed close behind.

"A hair shy of 231."

Mack's stomach dropped. She'd used every muscle and tool available to wrestle the car on her last go-round, and she wasn't sure how to eke more out of the rebuilt machine, even if her hand wasn't throbbing. Mack pulled gas-tinged air into her lungs, then puffed out her cheeks, exhaling in an even stream as she tried to calm her shaking body before pulling on her helmet with one hand.

To Mack's surprise, Janet reached around and buckled the HANS device to her helmet. "This is ridiculous," she muttered.

"We have to try," Mack argued, as she unwound the tape from her fingers. Pain zipped up her arm as soon as it was released and Mack sucked in the acrid air between her teeth. The throb was now radiating up her forearm and zinging through her elbow.

Her boss shook her head vehemently. "That's not what I mean. What I'm about to say is ridiculous, especially when that"—she pointed at Mack's hand—"is clearly broken. My first time here, I was slow as shit. Partly the car, partly not knowing what the hell I was doing. It was the early eighties and Little Al Unser was as green as I was, but he taught me something I've never forgotten." Mack nodded impatiently, irritated and surprised Janet was indulging in story hour now of all times. "I was lifting too early. When you think you should lift for the turn, wait. Only the smallest microsecond. It feels like you'll drive straight into the wall, but you won't. It will extend your line through the corner and cut time."

There was no way. Mack was already pushing as late as she could. Any later and she'd drive straight into the wall.

"It's fucking insanity for me to tell you this right now, I know. If anyone can make it work, it's you." Janet's raspy voice quaked. "Do what you can, Rookie."

"And if I crash?"

Janet scowled. "You already tried that." She pulled on her headset and leaped onto the team's timing booth, leaving Mack to climb in the car and start connecting her cords.

Several stalls away, Mack could see Roethlisberger's team scrambling to get on track, and on her other side, the scoring pylon showed eight minutes exactly left in qualification. A race to line up was on.

Before she'd even finished buckling in, Mack felt the engine roar to life behind her. She was struggling to pull her glove over her mangled hand when the crew chief motioned his thumb in the universal signal for *Go!* Forgoing the glove, Mack peeled out of her pit stall at the same time she saw the black of Roethlisberger's car in her peripheral vision. He whizzed past her pit box and pulled into the qualifying lane two car lengths ahead of her.

Except he pulled into the slow lane.

What the hell? He had no time to forfeit, nothing to lose from using the fast lane.

Mack didn't think. She didn't calculate time or have a strategy or even know why she swerved around him and pulled into the fast lane.

And instantly lost her previous qualification time.

In the turn of a wheel, she'd gone from an Indianapolis 500 qualifier to quite possibly the dumbest person who ever lived.

She'd given up a spot in the field—a precarious one, but a spot—in order to play a game of time and speed. She could have stayed safe, crossed her fingers that Roethlisberger didn't have the pace. She should have followed him into the slow lane and prayed that there'd be enough time. She should not have taken the risk.

"Williams, do I see you in the priority lane or am I having an episode of what-the-actual-fuck?"

Over the radio, Janet continued her diatribe, but Mack tuned her out. She'd made a choice, possibly a terrible one, but there was no going back now. Janet said a woman in motorsports had to be sexy or have a good story, and Mack supposed she'd made her own legend.

She wrestled her glove over her sore fingers, timidly tucking it down as far as she could, muffling her yelp on the radio. In the afternoon sun, the internal temperature of the car was over one hundred degrees, and Mack felt sweat trickle down the length of her back while she waited for the signal to take to the track. Her hand throbbed at the bare touch of the wheel.

What the hell had she done?

She flicked a glance at Roethlisberger, and realized every second they sat on pit lane was one second less he had to qualify. In the past, she'd been ruthless and willing to do whatever it took to win. She hadn't been afraid to take chances. She'd fought for the win even if she started dead last.

She'd refused to quit.

Maybe pulling into the fast lane wasn't an error in judgment, an impulse, or a stupid mistake.

Maybe the deepest core of her, the part that loved a battle, had done it on purpose.

There are a dozen ways to win a race, Williams. You have to find the right lane.

She was deep in her head when she saw the track official wave her out. There was nothing to do but put the pedal on the floor.

Mack gasped at the ache in her hand as she grabbed the wheel. She reminded herself that she could push through anything for four minutes, that she had to, that she'd pushed through worse. She'd had her fair share of wrecks in life: never knowing her mother, giving up a normal adolescence to chase races, Laurie leaving, unplanned pregnancy, Shaw's colic, Wes's accident, almost losing the family business during 2020. Yesterday, she'd crashed out and lost the Indy 500, then her house and the only job she'd ever had. Kelley threatened to take Shaw. She'd even lost her dad, in a way, as he steered toward new adventures. But she'd managed to still be here, still fighting. She could handle a little pain.

Upshifting, she sped onto the main track, careful not to hit the throttle too hard on cool tires, and did a little zigzag down the backstretch before accelerating into the final turns before her qualification run officially started.

Maybe it wasn't that Mack *could* survive something, but that she got the chance. She had the choice to take risks and go for broke. Mack couldn't control Kelley, or Laurie or Leo or Wes, and not even Shaw, who was her child but not her pawn to maneuver. But Mack could choose her own path, her own attitude, her own destiny. She'd let the past and setbacks and excuses and other people define her instead of taking charge of her own life. If Mack stayed in Haubstadt, or moved to Indianapolis, or went back to racing sprints and chased checkered flags around the country, there would always be something that could go wrong, a reason to stop trying. If Mack wanted to live a big damn life, she had to stop hiding behind her shame and fear, had to stop taking herself off the roster before the race even started.

She had to let go of what had happened and embrace what could be. And the time to do that was right now.

She drove under the green flag and her mind and body clicked into place as her qualification run officially started. She tuned out the pain in her arm and the radio in her ears. The high whine of the engine became the white noise behind her focus, and as she steered into turn one, brain, body, and car melded into one machine. She approached turn two and considered Janet's suggestion about holding out for the turns. It was pure folly; she was already driving on the razor's edge of control and her hand was growing weaker by the second. One small distraction, or debris, or miscalculation would have her back end spinning around and into the wall again.

Yet she knew, felt it down in her toes and up through her spine, that she had more to lose from playing it safe than going for glory. She'd told Shaw that sometimes taking a risk was worth the possibility of getting hurt, and today, Mack would make the field or go out on her own terms.

On her next pass down the front stretch, she prepared herself for how she would take the turn. She thought about the reality of a quarter of a second, the mere millimeters she would move her hands to make a ninety-degree turn, how low she could let her left tire drop below the inside white line without hitting grass.

And then she did it.

It was terrifying at first. She entered the first turn of her second lap sure she'd barrel straight into the wall instead of gliding through the long, acute angle that made up the corners of Indianapolis Motor Speedway, but she swooped through the turn with only the tiniest wiggle. She caught the back end and popped onto the short chute on an entirely different line, this time so close to the exterior wall that a quarter could not fit between her right tire and the painted concrete. She forced herself to take turn two the same way, once again driving down so low on the bottom of the track that she flirted with the grass and exited on a trajectory that would end in a tank slapper if she wasn't careful.

For four laps, she held the car on the edge, dipping her left wheels low as she entered the turns and pushing her right wheels high when she exited. Through the laps, she held the throttle down, never lifting even for a fraction of a second. The pain of her hand had morphed into a numb, unfeeling grip.

In her flow, Mack felt it: It wasn't too late. It wasn't too late for her to take on new challenges, to chase whatever finish lines she wanted. As easily as she chose to try the new driving line, she could decide to un-pause her life and move forward instead of rewinding the past. She thought her life ended the day she called Wyatt Venter to cancel her IndyCar test, but she'd already started over the minute she'd said yes to Janet Joyner. The deepest, most honest, most vulnerable part of herself answered Janet when they were still standing in the dark of the dirt track.

Yes, I want this.

Yes, I believe in myself enough to try.

Yes, I can choose to begin again because it's not too late.

Mack passed the yard of bricks and saw the checkered flag flutter over her, but there was no sound. No buzz from her radio, no Jimmy or Janet in her ear, nothing. An eerie silence hovered over the track, the usual din of the announcer and cheering fans absent. Mack eased off the accelerator for the cooldown lap and was heading onto the backstretch before her radio crackled.

"230.811," Jimmy announced in her ears.

Outside the car, Mack heard a distant hum, and she was through turn four before she realized the sound came from the fans, cheering and clapping for her.

"How much time does Roethlisberger have?" Mack radioed as she ducked into the pits.

Her voice was lost in the *BOOM!* of a cannon, the traditional ceremonial closing of qualifications.

"We're in!" Janet shouted.

"You'll start thirty-first next Sunday. Well done." Mack could hardly hear Jimmy on the radio from the dull roar of the crowded grandstands above pit lane.

She was a rookie with no logoed sponsorship, the only woman in this year's field, the final qualifier for this year's race, and she was in the Indy 500 for good this time.

From: Ruth@LeftoverLeggings.com
To: Tinsley@LeftoverLeggings.com; Umberto@ LeftoverLeggings.com
Subject: Mack Williams/Indy 500 [May 17, 7:06 p.m.]

T & Berto,

Did you see Indy 500 qualifying today? The only woman attempting the field qualified in the final moments. It was electric and perfectly drama filled, the way racing should be.

Her name sounded familiar and a quick search shows Mack Williams solicited us for sponsorship recently. How did this one not make it to my desk?? Between the reach of the Indianapolis 500 and the attention she's getting for her dramatic qualification, I suspect the ROI value is high but I want to see it in numbers. Today.

Ms. Williams is a female athlete, a mother, and a changemaker, like our customers. Her team is also run by a woman. She's a perfect candidate for our next campaign and I want her on our radar, and us on hers, NOW.

RBE
Ruth B. Evans
Founder and CEO
Leftover Leggings
Indianapolis, Indiana

To: MWilliams@email.com
From: FatimaAnwar@ESPN.com
Subject: Interview request [5/17, 6:04 p.m.]

To: MWilliams@email.com
From: JMS@RacerMag.com
Subject: Interview [5/17, 9:11 p.m.]

To: MWilliams@email.com
From: DOssie.S.Green@SportsNews.com
Subject: Time for an interview? [5/17, 10:12 p.m.]

To: MWilliams@email.com
From: Eliana@WomensHealthMag.com
Subject: Quick interview? [5/17, 10:22 p.m.]

CHAPTER 37

1 week until the Indianapolis 500

Mack barely touched the kill switch before she was swarmed by a dozen crew members. She unbuckled her harness as the crew slapped her helmet, reached through the aeroscreen to shake her hand, and shouted congratulations. In the chaos, she struggled to remove the steering wheel, disconnect her cords, and extract herself from the car as the team continued to celebrate. All down pit lane, crew members from other teams clapped and cheered for her, and she heard her name over the loudspeaker. *Mack Williams, the rookie driving for Janet Joyner Racing, will start on the inside of row eleven.* The back of the field wasn't ideal, but some of the greatest IndyCar drivers started at the back at some point in their career. Before a driver could battle for the win, first she had to make the race.

Mack felt golden inside, like the warm light of an Indiana summer sunset swirled in her body. Radiant beams of relief, gratitude, and pride bubbled through her veins. Even the pain in her hand as she yanked off her sweaty driving gloves couldn't dampen the euphoria.

Cameras and reporters hovered outside her car but Mack ignored them for now. Still in her helmet, Mack dove right into the middle of the celebrating crew. She'd put in the drive of her life, but she hadn't done it alone. Every mechanic, engineer, pit crew, and even all the folks in Janet's business office had put in countless hours so they all could stand and celebrate this moment. These people cared more about the team than what Mack had under her coveralls, and she knew that hadn't been the same for far too many women in motorsports.

Jimmy thumped her helmet. "The work is just beginning. We'll do a full engineering meeting tonight and fine-tune the car for race day. Gotta set you up to pass some cars."

"I can't wait." They laughed together, remembering her misery at the engineering roundtable.

Leo appeared in the crowd, his grin as wide as her own. She didn't think as she flung herself into his arms and gave into the embrace he offered, cameras and online creeps be damned.

She hadn't even unsnapped the HANS device when Janet pulled her into a shocking squeeze. Mack returned the hug, relishing comfort and softness from a person who rarely gave either.

"Hell of a run, especially considering that." Janet pointed at her throbbing hand.

High on the moment, Mack was honest. "I wasn't going to let a broken hand be the thing that kept me out of the race." Her adrenal system was still overloaded and everything felt warm and heightened, the pain forgotten in the excitement. "I will fight for every position."

Above them, she could still hear the cheers of the crowd, and she looked up into the grandstands and waved at the fans, trying to imprint the image into her mind. Whether they rooted for her individually or the excitement of the day in general, it didn't matter. The moment was the stuff of dreams, her dreams, made all the sweeter by the years and heartaches and despair.

"Of course you will," Janet said firmly. "I didn't pick you to be the token woman in this race. I picked you to win. It won't be easy, but the good things never are." Janet pointed behind her. "You've got some people who want to join this celebration."

In the middle of all that joy, her heart soared even higher when she saw Wes, Laurie, Shaw, and Billie standing behind the low concrete wall of the pits. Shaw jumped up and down, unable to resist the excitement of the moment and Mack motioned her forward, then wiggled through the crowd to pull her daughter into her arms.

"That was so cool! Aunt Laurie says we'll get to watch you in the big race! And I want to watch it for real, not on a screen."

Mack held Shaw close and marveled again at the resilience of children. She'd let Shaw down, she'd scared her silly, and yet here she was, Mack's cheerleader. She'd do anything to keep earning her daughter's trust, but now she knew she needed to introduce her to adventure, too—the risks and rewards, the highs and heartbreaks.

Releasing Shaw, Mack stood and faced Wes, whose eyes were thick with unshed tears. Unable to stop herself, Mack began to cry when Wes held her face in his hands and rested his forehead against hers. So what if she was the girl driver who cried? She could be both the woman with tears on pit lane *and* the woman who just made the greatest American race. She could be with Leo and be good at her job. She could be any damn thing she wanted to be.

Her throat was thick and snot began to pool in her nose, but she knew Wes understood what she could not say. He held her tight and whispered, "It's your time now, Spec."

Wes released her into Laurie's arms and her sister scooped her into the kind of soft yet firm embrace only sisters can give. They held on to each other long enough to silently say the things they couldn't say out loud yet. Over Laurie's shoulder, Mack saw Billie hovering beside Wes. She released her sister and turned to the woman who'd dressed her family in matching blue T-shirts emblazoned with large checkered-flag-patterned elevens. "I like the shirts."

Billie beamed. "Thank you. I know it's a bit much, but marketing is everything and we've got the best product at the track."

Mack bit her lip. She wouldn't have picked Billie for her dad, but maybe that's why she was so good for him. For them. "Thank you. For . . . for lots of things."

Billie pulled Mack into a lily-scented hug and Mack let herself lean in. And dammit if Billie didn't give good hugs.

"Mack! An interview?"

Hana Park vaulted the pit wall in a single smooth move, motioning the cameraman to start filming before he'd even cleared the concrete. "I'm here with Mack Williams, who qualified in thirty-first for the Indianapolis 500. Mack, you not only put up a dramatic last-minute run, you bumped Formula 1 star Mick Roethlisberger. How does it feel?"

"Like a dream come true." She knew her words sounded childish, heard the wobble in her own voice, knew she was still crying but she didn't give a shit. "My dad brought me here when I was a kid, and from that moment on I wanted to be right here. I think I broke his heart when I wanted to drive on asphalt instead of dirt." Hana laughed with Mack. "I wanted this so much. And I lost sight of that for a while but my dad never did. He never gave up on me. And my sister and my daughter. My daughter, Shaw, my biggest win. I cannot thank Janet Joyner Racing enough for this opportunity. And the crew." Mack gestured at the chaos around her. "These people behind me stayed up all night to rebuild the car. They're the real stars here. I'm so grateful. It's all so overwhelming."

Hana smiled patiently, letting Mack cry and gush without making her feel silly or rushed. "It's a big moment, not only for you but in the history of this race. You're only the tenth woman to ever make it into The Greatest Spectacle in Racing. What do you want to say to all the girls and women watching right now?"

Mack took a deep breath, wanting to not just say the right thing, but the truest thing. "We deserve to be here. Whether we call ourselves she or he or they. Anyone who loves this sport and is willing to do the work. Anyone willing to work as a team. If you're used to driving on dirt, or you have a kid, or even if you lost sight of your dreams for a bit. The Indy 500 is about faith and hard work. Do the work, pray for luck, and don't ever, ever give up hope."

Hana's eyes were suspiciously shiny. "One more question, Mack. You were on the bubble but you had a spot in the race. Why did you go back out, and why did you use the priority lane? Why take the risk and give up your qualifying time?"

Mack looked around. She saw her daughter, happy and right beside her. Her father, alive and always, always there for her. Her sister, standing next to her after so many years apart. Even Billie, who maybe was the fresh air their family needed. Janet and the crew, who'd brought her into a tight-knit system and made room for her. And Leo, a friend right when she needed one the most, someone who let her be her best and worst self and still saw value in her. The fans, the track staff, the other drivers who treated her like any other rookie. Somewhere, perhaps in an afterlife, her mom was watching and proud. She didn't need to be a martyr. She simply needed to be herself, and allow other people the same grace.

She couldn't sum all that up for Hana so she simply said, "I wanted to live big."

To: Kelley@KelleyCaruthersRacing.com
From: Laurie.Williams@StoeppelEvansFirm.com
Subject: Mack & Shaw Williams—new communication plan [May 20, 4:22 a.m.]

Mr. Caruthers,

In regard to your email dated May 16 concerning custody for the minor child, Shaw Westly Williams, all future communication should be sent through me. I represent Ms. Williams, and we reserve the right to bring additional counsel on board. Pursuant to Indiana Rule of Professional Conduct 4.2, do not contact Ms. Williams directly regarding custody, child support, or visitation for the minor child, Shaw Williams.

The attached Petition for Custody was filed today in Gibson County Juvenile Court, pursuant to UCCJA, Indiana Code §31-21-2-8. Additionally, a Petition for Child Support has been filed, including a request for support dating back to the birth of the minor child. A copy of both petitions is attached for convenience, with proper legal service to follow.

We are vehemently opposed to jurisdictional filings outside the United States and will object with the full force of the UCCJA and international law.

Laurie Williams
Partner, Stoeppel Evans PLLC

To: Laurie.Williams@StoeppelEvansFirm.com
From: AirekDystsel@SklootWattFirm.com
CC: Kelley@KelleyCaruthersRacing.com
Subject: RE: Mack & Shaw Williams—new communication plan [May 20, 2:16 p.m.]

Ms. Williams,

We have received your Petition for Custody, despite the cruel timing of filing in the middle of Mr. Caruthers's race season. Mr. Caruthers is not seeking permanent custody of the minor child, but adamantly reserves his right to visit his daughter whenever he chooses, without the constriction of a schedule due to his unusual job. Additionally, he denies all financial culpability for the child. Counter petitions are attached, with service to follow.

Cordially,
Airek Dystsel
Partner, Skloot & Watt

To: AirekDystsel@SklootWattFirm.com
From: Laurie.Williams@StoeppelEvansFirm.com
CC: Kelley@KelleyCaruthersRacing.com
Subject: RE: RE: Mack & Shaw Williams—new communication plan [May 20, 3:11 p.m.]

We look forward to seeing you in court.

LW
Laurie Williams
Partner, Stoeppel Evans PLLC

CHAPTER 38

1 day until the Indianapolis 500

"Can you imagine being squashed in the Snake Pit? I'd probably hyperventilate."

"Nah, it would be fun to rave with all those people."

"Why are we even debating this?" Leo asked. "Isn't the goal to never have the last Sunday in May free? We don't want to party in the Snake Pit. We want to race."

"That's right. We're the Track Pack, or whatever dumb shit they're calling us online now."

Mack, Boomer, Leo, and Jericho all rolled their eyes. They sat on the cold bleachers of turn three, looking down at the wide expanse of empty track and infield. In a dozen hours, these grandstands would be packed full of fans with coolers and sunscreen, but tonight it was just the four of them under the black sky.

Tomorrow, they'd challenge each other and twenty-nine other drivers to win the biggest race in the world. They should be doing yoga or hydration IVs or spending a quiet evening with their families, not breaking into the empty track and freezing their asses off, but Jericho insisted it was a tradition.

"Okay, but here's the real question." Jericho rubbed his hands together. "Who will be the first to piss in their seat tomorrow?"

"Adam Weston," Leo and Boomer shouted at the same time.

"He told me it's a Pavlovian response. The engine starts, he pees," Leo said.

Mack wrinkled her nose. "Well, this is my one shot, so as long as I don't pee tomorrow, I'm good." Men were animals, peeing wherever they wanted because they could.

"You never know what could happen," Leo said, flashing a quick look at Boomer.

Mack shrugged, not wanting to ruin the moment by pointing out that it was easier for men—especially an Indy 500 winner, an influencer, and the child of racing royalty—to find a team. Tonight, she didn't feel bitter; she felt determined. There was a strong chance she'd watch next year's race from the same bleachers under her butt right now, but she'd make the most of the one race she got. She would push hard in the off-season to find sponsors, or find opportunities in other racing disciplines that'd keep her on the radar, and maybe, just maybe, she'd be back here again. As Mack looked down the short chute and through the wide flat of turn four, she gave herself permission to hope.

"You can't leave, Rookie." Boomer pointed at her splinted hand. Leo's engineer, Lucie, had created a carbon fiber splint from a piece of bodywork, strong enough to hold her broken bone in place but flexible enough that she could still drive. "First that photo with your dad, and then the story about driving with two broken bones in your hand. You got more interviews than anyone else this week. You're IndyCar famous now."

She rubbed at the hand in question, picturing the news story that had run the day after her qualification: Williams Family Back on Track, with a quarter-page photo of Wes holding her face after qualifications, both of them crying. The media loved the daughter-of-a-legend story, and Mack had done interviews, including a Zoom with *Good Morning America*, on top of the regular series promos that kept them all busy. Laurie stayed by her side at every moment, a makeshift assistant keeping her hydrated and on time.

"And," Jericho said with a mischievous grin, "can't forget that photo of you climbing Leo like a koala."

"Stop," Leo demanded.

"Look at him blush!" Boomer taunted.

"I'm not embarrassed, jackass." Leo glared at Jericho. "The way people treated that photo was sexist bullshit. No one gave me shit. Just Mack."

"Put down your sword, Sir Leo." Mack rolled her eyes. Her performance on track had nothing to do with Leo, and screw anyone who thought it did. She was tired of caring what anyone else thought, except maybe Janet, who had lectured the two of them on optics and making the crew uncomfortable but hadn't forbidden anything. "I will let my driving do the talking and fuck the gossip."

"Amen," Boomer said softly. Mack hoped one day soon racing would be progressive enough to show Boomer celebrating with his boyfriend. She lightly tapped her nonbroken pinkie on top of his and flashed him a quick wink.

"One of the Track Pack is going to win tomorrow. I feel it in my bones," Jericho said, his brogue thick. He looked up and down the track, as if watching tomorrow's race happen in his mind.

"He feels it in his *buns*." Mack did a bad imitation of his accent and Leo and Boomer burst into laughter again.

Jericho looked at her with wide, serious eyes. "I can't explain it. I felt it last year, too. I mean I physically felt it in my body from the starting line. It was my year, if I didn't jack it up. Even when Leo came close on the last lap, I knew it was my year."

"They say this place picks the winner." Fans whispered that Boomer had The Curse, destined to come so close to winning the Indianapolis 500 and yet never crossing the bricks first despite having significant wins at all the other tracks in the series.

"Hey," Mack said, nudging his elbow. "If I can take ten years away from racing and make the Indy 500, anything is possible. I know it's cheesy, but . . ." A month ago she'd been sure she'd never push a throttle again, but tomorrow all of them would floor it to 230 down the very track in front of her. "Never count yourself out."

A moment of silence, and then Leo whistled long and low. "Life lessons from a rookie."

"No," Jericho said, reaching into a bag at his feet and handing Mack something small and soft. "Life lessons from *The Racing Mom*."

Mack shook out a T-shirt emblazoned with the nickname the media had given her, and barked a laugh to cover the sting of emotion in her throat. Her life in Haubstadt had been so lonely and small, and she vowed never to take for granted the simple gifts of friendship, the teasing and laughing and ridiculous T-shirts.

Jericho grinned and pointed at the infield dirt track nestled inside of turn three. It was the same size as the one in Haubstadt but looked positively tiny from the grandstands. "After I win tomorrow, you gonna show me how to race on that, Rookie?"

Mack arched her brows. "After *I* beat *you* tomorrow, I'm happy to kick your *rookie* ass on the dirt."

Boomer and Leo almost fell off the bleachers with laughter, and Mack felt warmth in her body even though the May night was chilly. She'd shut people out of her life, thinking it would keep her from getting hurt, but sitting sandwiched between her new friends, she knew she'd only hurt herself.

"I can't believe the sprints don't have gears. How do you even take the corners?" Boomer looked at the track skeptically.

"Real fast." Mack grinned. The clouds shifted above them, and almost as if the sky was listening, illuminated the infield dirt track. "Maybe I'll try the dirt race here this fall. Show you jokers how to sling mud."

Leo nodded. "You could get big sponsor attention if you ran the 500 in May and dirt in September. Would you be able to stay with your sister again in the fall?"

"Actually, Shaw and I are moving to Indianapolis." Mack kept her eyes on the infield, but she felt Leo's gaze on her face.

"Hell yeah," Jericho cheered. "I expect to see you at Body Work, making us all look bad."

"Can't wait." And my god, she couldn't. Moving to Indianapolis wouldn't magically solve her problems, but she was ready for a change and a new challenge.

Wes and Billie planned to rent space for the motor home nearby when they weren't traveling, and as much as the distance from her dad scared Mack, she also knew it would be good for them. Selling the track would be good for them, too. Wes was right that neither of them had a great head for business, and while dirt tracks weren't popular or lucrative, the land itself was valuable enough that it might give them a financial cushion they'd never had before. Mack supposed she should feel sad to see the track possibly torn down, but there were too many negative memories attached to the track for her to feel more than bittersweet relief. With Laurie attacking the issue of Shaw's custody, Mack felt less afraid of the future than she had since her daughter was born.

"Well laddies and lass, it's bedtime. Gotta get rested up to kick ass tomorrow. Same time and place next year?"

"I'll bring my winner's ring," Boomer boasted.

"Next year and every year," Leo said.

They all looked at Mack expectantly.

She didn't know what would happen tomorrow or what next year would bring. She'd try her damnedest to be back in a car, but if she was here in the bleachers . . . well, she'd survived worse. She had Shaw and Laurie, Wes and Billie, and now the jokers sitting beside her. Maybe even Leo, if it worked out. She'd find a way to keep racing, and no matter if she was a driver or a spectator, she'd spend the last Sunday in May at this track until she dropped dead.

"Yeah," she said. "I'll be here next year."

INDIANAPOLIS COURIER-JOURNAL

May 23

A Racing Paddock That Looks Like America

By Emily Ales

After twenty years in racing journalism, I still get asked one question more than any other: *Why aren't there more women and minorities in racing?*

Racing is a sport in which body composition has very little to do with success. Drivers must be fit enough to withstand double-digit g-forces and long hours in hot, uncomfortable conditions. They need quick reflexes and excellent spatial awareness. And of course, they must have a love of speed. None of these things are related to gender or race. A recent study even determined women have the physical and psychological ability to be as competitive as men on the racetrack (a conclusion shocking only to dinosaurs and incels).

So why aren't there more women and drivers of color on track?

The answer is both as simple and complex as history and money.

While women have been driving since the horseless carriage was invented, they were excluded from most sanctioned racing events until the mid twentieth century. The first woman to compete in the Indy 500 was Janet Guthrie in 1977. A Black man did not race at Indianapolis until 1991 (Willy T. Ribbs), and it was 2017 before an AAPI driver won at the Brickyard (Takuma Sato). In the history of Formula 1, only four women have started races, and no woman has started in F1 since 1992. Sir Lewis Hamilton was the first, and remains the only, Black man in Formula 1, making his debut in 2007. NASCAR has an equally abysmal history. These barrier-breaking racers received (and modern "only" drivers still receive) death threats and some competed with equipment so subpar that it was dangerous.

Today, there are no women with full-time seats in any of the highest levels of Western racing (IndyCar, NASCAR, and Formula 1). Women make up less than 10% of global racing participants. Black and brown drivers, even less.

The most significant factor in the ability to race is sponsorship money. Racing is expensive (a single IndyCar has a price tag of $1 million, and that's only for the vehicle itself), and with teams in constant competition for sponsorship, drivers who bring money to the table are given greater consideration than those who do not. The biggest sponsorships go to the most successful drivers—or those with famous last names—but even smaller sponsorships can be hard to come by for young and unknown drivers.

In any sport, talent cannot overcome a lack of practice. Without consistent time to acclimate to the car and learn the minute ins and outs of particular tracks, a driver struggles to be competitive in a racing series or even a single event. And lap time costs big, big money.

It's the snake eating its own tail: Companies don't want to give sponsorship dollars to unproven drivers, but those traditionally kept out of racing—women and minorities—aren't able to prove themselves on track without financial support.

And yet, women make up 40% of racing fans. Sir Lewis Hamilton, the only Black driver in Formula 1, has almost forty million followers on social media and was recently voted the "Most Marketable Driver in Motorsports" for the twelfth time.

Research shows that sports fans tend to be loyal to sponsored brands of their favorite athletes, and women even more so. I'm no economics expert, but if women are almost half of all racing fans and are often loyal to a favorite driver's brand . . .

And yet. Here we are.

There are groups working to close this gap, like women's beauty brands e.l.f. Cosmetics, Fenty, and Charlotte Tilbury, who sponsor female drivers in various disciplines. Organizations like Shift Up and More Than Equal are working to bring sponsorship and support to women drivers, and the Hamilton Commission and Force Indy support drivers of color. But none of these organizations alone, or even together, is enough to overcome the drastic gap in funding between the white men who have always been in racing and the women and minorities who are as good, if not better, behind the wheel (for example, see Lewis Hamilton's multiple F1 records).

It must start at the top, with racing series requiring more diverse representation from teams, and from the major teams putting their sponsorship efforts—purposefully—behind those historically shut out of racing. Will efforts at incentivizing nontraditional drivers anger some in the paddock? Of course. Will it make a difference? If teams truly want to see "pure racing" as they claim they do, it's worth trying.

Until historically excluded drivers are given financial support to participate in racing at every level, from junior karting events to the Indy 500, we will continue to see an "only __ in the race" in the Indy 500 every few years, often in a one-time opportunity ride with little ability to be truly competitive.

Which brings me to the real question: Do racing fans want to see the very best drivers in the world, or are they content watching the people who have had obvious pipelines to get into the driver's seat?

I know which one I prefer.

CHAPTER 39

The last Sunday in May

Mack stood on the dais as her name was announced over the loudspeaker and waved to the three hundred thousand fans spread across the grandstands and infield. Sponsor logos peppered her new fire suit, including an Indiana-based company that converted plastic bags into designer leggings and a giant Engine Starters patch for her angel investors. Mack held Shaw's hand and encouraged her to wave to the crowd. From behind, she heard Laurie, Wes, and Billie cheer loudly for her.

As she stepped off the stage, she saw Leo waiting for his turn. He'd qualified fourth, an excellent spot to stay out of trouble and vie for the win. He pushed his Ray-Bans off his face and gave her a smile big enough to show that perfect snaggletooth. He and Shaw bumped knuckles, and Mack couldn't help but match his wide grin. "You ready to do this, Rookie?"

"I've been ready for a long time." She looked out at the grandstands and knew Leo felt the same sense of awe as they stood together and stared out at the sea of people, vehicles, sound systems, and equipment. The Indianapolis 500 was truly a spectacle. It was more than a race. It was the carefully orchestrated routine of traditions: the Purdue University marching band, the Memorial Day tribute, singing "Back Home Again in Indiana," the final parade laps of thirty-three precision machines gearing up for the biggest spectator event in the world.

The Indianapolis Motor Speedway was a track, the Indy 500 was a car race, but *Indy* was a feeling.

"Congrats on the Penske contract," Mack said. "You'll be drinking champagne out of crystal flutes for breakfast." When she read about Leo's move to the elite team, she'd been genuinely thrilled for him. She told herself it was stupid to feel hurt he hadn't told her himself, that they'd only known each other a few weeks.

Leo's face fell a little. "It's a dream team, for sure. But it's hard to leave JJR. Janet and I have been together a long time. I owe her everything."

"You know the phone will still work, right? She'll act annoyed but secretly love having you call to chat."

"I already gave Janet my replacement recommendation." When she read about Leo's move to Penske, she'd wondered about the newly open seat at JJR but hadn't let her hope extend that far. Leo flicked his gaze to Shaw, who was preoccupied with the spectacle, and lowered his voice. "I'll still be based in Indy. I wanted a change, but . . . well, hopefully it creates an opportunity for you."

Pursuing something with Leo was like the line she'd run in qualifying—dangerous, with a high probability she'd crash into the wall, but worth the payoff if it worked out. Watching him watching her, his face an intoxicating mix of sweet and intense, she knew it was a risk she was willing to take.

"Rookie! Let's do this!" Jericho Blair's unmistakable burr echoed around the busy backstage as he and Boomer made their way to Mack and Leo. He whistled at a nearby photographer. "If these people online want to call us the Track Pack, let's give 'em some pictures. Smile, assholes."

Mack pulled Shaw into the photo and stood between the friends she'd never expected to have. Two more photographers pushed in for the shot, and then another and another. Mack hoped it made every racing outlet.

"You've got this, Rookie. All you have to do is cross the yard of bricks and you won't have that little *R* by your name next year," Boomer said.

Her veins zinged at the possibility of returning here next year. Mere weeks ago, she'd have berated herself for the moment of desire, but she understood now that wishes, even if unrealized, wouldn't break her. Hope could keep her going.

Mack turned to find Leo hunched over, listening to Shaw. Shaw bounced on her toes, braided pigtails bouncing. Billie had outdone herself on race day, with lots of glitter and checkered bows. "You used to be my favorite driver but now it's my mom. You can be my second favorite driver. I want my mom to win!"

Leo grinned. "I hope I win, but it's okay if your mom beats me. She's worked really hard to be here."

Shaw preened as if Leo had complimented her. "Oh, she's definitely going to beat you. She can drive different types of cars *and* with a broken hand."

Leo threw his head back in laughter, and Mack glanced toward the dais so she wouldn't keep watching Leo with her daughter. She motioned toward pit lane. "Good luck, Leo. If it's not me, I hope it's your win today."

"Back at you, Rookie." Leo leaned in. "I'll see you . . . tonight? To celebrate?"

She couldn't look away from him, even with the chaos carrying on around them. He was unlike any man she'd ever known. Leo wasn't threatened by someone else's success, or afraid to be honest, and he kept his word. He was confident but never arrogant, gentle but not soft. He made her heart want one thing even while her head argued against it.

She went with her gut.

"With Shaw?"

The surprise on his face delighted her, and she grinned as his smile widened to match her own.

"Absolutely with Shaw," he said, dark eyes sparkling.

His name blasted over the loudspeaker for his driver intro, and Leo took a few steps backward, grinning big enough that his dimple appeared under his beard. "Good luck, Mack. See you right here after the race."

He'd laughed at her puzzled frown as he jogged up the steps to the podium, and when Mack finally turned, she realized they'd been standing at the entrance to victory lane.

As she walked through the paddock, Mack soaked in the electric energy of the last Sunday in May. The heartbreaking years she'd spent watching other people race here, wishing it was herself instead, were worth this moment. Standing in the shadow of Gasoline Alley and the iconic Pagoda, Mack knew she wouldn't change one moment of her journey. It wasn't what she had planned and wasn't how she would do it if she'd had a full range of choices. It wasn't an easy path. But it was *her* path, and it wasn't over.

She'd needed those dark days to fully appreciate the lightness of finally being *here*. To know that whatever happened today, she'd taken a risk and the reward wasn't just the racing, it was the pride she felt inside.

If she was lucky, she had a lot of life left ahead of her, and she planned to live it instead of surviving it.

After the driver introductions, a parade of thirty-three convertible Corvettes looped the drivers around the track, and Mack and Shaw waved at the massive crowd gathered to watch The Greatest Spectacle in Racing. As long as she lived, and as many times as she earned the opportunity to participate in this race, Mack would remember watching women and girls stand and scream when she passed the grandstands. She lifted her eyes to the perfect blue Hoosier sky and asked the universe to let her show those girls a victory. One day, she'd stand on the podium with the winner's wreath around her neck and dedicate her win to Shaw and the little girls who cheered her name. Maybe Leo would be next to her, like he'd said, but she knew she'd be fine if he wasn't. She controlled her own joy.

Time accelerated into hyperdrive and Mack tried to memorize each second. She squeezed Shaw's hand when a priest delivered an ecumenical invocation, stood tall as "Taps" played to honor fallen soldiers, and sang “Back Home Again in Indiana” with Billie, Wes, and Laurie. Around them, most of the drivers shared last-minute conversations with their engineers, tugged on helmets, or made a final dash for the toilets. But Mack inhaled and exhaled, trying to imprint this feeling into the very core of her body. If she never experienced this moment again, if this was truly the only chance she ever had to race Indianapolis, she would be okay. She was in control of her own life, and if she felt stuck again, she knew now that she could be honest with her dad, and Laurie, and they would listen. Like a cardinal trapped on a sunporch, she had to find the door and fly through.

Laurie pulled Mack into her arms. “Go show your daughter and all those little girls out there”—she waved up at the grandstands—“that it’s time for a woman to win this damn race.”

Mack bit her tongue to stop tears from clouding her eyes. She squeezed Laurie tight, like they had as children. “Go fast, be safe,” they said in unison.

Wes was waiting for her next. Mack hoped the press of her arms around his shoulders conveyed her love and gratitude. “Go show ’em how a Williams drives. See you soon.”

She leaned down and kissed Shaw, told her how much she loved her, hugged her tight. Her daughter’s sweet smile was the perfect send-off.

The clock ticked down as Mack bumped fists with the crew one last time, listened to Janet’s final instructions, and pulled on her helmet. She slid into the driver’s seat and fastened her belts while doing one final radio check.

“All right, Rookie. Let’s show these boys how it’s done.”

Safe in the quiet confines of the car, Mack began her pre-race ritual. *Ray Harroun. Louis Meyer. Wilbur Shaw. Parnelli Jones. Jim Clark.* She mentally ticked her way through the names of all seventy-six men who won the most famous race in motorsports, but this time she added a woman. *And soon, Mackenzie Williams.*

“Drivers, start your engines!”

Behind her, the starter engaged and the now-familiar growl filled her mind and body. She checked her clutch and brakes, flexed her hand through the specialized splint, and exhaled as she slowly accelerated forward for the three parade laps before the green flag.

As she pulled alongside the other cars in her row, driving around the track in the traditional formation of eleven rows of three cars across, she glanced up at the hundreds of thousands of fans and wondered who else was out in the crowd, dreaming about racing around the most famous racetrack in the world and showing the boys how to win. Who out there was brimming with ambition and determined to take on the ol' boys club of racing. Maybe it was her own daughter. Maybe it was a teenager, or maybe even a mom like her.

It wasn't too late for any of them. There was time. There was always enough time for dreams.

"Green green green!" Jimmy cried into her radio.

Mack throttled up and crossed the yard of bricks, full send.

Acknowledgments

First, thanks to you, reader, for picking up this book! A debut author is a bit like being the new kid in school, and if you've chosen and read this book, you've made me feel welcome and included on my first day. Thank you from the bottom of my tender heart for spending your time and money on this story. I'll never take that for granted.

In May 2017, I held my infant daughter while complaining to my best friend that yet again, there was no woman racing in the Indy 500. She calmly said, "Someone should write a book about that. A woman who loves racing. A woman who said she's going to write a book someday." Lucie, thank you for kicking off this wild ride, for always believing in me as a writer, and for being the best best friend. There were so many days you talked me out of quitting. Sushi Sherbet.

Claire Friedman, thank you for reading my rough book and seeing its potential. You were right about Leo! You're a dream agent and I'm grateful you took a chance on me. Nancy Holmes, you got Mack from the very beginning. Thank you for pushing me to make this the best possible version of the story. Welcome to Team Girl! Jodi Warshaw, thank you for your gentle, thoughtful guidance and eagle eye. Thanks to the Lake Union team, Angela and Jo; editors Tara, Ashley, Nicole, and Jessica. Thank you to Emily Mahar for the brilliant and beautiful cover design! Thank you, Kaitlyn Kennedy and your Midwestern team.

Love and thanks to Shauna, Meghan, Ashley, and Erin, who said, "Of course you did!" when I confessed that I'd written a book about the

Indy 500. Sara, Rachel, Sarah, and Leslie, thank you for the countless walks, phone chats, and coffees. WWAG, thank you for the accountability! Sandy at Rockvale Writers' Colony, thank you for the haven you've created for writers and the years of support. Mary Adkins, your class and your books taught me to be a better writer and to actually finish the book—thank you!

Every writer deserves the support and enthusiasm of my in-laws.

Emily, my own Laurie, thank you for responding to my random texts about Indianapolis and suggesting the St. Elmo scene. I love you like I love Indiana: always. Brian, I won the brother-in-law lottery. Thank you for renewing our tickets each June, and for taking a long walk with a beer can around the Speedway.

Mom, you've always believed in me as a writer. Thank you for being a babysitter, chef, taxi driver, ballet and baseball grandma, and all-around indispensable help. Thanks for reminding Dad to bring sunscreen to the race.

Andy, I don't have the right words to tell everyone why you're the best: best friend, best husband, best dad, best person. I'm so glad we didn't screw it up. I love you.

Jasper and Genevieve, on days when I didn't feel like writing, you inspired me to do work that would make you proud. I love you forever, I like you for always.

My dad took me to my first dirt track race—in the real Haubstadt—when I was so young I only have hazy memories of loud engines and coming home covered in flecks of Hoosier dirt. I was six when he took me to my first Indy 500 and we attended the race together every year until his last race in 2022. He didn't live to read the final manuscript, but he's on every page. Thank you, Dad. For everything.

About the Author

Photo © 2024 Sarah Unger

Kate Clark Stone attended her first Indianapolis 500 at six years old and wrote her first book at eleven. A former attorney, Kate relishes watching fast cars, swimming, paddleboarding, and spending time with her two very good dogs. Forever a Hoosier at heart, she lives with her family in the mountains of Tennessee.